CU00847633

GIRL

OF THE

ASHES

Biography

Hayleigh Barclay, born in 1987, is a Scottish writer with a Doctorate in Creative Writing from the University of Glasgow. Her research involved 19th century Gothic Vampire literature and contemporary female Goths. Lover of all things witchy and magical, when she is not liking pictures of motorcycles on social media, she is watching supernatural shows on Netflix or plugged into her iPod.

GIRL

OF THE

ASHES

HAYLEIGH BARCLAY

Garmoran Publishing

First Published in Great Britain 2020
Copyright © Hayleigh Barclay 2020

The moral right of the author has been asserted. All rights reserved. No part of this publication may be reproduced, in any form or by any electronic or mechanical means, including information storage and retrieval systems, without the prior permission in writing from the publisher.

All characters and events in this publication, other than those clearly in the public domain, are fictitious and any resemblance to real persons, living or dead, is purely coincidental and not intended by the author.

Cover Designer: Gary Coventry, Instagram@woodland_92

ISBN: 978-1913510091

A CIP catalogue record for this book is available from the British Library

Printed and bound in United Kingdom by Biddles, King's Lynn

Published by Garmoran Publishing
Ardnamurchan, Scotland

www.garmoranpublishing.com

CHAPTER ONE

PRESENT DAY

Somewhere, about six hundred miles from here, there is a gravestone with my name on it. Elise de Volonté: 11th March 1879 – 7th November 1897. May she rest in peace.

A century on, and the peace inscribed on the stone has yet to find me. I have hunted through decades, seeking revenge against those mortals who torture others like me. They kill us for following the Old Ways; they would have us chanting and kneeling in front of the statue of their Idol.

Three hundred and fifty years ago, the Councillors of the Inservium overthrew the Government and Church of my home town, Loch Fala. Claiming divine right and ordaining themselves as rulers, the Councillors rose to power, and reached out to the common man by promising to ease their suffering in exchange for faith and devotion. Impalement awaited any man or woman who did not bow to the power of the Inservium, and their corpses were paraded along the roadsides. The starving collected scraps of bread and widows and orphans sought sanctuary, all while the blessings and taxes of the Councillors "protected" the citizens from unholy horrors such as vampires, witches, and Pagan gods.

I was seventeen when I first witnessed the evil of the Inservium. Until then, I'd lived in considerable ignorance in Loch Fala. Situated north of mainland Scotland, between Thurso and Ben Hope, sits the isolated town of Loch Fala. Despite the inhabitants' reclusive natures, migrants who stumbled upon the settlement received welcome; Scandinavian, German, and

Dutch victims of the 1717 Christmas Flood, French aristocrats escaping their Revolution, and Irish farmers hoping for a new start after the Great Famine all found refuge. The townspeople lived under the delusion of goodwill and tolerance. Blackmail, torture, corruption, fraud, and murder all served to keep the Councillors in power. Death was evoked in the name of religion, but little did the Councillors know, death was laughing and taunting them whilst blessing their enemies.

I was one who survived.

I travelled the ends of the earth, hunting, interrogating, and killing with the sole purpose of avenging my coven. Every time I was close to finding freedom, the Inservium found me instead. But, this time, I hoped to find my other half, Jacque.

For the foreseeable future, my residence is London, England.

Four days ago, I arrived by train from Paris and headed straight to the address supplied by my sister, Amelie.

Leaving St Pancras station, I walked along a secluded cobbled alleyway, hidden behind a row of restaurants. The smell of rotting cabbage, hamburgers, and sour milk seeped into the damp mouldy brickwork. An overflowing gutter dribbled onto the street and gurgled in the drainpipe. A group of rats scuttled behind dustbins, eating scraps – two of them were fighting inside an upturned lid. Behind, the sound of footsteps edged towards me. Slowing my pace – it seemed only polite to give them a chance – I looked around for any witnesses. A CCTV camera sat about twenty feet ahead and kitchen staff clattered away indoors, listening to a radio.

The footsteps quickened but I kept my pace steady, allowing them to come within arm's reach of me. I halted and spun around to face them.

"You must be new," I said to the young man standing in front of me.

He didn't reply. Instead he removed a long dagger from

under his black cloak and aimed it towards me.

"Nice necklace," I added. "It's so shiny. Have you been a very good boy?"

In the man's gold medallion hanging from his neck, the embossed image of their Idol stared back at me.

"You are an abomination!" the man said, gritting his teeth.

"And you are a pain in the arse," I replied, smiling.

Before he could answer, the sound of a glass smashing from one of the kitchens distracted him.

I removed a dagger from my belt and tossed it towards the CCTV camera, slicing the wires.

"We wouldn't want evidence, would we?" I said.

As he thrust his dagger towards my chest, I twisted his wrist until the bones snapped, and his blade fell to the ground. Before he had the chance to scream out, my hand grabbed him by the throat, and pinned him against the wall, causing the radio perched on the windowsill to topple over.

"Shhh!" I whispered, winking at him.

I reached over to turn up the volume, and the warbles of a bubble-gum pop princess masked the henchman's cries, whilst my knee plunged a series of strikes into his ribs and groin. Before his body slid down the wall, I threw him to the other side of the alley, where he collapsed onto the cobbles.

"It's worth it," I heard him splutter whilst struggling to breathe.

I moved forward, and kicked him in the face, gouging his cheek with my boot buckle. Trying to regain his composure, he threw a few limp punches in my direction.

"We'll never stop. You're making it worse for yourself," he added.

I rolled my eyes, withdrew a poignard from my trousers, and smoothly pulled the blade to sever his jugular.

One more dead Councillor.

Without a second thought, I dumped his body into a dustbin for the rats to feast upon. The reflection in the metal lid showed my face covered in blood.

"Every time!" I said, smudging it across my cheek.

Wiping my blade along the purple fabric, a red stain appeared on my coat. I placed the poignard back inside a pocket, retrieved my dagger from the cobbles and carried on with my journey – without glancing back.

The streets buzzed as zigzagging corporate suits babbled into their mobiles, tourists hauled novelty suitcases out of black cabs, and homeless men and women begged in doorways with empty plastic cups. I stopped and placed a few coins into a young girl's hand.

"Thanks, love," she whispered, pulling her sleeping bag closer.

"You take care," I replied, squeezing her hand.

Long ago, I had been in her position, and hoped her fate proved happier than mine.

As I continued towards my destination, the tide of passers-by parted as people stared at my blood-stained appearance.

"Street theatre," I said.

A little boy grabbed my coat sleeve. "Can we see?"

"I'm contractually obliged to say no."

"Oh, go on!" he replied with his brown doe eyes full of mischief.

"Do you know Equity rules?"

His brows furrowed. "What's Equi—"

"Didn't think so! Goodbye," I said, running away as my weapons rattled against my pockets.

Passing signs for Phoenix Road and Camden Town, then crossing the canal, I arrived at Gloucester Avenue and found Jacque's residence.

It was a still autumn evening, but as the violet and magenta hues of the sky turned grey, a storm brewed overhead.

I stood in front of the black doorway, and studied the little white button beside Jacque's name.

What would I do if he rejected me? I thought. Perhaps his life was better in London, and that's why he never searched for me. For all I knew he may attempt to kill me. Reality never lives up to anticipation.

As my fingers hovered over the metal panel, an electric shock from a loose wire shot up my hand, causing me to inadvertently press one of the other buzzers.

"Shh!" I pleaded with the droning tone.

"Hello?" proclaimed an Eastern European voice out of the speaker, "Who is it?"

"What? Nothing! Nobody!" I stuttered.

"Who is it you're looking for?" the man demanded.

I hesitated, attempting to think of a logical answer. "I'm delivering a parcel."

The man grunted. "I've heard that before. For who?"

"Jacque. Jacque Angou."

"He's not in. I saw him leaving with a redheaded woman last night."

I felt foolish for believing he would have remained faithful to me. Before regret fully set in, I backed away from the doorway.

The man's voice continued, "Your accent sounds familiar. What is that? Scottish?"

I ignored him.

"She sounded the same as you. Although her accent was a little different."

It dawned on me who he was referring to, "The redhead was Scottish?"

"Yes, I believe so."

"Are you sure?"

"Definitely."

A click indicated our conversation was over.

To face Jacque would be one thing, but to face the redhead would be problematic, to say the least. Nothing could persuade me to wait outside those flats any longer.

Perhaps to catch a glimpse of Jacque's life without me, though, I decided to stay in London. I found myself searching for him in places I thought he might frequent. I skulked in bars which offered two-for-one deals on Tequila shots, peeked through windows of dilapidated books shops, and loitered around a steak house claiming to have the best rib-eye in town.

The first time I caught sight of him was an accident. I think.

Sitting outside a café in Camden Market, I read through my emails and savoured a pumpkin spiced latte. Have you been mis-sold PPI? Delete. Twenty percent off car insurance. Delete. Two-for-one on meal deals. Save for later. Just as I was about to put my phone away, a message popped up from Lana Percival.

We've found her. Inservium tracked us before we got the go ahead. The Garcias and Riccis are coming. Be ready. L.

Forward to Natashka. We needed to leave. As I flung a ten-pound note on the table and prepared to disappear, that's when I saw Jacque, coming out of a vintage clothes shop on the opposite side of the road. His dark hair was short and messy and his eyes still had their icy blue stare. The obsession with tattoos hadn't waned over the years, although the black blazer and ripped jeans were a reinvention of the style he'd once sported. When I saw him, the noise of the traffic ceased and the bodies stopped dead around me. I wanted to run but couldn't breathe let alone persuade my limbs to move.

Jacque didn't see me.

My phone pinged with a direct message from Natashka:

You can't go anywhere. We're going to need him.

That night I snuck back to his whitewashed maisonette. Trying to avoid confronting the buzzer system, I chose instead to climb a drain pipe and dismounted onto a balcony outside Jacque's bedroom window. I'm always grateful that city neighbours take very little to do with each other's business – unless it involves going out with redheads.

I unpicked the catches on the window and stepped inside to find the flat empty and dark.

"Same old Jacque," I whispered, flicking on a side lamp. It was a generic minimalist room, containing only a bed, a wardrobe, chest of drawers, and a stack of books sitting in the corner.

No photographs. No unopened letters. No takeaway containers piled to the ceiling. In fact, the flat gave no indication as to who lived there at all.

I rummaged through drawers to find more clues. Not that I needed any, but after a century of trying to track the man down, a good nosy felt justified.

"A decent pair of Calvin Klein's. Good choice!"

A pair of black socks. Two pairs of black socks. Fifteen pairs of black socks. Twenty-three pairs of black socks.

"That's a wee bit obsessive."

Phone chargers, black t-shirts, a Kindle, an iPad, more black t-shirts. Then I found it.

Hidden amongst the second sock drawer lay an oval portrait of a young girl from 1897. Me.

The phone inside my jacket pocket vibrated. Upon answering the low thumping sound of night club music overpowered a familiar Russian accent.

"Elise, it's Natashka. Have you done it yet?"

"I know it's you. And not yet."

"Are you sure you want to do this?"

Looking down at the girl in the frame, all doubts left me. "I do."

"Very well then. I'm sure it will be very melodramatic. I'm going to need every detail later! That's if you two aren't too busy."

"Is your mind ever out of the gutter?"

"No. I'm starving, I will meet you back at our usual haunt."

"We don't have a usual haunt. We don't even live here."

"Minor detail! Remember to at least crack a smile when he appears. I know you have been practicing. See you later, *Zaya*."

Natashka blew a kiss down the phone and hung up. I still didn't know where I was to meet her.

Clutching the portrait, I thought back to those innocent days of 1896. The girl was smiling. A mass of dark ringlets hung beyond the shoulders of her coat and strayed into one of her eyes, rimmed with black kohl. The artist hadn't been too impressed by Jacque and me that day we entered his studio, but he took our money anyway.

That girl in the portrait had dreams and summer sweetness. But this girl, now holding it, has witnessed a century worth of change: the Orient Express journeyed across Europe, the symphonies of Brahms, Tchaikovsky, and Bach played in concert halls across the world, and the Inservium launched the Second Cleansing of my kind, killing entire families.

Queen Victoria celebrated her golden jubilee, Jack the Ripper terrorised the streets of Whitechapel, France finally permitted women to study at the École des Beaux-Arts, and Bram Stoker published Dracula.

I died.

Edward VII took the throne only to be dead nine years later. The Titanic sank. World War I promised to be the war to end all wars. History taught us otherwise. The Suffragettes won their vote.

Gas lamps gave way to electricity and the darkness of the cities transformed into strip lights of neon jazz halls. Skirts grew shorter as heels got higher. Women put away their baking trays and vacuum cleaners, choosing instead to burn their bras for the sake of equality.

The financial world collapsed and was rebuilt only to collapse again.

My sister tried to kill me. I returned the favour by actually killing her. Or so I thought.

The Second World War came and went, rationing everything except blood.

The 50s saw the rise of the Civil Rights Movement. The 80s protestors rallied for Gay Rights. The 90s swore equality for disabled people.

Union strikes. Recessions. Threats that the end was nigh. Still the world carried on.

Nothing really changes; everything remains the same. Some scars do not fade, and some memories should not be left untold. Whilst the world replaced one leader with another, invented one miracle after another, or advertised the newest fad, I was in the background, wandering the streets between lives. Any human I came into contact with quickly forgot my name. The only trace left of me is that gravestone six hundred miles away.

I tucked the portrait back inside the drawer, removed my diary from my coat pocket, and placed it on a pillow.

Hiding on the balcony, I awaited Jacque's return and promised myself to sit as he read every word. As night descended, the waxing moon materialised behind the clouds. Natashka would call it a good omen for regaining what is lost.

The street lamps shone on a man crossing the road towards the house. Jacque. A crack of lightening flashed in the distance as spots of rain tumbled from above. Jacque quickened his step, but I dared not watch him too long for fear of courage abandoning me. As I crouched against the cold brick wall, I heard his keys rattling at the doorway. He may not forgive me. He may not love me.

But it is time for him to discover how many people I have killed for him.

Chapter Two

October 1897, Loch Fala

The sky turned grey. Rain started to fall. Thunder threatened in the distance. I stood outside the Inservium's gate and watched the townspeople stepping out of the large, white, wooden building, having finished their morning prayers. The bell in the clock tower struck eight o'clock.

Today another person would die.

"Isn't that Marius de Volonté's daughter?" whispered one woman, as I walked along the path, between rows of gravestones.

"Aye," the second answered, with her hand concealing her mouth. "Just look at the state of her."

"She looks like a boy in those clothes," piped up a man, in a tweed coat and a bunnet.

"And her hair is down," added a third woman, holding his arm. "In public!"

"She'll be the next one getting murdered in her bed," said the man. "Wait and see!"

"I'm surprised it's not happened already."

"Well, I read in the Daily Alba…"

All four paused just briefly, and aimed sickly-sweet smiles at me as I walked past to enter the building, shutting the door in their faces.

Dozens of white tapered candles lit the sanctuary, and a blazing fire pit flickered against a statue of their Idol, which hung menacingly on the wall. As I made my way up the centre aisle, an eerie silence breathed throughout the room.

Huddled in a corner, a group of Councillors glared at me whilst I sat in a pew and rifled through the pages of a prayer book. From a back room, the muffled sounds of chanting drowned out the prostrations and sermons of the trainee Councillors.

The ground shuddered as a stone slab receded from the floor, causing the candles to flicker against a gust of wind blasting through the sanctuary. From the vaults beneath, emerged a tall figure in a black cloak. As his footsteps grew closer, I turned around to face their Idol, and slid along the pew to make room.

A shadow cast over me and a wrinkled hand appeared from under the cloak to snatch the prayer book.

"Here for morning prayers?" came the familiar voice of Councillor Bothwell.

"You know I don't do that anymore," I replied, avoiding eye contact.

"It's such a pity the boy turned you against us," Bothwell said, taking a seat beside me. "You used to be so devoted to the Idol."

"Hmm."

"I remember you as a little girl, singing in our choir," he said, patting my knee.

I didn't reply.

"Not the most glorious of mornings," he continued.

"How is Jacque?" I asked, ignoring him.

Bothwell lowered his hood, and his cold, black eyes stared at me. "It's good that you got our letter this morning. We are never sure if that landlady of yours is reliable."

"She's suspicious," I said, removing an envelope from my pocket and handing it to him. "She was fine when it was a letter every month, but two and three a week is drawing attention."

His thin lips curled into a sneer. "Do you not want Jacque back?"

"Of course I do."

"These are righteous missions we send you on. You are proving to us that you are worthy."

I straightened up, and stared at the statue of their Idol, wishing I could tear it down and burn it in the fire pit.

Bothwell scrunched up the letter, and tossed it onto my lap. "Besides, we have sent you to some rather nice places."

"How is Jacque?" I said, brushing the ball of paper off my knee.

A young man – jolly-looking, with rosy cheeks, shiny skin, and wearing a brown cloak – approached and stood beside Bothwell. "Excuse me, sir. When you have a moment, could you help me with deciphering the Prayers for the Wicked?"

"Of course, my son. I'm always happy to help our Initiates," Bothwell replied, grinning. "I'll meet you in the vestry – we can practise the one forgiving fornicators, liars, and murderers. Do you use that one, Elise?"

I frowned and kept my eyes fixed to the floor.

"She's very shy," Bothwell continued.

The young man tutted and kissed Bothwell's hand before leaving.

"He seems eager to please," I said.

"He's from a good family," Bothwell replied. "Like you were. Pity you ruined it!"

"I had Jacque."

Bothwell sniggered, deepening the lines on his face, and handed me a piece of paper. "Here, I have written down a name for you. You know what to do."

"Are they in the Records?" I asked, placing the paper in my pocket.

"Yes, this one is nearby," Bothwell replied, standing up. As he moved to leave, he turned his head to me and said, "Don't make this one so messy. You're showing off now."

"It wasn't my fault. He put up quite a struggle," I said, shrugging.

Bothwell held up his hand, not wanting to hear any

more. "Do as you're told, and you'll see Jacque."

After he left, I waited for the sanctuary to clear. One by one, the Councillors and trainees came and went – wafting incense, collecting prayer books, emptying the donation box – until I was finally alone.

The clock tower bell struck ten. I walked behind the pulpit and pulled down on a hidden wooden lever, which opened a safe in the wall, containing a large, silver box. When I opened the lid, a streak of sunlight burst through a stained-glass window, onto a treasure trove of weaponry – hatchets, iron chains, whips, razors, and blades of every shape and size – some engraved with runes, others encrusted with jewels.

"Earth-stars-moon-sun-I-choose-that-one," I repeated, selecting two daggers. Before closing the box, another – with rubies around its hilt – caught my eye. "You're just a bit too tempting. The others will think I'm playing favourites!"

As I slid the three daggers down my boots and closed the safe, a group of Councillors appeared from the vestry.

"Leave!" said Councillor Boyd, glaring at me.

"I need to check the Masses Records," I said, edging towards a corridor.

"You have five minutes," Boyd replied, pointing at me with a prayer book in his hand. "Or I'm reporting you to Councillor Bothwell."

Nodding, I dashed past the Councillors, keeping my head low.

Sunlight turned to shadows as I descended through the Inservium passageways, past portraits of deceased Councillors and murals of sacred images. After reaching the golden statue of their Idol, I made my way into an underground chamber, no more than six feet wide. The dark, damp, claustrophobic room contained one item – The Masses Records, the sole purpose of which was for the Councillors to keep track of every citizen of Loch Fala. Nothing was hidden – except the records of the Councillors themselves'. Reading the piece of paper that Bothwell had given me, I heaved open the pristine book, covered in gold filigree.

Page by page, I searched until I found the matching record:

Viktor Auldwyrd – Address: 74 East Row.

According to the Inservium, his estate far exceeded his position as a schoolmaster; he had committed no known crimes and his family tree only extended to his wife – a blot mark on the page concealed her name – his mother, Juliska Bavos, and father, Alexander Auldwyrd.

Nothing suggested a reason as to why the Councillors would take a disliking to such a boring man.

After closing the book, I made my way back to the sanctuary, where Councillor Boyd was sat in a pew.

"That was ten minutes," he said, looking towards the statue of their Idol. "I will forgive you. This time."

As I opened my mouth to reply, a young man and woman, walking arm-in-arm, entered the Inservium. The woman radiated a warm glow as she hurried towards the Councillor.

"Ah, Miss Adair," Boyd said, taking her hand. "Here to discuss wedding plans, I assume?"

"Oh yes, yes we are," the woman replied, all smiles and bright eyes. "John and I are beyond excited."

The young man almost tripped over himself as he rushed down the aisle to join his fiancée. The pair giggled and gazed at each other when he moved a strand of hair from her face.

"It won't last," I muttered under my breath, whilst walking past.

The woman, oblivious, pulled a bunch of blue ribbons from her bag, tied them along the pews, and nodded in approval. Boyd, however, growled under his breath at me and kept a fixed stare as I stormed out the door.

Thunder rolled in the distance as I made my way towards the town square, and the faint smell of rain clung to the air.

Along the streets, market vendors paced up and down the cobbles waiting for customers, men sat on stools reading newspapers whilst getting their shoes polished, and women stepped out of carriages, lugging behind whining children.

"Oh!" said a little girl, pointing at me. "Nanny, look!"

"Shh!" the nanny replied, slapping her hand.

"Shouldn't you be in school?" I said, narrowing my eyes at her.

The nanny looked at me, appalled, and ushered the little girl away.

Continuing along the road, I passed a large house where a young woman, wearing a straitjacket was being escorted outside by two gentlemen. As she collapsed to the ground, screaming for help, one of the men turned to the other and said, "Ignore her, it's classic hysteria."

"Will she ever be normal again?" said the second man.

"Oh, yes, we'll take her to the institution," replied the first, with a chuckle. "It's just a small operation."

Feeling the sickness rise in my throat, I ran around the corner and hid. It reminded me of the times my father told me he had put girls like me in asylums. That was before I lived out of wedlock with Jacque, turned into a murderer, and developed supernatural abilities.

Hearing the woman pleading to her husband, I sneaked around the corner just in time to see her being manhandled into a carriage and then driven away.

Her high-pitched screams still resonated in my head as I passed Poska's Inn and watched the drunks attempt to drag themselves from the streets, leaving behind puddles of vomit. Finally, I arrived in Linton Road.

"She's absolutely baying for your blood," said Peter, as he passed me on the street. "You'll be the next murder victim we read about!"

"For crying out loud, she'll get her money!" I replied, walking up the path towards the front door of the manor.

"Well, if I hear any shouting from upstairs, don't expect

me to come save you."

"You're such a good neighbour," I called over my shoulder. "Arsehole!"

When I opened the door and stepped into the hallway, a sour, damp smell from a pile of wet clothes hanging over a winter-dyke, hit me. It just about disguised the foul odour of the rotten woodwork along the staircase, and the 'old woman' fragrance of shit and urine. As I checked for signs of my landlady and closed the door, a woman's voice called out behind me.

"What are you wearing?"

"Oh, not you again," I said, turning round to find Katie Norris, standing outside her door. "I told you, I'm not interested."

Katie grabbed my hand and dragged me into her small garret, overflowing with mannequins and sewing tables. The room was crowded with satin and velvet evening gowns, morning dresses in florals and pastels, and button-down blouses finished off with ornate brooches and pins.

"Can you believe I made all of this in a week?" she said, making a pathway through the hoard of leftover fabric. "I'm sure we'll find you something."

"We won't!" I replied, turning to leave. "Save it for your shop. I have to get upstairs before Miss Agatha finds me."

"Oh yes, she was here about an hour ago, asking if I'd seen you."

"What time is it?"

"10:30," Katie said, glancing at the carriage clock on her mantelpiece.

"Hmm, I'll wait another ten minutes, for her nap time."

"You'll have to pay her eventually," Katie replied. "You and Jacque should have known that nothing comes for free when you rent a room here."

"The Misfits' Manor," I said, rolling my eyes.

"Charming!"

As a reply, I stuck out my tongue.

"Just stand here a moment," Katie said, placing me in

front of a full-length mirror, and motioning towards me. "What was one thinking when she put on this morning's attire?"

Looking at my reflection, it was a sharp contrast to the woman standing beside me, with her tailored skirt, jacket with puffed-out sleeves, rosy cheeks, painted lips, and blonde hair twisted perfectly high in a bun.

"There is nothing wrong with me," I said.

"Your hair looks completely wild," Katie replied, ruffling my long, dishevelled black curls. "And your eyes-"

"What about my eyes?" I asked, examining the deep layer of smeared kohl around them.

"Oh, don't get me wrong, they're a lovely shade of grey, it's just this black muck makes your skin look even paler."

"That's none of your business!"

"Actually," she continued, "you always seem to wear black."

"Have you nothing more interesting to say to me? I do have a brain, you know."

"Sure you do," Katie replied, stroking my cheek.

"Excuse me," I said, swiping her hand away. "I am fluent in French, Italian, and Spanish, can recite passages from Shakespeare and Dickens, and know how to dissect a man's body from head to toe."

Katie laughed. "Oh, what's the point of a woman having a brain when you don't have a husband?"

"You don't have a husband."

"Not yet. I will one day."

Lifting a green feathered hat, I ran my fingers across the delicate appliqué around the rim. "What about your shop?"

"It's father's shop, really," Katie replied, taking the hat from me. "Once I'm married, I won't need it. Besides a lady has to be careful around these parts. Just think of all those murders. It terrifies me."

"Well, these are very difficult times."

"What kind of a man goes around slicing people to bits?

It was decapitation last week."

"How do you know it's not a woman?" I said, giving her a sideways glance.

Katie laughed. "A woman isn't able to do such things."

Not interested in listening to her nattering on about my murders, I decided to change the subject. "And what about all your hard work? That hat alone must have taken weeks to make."

"It's a sun bonnet," she said, "and stop avoiding the truth, a woman needs security, Elise. Remember that."

Aware of the daggers hidden inside my boots, I replied, "But we are capable of so much more."

Katie scowled and walked over to a drawer to remove a pale pink, chiffon dress, with bows at the collar. I took it as the perfect opportunity to hide my necklace, containing a vial of Jacque's blood. "What about this?" she said, holding the dress in front of me.

"No."

"It's very popular," Katie replied.

"I said no!"

"But it's far more elegant than this," she said, pulling at my coat.

"Don't touch it!" I snapped. "It has sentimental value."

Waving the dress at me, Katie sighed and said, "But maybe this will make Jacque come back to you. Men do like beautiful women."

"Jacque bought this!" I said, tracing my finger along my coat's ivy pattern embroidered on the purple velvet.

"Oh," Katie replied, with an awkward smile, placing the dress on the chair. After a brief pause, she continued, "Do you know there's a stain on it?"

"I cut my hand."

"Didn't you think to clean-"

"Goodbye, Katie," I said, running out the door.

As I went upstairs, I heard the sound of snoring coming from Miss Agatha's room.

"You're lucky, Elise," said Mr Mills, poking his head around his door. "You know she's looking for you?"

Ignoring him, I raced to my room in the attic. The air within was cold and dank, making me curl my toes, and hold my arms close to my chest. As I crossed the room, the floorboards creaked and a spider crawled out from underneath, looking at me, I suspected, with confusion.

"Don't ask," I said to it, holding my hand up. "It's been some morning."

Removing the daggers from my boots, I tossed them onto my bed, where they landed on a set of blackened bedsheets, ruined by massive patches of scorch marks. Again.

"I see you haven't changed the bed," I said to the spider, as I took off my coat, and wandered to the wardrobe, opening the doors. "I've done it for months, now. Surely it's your turn."

The spider scurried beneath the desk in the corner.

As I hung up my coat, I caught the faint smell of Jacque's aftershave lingering on his shirts. Taking one off the hanger, I held it close to me, and inhaled his scent. My Jacque.

After wrapping the shirt around my waist, I removed a pocket knife from a pair of trousers folded on a shelf.

Five… ten… fifteen… twenty… all the way up to three hundred and four, I counted, carving another tally mark into the wall above my bed. Three hundred and four days since Jacque was taken from me. As I stood back, the ruined bed sheets caught my eye, distracting me from admiring my handiwork. Tossing the knife onto the desk, I walked over to the wardrobe and took out one of the last sheets remaining on the shelf. Stripping the bed, I thought of the woman being forced into the carriage and what she might have done to get carted off to the asylum.

Had an affair?

Took no interest in motherhood?

Read too many novels?

If that's what they did to her, then what would they do to

a girl who bursts into flames while sleeping?
Something was happening to me.

CHAPTER THREE

In the distance, the clock tower bells struck ten o'clock. It was time.

I finished my last bite of stale bread and cheese before retrieving the daggers from under my bed and leaving.

Downstairs, the high-pitched screeches of my neighbours arguing echoed through the walls. (Mrs Mills has accused her husband of pawning her wedding ring to pay for his gambling. Mr Mills has responded by reminding her of the promise to bear him sons, but instead, all he got was two stillborn daughters.) Across the landing, Miss Agatha opened her door to poke her nose – along with the stench of patchouli – into other people's business. The baby on the second floor started to cry from all the disturbance, followed by his mother's boots scampering across the floorboards; the struggling poet on the ground floor bounded up the stairs, muttering profanities, and banged on the offending neighbour's door. As I passed him on the stairwell, he called to me whilst tapping his foot on the skirting board, "What do you make of this?"

I shrugged and left the house.

Dense clouds eclipsed the black sky. I wandered along the cobbled streets, passing Poska's Inn, Dante's Café, and a pack of men fawning over the scantily-clad ladies outside Mistress Lucille's "establishment". Keeping to the shadows, I lifted my hood and continued. One of Lucille's women approached me, patting my shoulder. When I turned, she withdrew her hand and frowned, looking down at my trousers.

"Sorry, little dear. I thought you were a man," she said.

I rolled my eyes and walked away.

"I didn't mean to offend you," she cried out.

"I know," I said, shuffling on quickly to avoid the on-lookers' stares.

As I crossed onto MacLeod Avenue, the rain started to pour, causing the streets to empty with rows of houses filled with silhouettes of men and women lighting lamps and drawing curtains. A sharp pain seared my ankle, as one of my daggers jabbed into it. Whatever occupied these families – eating supper, making polite conversation, or falling asleep, trying to ignore their spouses – at least I wouldn't be murdering them. Yet. I leaned down, readjusted my boot and ran across the road, traipsing through puddles, and slipping on cobbles. Gusts of wind blustered through the streets, almost knocking me off my feet, and rain battered across my face. Nothing could make me turn back. Numb, my fingers trembled inside my coat. Lightning struck the chimney of the house across the street, causing the bricks to plummet and smash the windows of a neighbouring house.

Shrouded in darkness, I took the quickest route past the slums and town square; broken street lamps and a howling dog welcomed me as I reached East Row. The clock tower bell struck eleven, and the storm settled, leaving me shivering outside Viktor Auldwyrd's three-storey house. A black cat crossed my path.

"Shoo!" I whispered, and it scampered behind a dustbin, rummaging for scraps.

With its crumbling walls and dilapidated roof, I walked towards the house's porch, searching for signs of easy entry. As I moved around the side, a figure, wearing an overgrown coat, appeared in the neighbour's garden and lit a cigarette. I crouched down, hid behind a rose bush, and kept watch.

"Did you find him?" said a woman, leaning over a balcony.

The figure, taken aback, took a quick drag before

stomping out the cigarette. From under a hood, a girl's voice stuttered, "Um, no, not yet."

"Oh, that little bugger," said the woman. "He'll be absolutely sodden."

"Rupert!" called the girl. "Rupert! Where are you?"

"Ah!" I grunted, feeling something brush against my leg.

"What was that?" said the woman.

I turned around to find the black cat nuzzling into my trousers.

The girl went inside the house, and came back out holding up a gas lamp. "I don't see anything, ma'am," she said.

The cat meowed.

"Rupert?" said the woman.

I grabbed the cat and tossed it towards the garden.

"Rupert!" the girl shouted, as the cat climbed through a gap in the fence.

"Nancy!" the woman said. "The neighbours. Be quiet, this instant!"

"Sorry, ma'am," the girl said, lifting the cat.

As the two women returned to the house, I sighed with relief, and sank into the wet grass. Once again, the street was silent. Out of the corner of my eye, I noticed a broken catch on one of Viktor's kitchen windows. Cautious of either of the two women reappearing, I crawled over a row of plants towards the window, and climbed inside. I stepped onto a worktop, and found the house in total darkness.

My boots squelched as they landed on the floor. I took the matches from my coat and struck one against the wall.

"Urgh!" I grumbled, removing the candle from my pocket. The wet wax disintegrated in my hand causing the wick to fall to the floor. "Bloody rain!"

Throwing the remains in the sink, I held the matchstick in front of me to search for a more substantial light. As I crept around the kitchen, the flame flickered against a shelf that was overflowing with utensils, cookbooks, and herbs. Ripping out a recipe page for Victoria sponge, I scrunched the paper and set it alight; better, but still not effective. Finally, as I entered the hallway, I found a paraffin lamp with just enough oil left to guide my way.

Room by room, I searched for Viktor with my dagger at the ready. Each room was elegant and pristine, with full china dinnerware covering the dining table, crystal chandeliers dangling from the ceilings, and gold, silver and porcelain figurines dotted throughout.

All except the library.

It was a large room, and unlike the other rooms well lived-in judging by the worn fabric of the chairs, stacks of newspapers, and a pipe and tartan slippers resting by the fireplace. Tables, cabinets, and windowsills overflowed with books and magazines, adding an antiquated smell to the already dusty air.

As I turned to leave the room, a magazine illustration of a shadow looming over a woman caught my eye. The scene was more humorous than horrific, with crude, cartoon claws drawing nearer as the woman fainted on a futon. I placed the dagger into my coat pocket, and lifted the magazine from the armchair, to take a closer look. On the opposite page, there was a poem – Little Girl of the Ashes.

Rest in peace in forgotten dreams,
Beneath where spirits dance between.
Here lies a little girl of the ashes,
With hunger born of blood-soaked sashes.
Wherever the bones and red rivers grow,
You'll find the girl, lurking below.
Where does she rise? Nobody knows.
A mortal life, how the death knell marches,
And grieving mourns for missing chances.
Upon the tomb where the reaper passes,
Here dies the little girl of the ashes.
(Written by N. Mikhailov)

Jacque would have liked it.

I tore out the page, and put it in my pocket, to give to

him when he returned.

After dropping the magazine to the floor, I left the library and went upstairs. Empty picture frames lined the walls with the remnants of slashed portraits scattered along the stairs. Reaching the landing, I tried the door handles of each room – all locked. As I walked through the narrow corridor, the floorboards creaked under my feet and a spider crawled along my boot, up onto my trouser leg. Swiping it away, within the darkness, I heard a door opening, so I hid in an alcove, waiting for someone to appear.

Nothing.

"I'm in here," said a man's voice.

I remained silent, refusing to move.

"Nobody else is here," the man said. "You are quite safe."

Removing the ruby-encrusted dagger from my boot, I crept towards the door. I checked the hallway ensuring no one was about to pounce, before stepping inside the room. On the floor, flies buzzed around plates of uneaten food and bundles of unwashed clothes. Cracked perfume bottles and a shattered mirror sat upon a dresser. The name "Emmeline" was scrawled in what looked like black ink across the bare walls. A torn, satin evening gown lay crumpled against the wardrobe.

"It's time then," said the man.

I raised the lamp, and saw him, lying on top of a mattress – a bald, middle-aged gentleman with an unruly beard and small round spectacles. Judging by his filthy shirt and waistcoat with his sweaty sour smell, he hadn't washed for more than a week.

"What is your name?" he asked, watching me circle around the bed.

I shook my head.

"I don't suppose it matters anyway," he said. "Are you going to kill me?"

"It depends. Are you Viktor Auldwyrd?"

"Yes," he replied.

"Then, aye. I am."

He smiled.

I placed the dagger at his throat. He didn't move or struggle. In fact, he didn't attempt to do anything.

"You can fight back, you know," I said.

He closed his eyes and sighed, as though already defeated.

I pressed the blade further into his skin, causing blood to drip onto my fingers. Viktor just stared at me, remaining still.

"Stop doing that," I said.

"What?" he mumbled.

"Looking at me. It's unnerving."

Viktor turned his head away from me. Confused, I removed the dagger and knelt on the bed.

"It's almost like you're begging me to do it," I said, shoving him.

"Why haven't you?" he said.

"It seems like an unfair fight," I replied, shuffling closer to him. "I'm used to punching, kicking, screaming – one woman even tried to decapitate me. But here you are, using emotions against me."

He ripped off a locket from around his neck and handed it to me.

"Open it," he said.

Dagger still in hand, I undid the clasp. Inside was a miniature of a familiar-looking, dark-haired woman with emerald eyes and a playful smile.

"What do you think?" Viktor said.

"She looks like she wants to haunt me," I replied, snapping the locket shut, and putting it in his trouser pocket.

"The dead often do."

"Hmm," I said. "I know."

"Did you murder her?" said Viktor, turning around.

The room fell silent, and I found myself unable to look at him.

"It's all right, I already know the answer," he said. "You

went all the way to Wales to kill her."

"That's where I was sent."

"Who sent you?"

"Don't ask questions."

"Why did you do it?"

"I said don't ask questions," I replied, gripping the dagger tighter.

"Her sister found her body. That's who she was visiting," Viktor said, his eyes filling with tears. "She said you made quite a mess of my wife."

"Her last words were about you," I whispered. "She said, 'tell him I love him.'"

"Well, I guess now you have," Viktor muttered. He frowned, reaching up to touch my hair. "Is it raining?"

"It was earlier," I replied.

"Emmy used to love the rain. She said it was good for the ducks. We don't even have ducks."

We both laughed.

"You must be frozen," Viktor continued.

"Oh, aye, maybe a little," I replied, wrapping my coat a little tighter around me.

He whimpered and I bent down to hear what he was saying. His dry lips brushed against my ear. "Do it. It will be a kindness," he said. "I just want to be with her."

I sat up and sniffed, gripping the dagger.

"Sorry if this wasn't more eventful. I'm just a fool in love," he smiled, holding my hand to guide the blade towards his throat.

"So am I," I replied.

He patted my arm as if to offer reassurance, and I sliced the dagger across his jugular. I had never seen a man, nor a woman, die with such a look of contentment.

CHAPTER FOUR

The next morning, I woke up to the sound of someone banging on my door.

"Elise, get out here!" said a gruff woman's voice.

I groaned and climbed out of bed. "Coming, Miss Agatha."

Bang. Bang. Bang.

"Elise, if you don't answer, I'm going to-"

"What?" I said, opening the door.

Miss Agatha pursed her lips and folded her arms, looking me up and down. "Good morning."

"Good morning," I smiled, keeping my bloodstained clothes hidden.

"Did you sleep in your clothes?"

"Aye."

The old, wart-faced woman narrowed her eyes and sniffed.

"How can I help you, Miss Agatha?" I said.

She gave me a letter, sealed with black wax.

"Thank you," I said, waiting for her to leave. Instead, she sucked her teeth and leaned against the wall.

"Aren't you wondering who it's from?"

"I know who it's from," I replied, starting to close the door.

"I want my rent money. You're three months behind already."

"I paid you last week."

"No, last week you said you were going to pay me this week."

"I did?"

"Aye! You owe me thirty-two shillings."

My nose started to twitch. I grabbed a handkerchief from Miss Agatha's pocket. "Ah-choo!"

After blowing my nose, I handed her the frayed, patchouli-soaked rag. "Idol, have mercy," she said, looking at it with disgust.

"I'll get you the money. Promise," I assured her, and closed the door in her face.

As I turned around, I saw a spider descend from a chair's armrest, and land upon the floor. "You are so lucky that you don't have to deal with annoying landladies," I said to it, then broke the seal on the envelope. The penmanship was instantly recognisable – Bothwell, summoning me to the Inservium. I ripped up the letter, and sneezed again. "Urgh! These murders will be the death of me."

I looked over to the bed, and saw scorch marks all over my bedsheets. In a desperate attempt to conceal them, I gathered all my pillows and blankets, and dumped them on top. It is a universal truth that if one does not see something, then one does not have to deal with it.

After washing, I changed into a pair of Jacque's trousers and a shirt, my boots, fingerless gloves, a scarf and coat – then left. As I turned into the stairwell leading to the ground floor, the weapons hidden inside my clothes rattled softly and reassuringly against my pockets. The poet was screeching away on his violin, and the distinct smell of absinthe wafted into the hallway. For once, the baby next door was quiet. I couldn't help but smile as I reached the bottom step. Despite the fact that three apartments had been advertised when Jacque and I first arrived, Miss Agatha had only offered us the dingy attic.

"Newlyweds can't afford to be fussy," she said.

"Oh, we're not marr-" I replied, but Jacque interrupted.

"It'll do nicely."

"No good having domestic sensibilities," Miss Agatha

added.

We agreed, if only to enable us to shut the door and get rid of the old woman. The furnishings might have been scarce and the walls and floor bare, but the attic space had been all ours.

Tucking my scarf into my coat, I stepped into the hallway, narrowly avoiding a pair of crusty wet knickers hanging over the banister.

"Elise!" came a familiar man's voice from behind the front door.

It can't be, I thought, watching the handle turn.

The door opened and there he was. Black hair, tied at the back, with stray strands around his face hiding the frown lines, icy blue eyes, smudged with kohl, and traces of scars under his collar.

"Jacque!" I cried out, running towards him.

"Don't," he yelled, holding out his hand to ward me off.

As soon as I wrapped my arms around him, he screamed out and collapsed against me.

"You were too late," he whispered.

Beneath my hands, I felt him being taken from me – dying – as his limbs and torso melted, and clotted into a mass of flesh and bones.

"What's happening?" I said, gripping him tighter.

"You were supposed to save me," Jacque replied.

"I can still save you."

Unable to breathe. Unable to speak. Unable to feel him, I clenched my fists desperate to keep him.

"I'm sorry," he said, kissing my cheek.

Bit by bit his body crumbled into a thousand tiny pieces of ash and hopelessness, until he disappeared. He left me. Again.

"Jacque?" I muttered, trembling as I fell onto a step.

Behind me, a door creaked open.

"You all right?" said Mrs Mills, coming down the stairs. "You're as pale as a ghost."

"I'm fine," I mumbled.

"If you're fine, why are you shaking?" she replied. "Has Peter been giving you opium? Honestly, he should stick to writing those ridiculous sonnets."

"No, really," I said, clinging onto the bannister and hauling myself up.

I offered Mrs Mills a half-hearted smile before running from the house towards the Inservium.

***

It was only your imagination, I told myself, approaching the large iron gate. Clutching at the bars, I watched a group of Councillors huddled in the graveyard. Jacque would be safe. He had to be.

I stepped inside the building, and was met by an obese middle-aged man with blond hair and two missing front teeth. Councillor Lennox. He grunted, and held out a folded piece of paper. As I reached to grab it, he released his fingers, allowing the paper to fall to the floor.

"Why was Viktor Auldwyrd expecting me?" I said. "He wanted me to kill him."

Lennox snorted, and walked away.

"You're getting rid of husbands and wives now?" I called out. "What next, whole families?"

The Councillor turned to fix me with a threatening stare, then left without another word.

I leaned down and placed the piece of paper in my coat pocket. As I stood, I felt a hand take a firm grip of the back of my neck, and force me into a dark corner. I turned around and the hand took hold of my shoulder. The sweaty palm and fingers moved up my throat, and towards my chin, squeezing tighter until they pinned my head against the wall. Despite not being able to see him, I felt the flutter of Bothwell's breath against my lips. His voice was low and measured.

"Should I tell Jacque that you no longer care about him? Hmm?" he said. "Do you not remember what happened the last time you asked questions?"

I nodded, and he pressed his fingernails into my cheeks.

"It would be a pity if that were to occur again," he said, before continuing. "The poor boy screamed for hours. And it was all your fault. Do you want that to happen again, Elise?"

"No," I mumbled.

"Why didn't you bring back the weapons last night?" Bothwell growled.

"There was a storm."

"And?"

"I thought it best to wait."

Bothwell laughed. "That was your second mistake. Poor Jacque."

"I promise to bring them back tonight," I said.

"Say you're sorry," Bothwell whispered into my ear.

"I'm… I'm sorry."

"Now, what was that about Viktor Auldwyrd?"

"Nothing. Nothing at all," I said.

"Good for you," he replied, slowly kissing both my cheeks before releasing me. "Now, go."

Feeling the sickness rise in my stomach, I ran from the Inservium. As I stepped outside, the warmth of sunlight washed over me. I walked across the graveyard and leaned against a willow tree. "Jacque will come back," I muttered, sweat dripping down my forehead whilst I struggled to catch my breath. In the distance, Councillors were toing and froing, flicking through prayer books, and prostrating to their Idol in the sky.

For the first time since I was a child, I climbed a tree and sat a while. With the branches and leaves wrapped around me, I felt safe knowing they sheltered me from the world.

I removed the piece of paper from my coat, and couldn't believe whose name was written upon it. Mhayree de Loire.

My mother's oldest friend. For the life of me, I couldn't fathom why the Councillors would want her dead? As far as I was aware, she posed no threat to society. She had done what was expected of her – got married, had a child, and kept a clean, respectable household. Although, perhaps the same could've been said for all my victims.

At least she would be easy to find.

The longer I sat, the more I found myself imagining her death. Strangulation. Stabbing. Decapitation. I considered the different options, attempting to settle on the most humane. Maybe I should have felt guiltier about the prospect of killing her. After all, when I was a child, she was the one who sneaked me an extra biscuit during teatime, let me play dress-up with her gowns, hats, and fur coats, and bought me my favourite porcelain doll.

But I didn't feel guilt.

My job was simple. Kill. Don't get caught. Save Jacque.

Dusk was setting in. I tore up the piece of paper and fed it to the wind.

***

Later that night, I had a small dinner of fish pie at Poska's Inn, and a dram of whisky at Dante's, before walking to the de Loire house.

The building was just as I remembered: cream stone walls, arched windows with balconies, and a red door with a silver crescent-shaped handle.

Finding the windows and door locked, I tightened the belt around my waist and scaled a large ivy-covered lattice fence, until I landed on the porch roof. Climbing onto the ledge of the first storey, I came to a balcony, whereby I attempted to open the window. Locked. No matter, a girl does what she must do. Wiping my brow and removing the stray ivy leaves which had got caught in my hair, I heaved myself onto another ledge and reached the second storey. Again, the windows were locked. Does nobody trust anyone these days? I thought. As my daggers rattled inside my coat pockets, I grasped onto the guttering and manoeuvred onto the roof. Unlike the houses commissioned by Councillors for the townspeople, the older ones always had secret hatches hidden in the rooftops. Crawling along uneven tiles, I grabbed onto the chimney, letting myself through the hatch and into the attic.

Waiting for me was Mhayree de Loire, holding out a cup of tea.

"It's either Earl Grey or a good thrashing. Your choice," she said with a Glaswegian lilt.

She hadn't aged a day in the past fifteen years. Not one speck of grey tainted her bright red hair and her blue eyes still maintained their youthful innocence. She stood in front of me with a hand on her hip, chin in the air and somehow not looking directly at me, as though daring me to make the wrong decision.

"I thought they might try to kill me," she said, with a sarcastic smile. "I didn't think they would send one of our own, though."

"One of your own?" I asked.

"Oh, that's right, you don't know," she sighed. "How very sad."

As she moved towards me, the pieces of fabric hanging from her white nightgown swept along the ground like tentacles.

"What do you mean?" I said, grabbing a dagger from my pocket.

"How are you sleeping? Any scorch marks yet?"

I held the dagger in front of me, and narrowed my eyes. How could she possibly know?

"Hmm," she said, raising an eyebrow. "I suggest you go home, my dear. Your mother misses you."

"I highly doubt that."

"What did you expect her to do, Elise? You know how your father is."

"Aren't you the slightest bit worried that I'm pointing a dagger at you?" I said.

Mhayree laughed. "I heard you got involved with some boy. Does he know you're doing this?"

"Don't talk about him!"

She tapped the blade with her finger, before smacking it from my hand, and leaned down to stare at me. "Is that how the Inservium got to you? Is that how they turned you into a murderer?"

"What would you know?" I said, slapping her across the face.

Without flinching, she caught my wrist. "Tell me, my dear, how good does a lover need to be to make you want to slaughter dozens of innocent people?"

As raw anger took hold of me, I punched her in the chest. She tutted, rolled her eyes, and tossed the cup of tea in the air before tackling me to the ground.

Within seconds, she stood up.

Not to be outdone, I kicked her in the groin, and she fell to her knees. She whacked the bridge of my nose, the impact causing my eyes to water.

I removed a bronze-gilded dagger from my belt and swiped at her throat. She swerved back and twisted my arm before the blade could touch her skin.

I hit her in the mouth and blood trickled from her lip.

"Aye, not bad," she nodded, and kicked me in the stomach.

Shocked and winded, I collapsed on the floor, unable to breathe. She pulled my hair, ripping out chunks, and slammed my head into the floorboards.

Every time we kicked, punched, and scratched, we crashed through furniture, or collided with the walls.

"Mama," shouted a young girl's voice from downstairs.

Mhayree stopped fighting and pinned me to the floor. "Darling, you shouldn't be out of bed," she called back.

"I heard noises," she yawned.

"Your daughter?" I said, as Mhayree climbed off me.

She lifted the broken cup and saucer from the floor and handed it to me.

"Noises? I didn't hear any noises," she said, whilst trying to hold me up.

"Is it the girl who was climbing up to the roof?"

Mhayree shook her head and took a deep breath. "Say something."

"What?" I replied, as a sharp pain shot through my ribs.

"Say something. She's obviously seen you."

"We're having tea," I yelled, wincing at what felt like broken bones.

Mhayree patted my back. "Earl Grey. Good decision."

"Thank you."

"Go back to bed, Freya," Mhayree said. "I'll be through shortly to tuck you in."

At the sound of the young girl's feet scampering away, Mhayree turned to me and whispered, "Mama has a family to protect!"

She gathered up my daggers, paying particular attention to the runes engraved on each one. "Nemes," she whispered.

"What?" I said.

Mhayree grabbed me around the waist, and dragged me from the attic.

"What is a Nemes?" I said, slamming into a wall to stay upright. By the doorway stood a brunette girl – no more than six years old – in her night dress, clutching a doll.

"Ask your mother," Mhayree replied, as we collided into the bannister. Down three flights of stairs, until reaching the front door.

Mhayree shoved me outside, after placing the weapons into my pockets.

"I'm guessing you won't be trying to kill me again," Mhayree said.

With a swollen lip, half-shut eye, bloody nose, possible broken ribs, and what felt like a dislocated shoulder, I thought it best to shake my head in agreement.

She walked me to the gate and whistled. Within seconds, a carriage drew up in front of us. When we stepped onto the pavement, the driver – with his black cloak, top hat, and black leather gloves – bowed his head to Mhayree. She spoke to him in a foreign language that I did not recognise, and he turned to face me. As I looked more closely, it was clear that he was no man, but a skeleton. Instead of eyes, two flames watched me as they flickered in his sockets. A maggot emerged from the right one and dropped onto my boot. He leaned down and sniffed me, then tilted his head towards Mhayree. She nodded, opened the carriage door and pushed me inside.

"*Tutta va illna dentka. Kusta na va tulan laupnoom. Pukktan?*" Mhayree said to the driver before turning to me. "And as for you, Elise. Tell the Councillors that death has blessed this house and given us a free passage. Their Idol may not be as merciful! Now. Go. Home."

She slammed the door shut and walked away. The crack of a whip made the horses rear up and bolt into the night.

CHAPTER FIVE

The next morning, I woke on my bed, with bandages soaked in yarrow and witch hazel leaves wrapped around my body. Beads of sweat dripped down my face as my temperature spiked, causing my eyes, cheeks, and chapped lips to burn. Above me, a spider descended from its web, and swooped towards the bed.

"Most peculiar," it said.

"Shh," I replied. "Spiders can't talk."

The little arachnid stared at me with its big red eyes. "You make the most peculiar choices."

I held my hand out in protest and saw my knuckles covered in blood.

"Most peculiar choices," said the spider.

As I looked down, the blood oozing from my flesh floated into the air. The spider's legs popped the droplets like bubbles, making them dissolve.

Landing on my chest, the spider carefully examined my wounds as a doctor would a patient. "Very interesting, Little Girl of the Ashes," it said.

The spider perched as though sitting at a spindle, rubbed its legs together, and produced a silk thread.

"What are you doing?" I mumbled, my eyes growing heavy.

"Being peculiar," the spider said, knitting together the layers of my flesh. "Goodnight."

"Goodnight," I said.

Then the room turned black.

Footsteps stomping.

"Who's there?" I whispered, still half-asleep.

The door creaked shut. Behind my closed eyes, I felt sparks sizzling, desperate to be released. I peeled back my blanket to let the cold air hit me and opened my eyelids. Instantly, searing hot sparks shot from my pupils, crackling and smouldering before fizzling out.

"It has to be madness," I directed to the spider, sitting on my pillow. "I'm resigned to the fact that I'm mentally unhinged. And will commit myself into an asylum once Jacque is safe."

The spider scurried up the wall.

On the other side of the room, I caught my reflection in the mirror. Strips of fabric from my torn clothes covered the bed, leaving me half naked upon the sheets. I ran my hand across my chest, bound with tight bandages. The yarrow and witch hazel's mushy leaves and white petals seeped through the cotton. The cuts and bruises on my face had gone. There was no blood on my hands. I unwound the bandage covering my shoulder and raised my arms one at a time. No pain. As each bandage was removed, the gooey, green plant mix slid off my body, leaving no trace of wounds, broken bones, or stitches – not one scar.

"Perhaps the asylum won't be so bad," I said to the spider. "Mrs Johnson just got released and she seems fine."

The spider didn't answer.

"Wait! The footsteps," I continued, reaching for a dagger under my bed. "Someone was in my room whilst I was sleeping."

As I sat upright, I noticed a scrap of parchment, scribbled with red lettering, stuck on the inside of my door with a knife. Straining, I climbed out of bed and fell to the floor. I never realised how bloody freezing this room was. Or how the rough wood grain of the floorboards made impressions of themselves onto my knees and hands.

Crawling across the room, every creak reverberated through the palms of my hands. Exhausted, I leaned against the wall and pulled myself to stand as the chipped ivory paint lodged beneath my fingernails.

With one swift move, I ripped down the parchment:

It has come to our attention that your lack of competence failed to ensure the success of the instructions imparted by those better than you. Your failings have forced us to spill another's blood. We have decided however, to show leniency towards you. Henceforth, you have until midnight to complete your holy assignment. Rest well, Elise.

B.

"Jacque," I whispered, tracing my hand over the red ink. "What have they done to you?"

Walking across the room, I ripped apart the parchment and undid the latch on the window. As I threw the pieces outside, the wind carried some away to far forgotten places and others landed in a puddle outside the house. A woman pushing a pram strolled past whilst a little boy trailed behind.

"Why is that puddle turning red mammy?" he said.

"Come along, Alistair," said the woman, ignoring him.

Jacque's blood seeped onto the street.

I closed the window, leaned against the wall, and slid towards the floor. At least this time, Bothwell hadn't sent a piece of Jacque's flesh – although who knows how he had gotten the blood. Maybe it meant Jacque was dead. Would Bothwell kill him without telling me? Maybe. Then again, perhaps all I needed to do was behave and he'd be safe. Not if he's already dead, though.

"No, no, that can't be possible," I said, twiddling the dagger between my fingers. "I just need to kill Mhayree before midnight and everything will be fine."

I ran to the wardrobe and opened it. Rummaging through

a pile of Jacque's clothes, I found, hidden at the bottom, one of his books – *Plantes Dangereuses*. I skimmed through pages filled with Jacque's notes and corrections, until reaching a page entitled "*Belle Mais Mortelle Femme*." Underneath was a sketch of a delicate, purple flower with tiny black berries – Belladonna. According to the author, Monsieur Boucher, ingestion of these berries would induce hallucinations, convulsions, delirium, and eventually, death.

Perfect. And I knew just where to get it.

I threw on some clothes, a pair of boots, and a scarf from the pile on the floor. Looking at the mass of herbs and yet another set of scorch marked bedsheets, I decided to leave the clean-up until later. I washed and dressed, grabbed my purple coat, and left with a plan already forming.

The sun was high in the sky, and the streets were crowded with gentlemen in top hats and ladies with parasols – the sort of people who used to stare at Jacque and me with contempt and make ugly comments under their breath. Packs of women were huddled together, concocting dinner party plans and little trysts that would keep the call of the embroidery needle at bay. The men congratulated themselves on their latest financial triumphs and made lewd jokes. The prostitutes were still in bed.

"Fresh apples! Five for a shilling!"

"Meat pies! Best in Loch Fala!"

"Nice juicy haddock! Caught this morning!"

"Milk! Cheese! Fresh from the farm!"

Walking past the market vendors, the smell of warm, newly-baked bread filled the street, causing my stomach to rumble. The baker's window was filled with rows upon rows of scrumptious cakes – lemon buns, vanilla slices, and custard patties – tempting me inside. Just looking at them made me all the hungrier, until I could almost taste them. A bell rang as I opened the door and hurried towards the cake stand. After picking out two almond tarts, I shovelled the first into my mouth – savouring each and every bite. Mrs

Lovell, the baker's wife, stood behind the counter, with a look of disgust on her face.

"Hungry, are we?" she said.

"It would seem so," I said, with pastry crumbs spluttering everywhere.

"And how do you intend to pay for those?"

Swallowing the last bite, I dipped my hand into my trouser and coat pockets, searching for coins. None.

"Umm…"

Mrs Lovell looked me up and down, as though concerned. "You've lost an awful lot of weight lately."

"Things are just a little difficult at the moment," I said, removing a ring from my hand and placing it on the counter. "Would you accept this? It's not much, but the silver should get you some money."

Mrs Lovell, without glancing at the old, tarnished piece of tat, placed it in her pocket. "Of course. Just this once, mind."

"Thank you, Mrs Lovell," I said, smiling. "How is Mr Lovell?"

"Oh, grumpy as always," she replied, laughing. "The damned brute locked me out of the house for three hours last week for eating one of his pastries."

"I hope you gave him what-for."

"Well, I didn't want to make a fuss," Mrs Lovell said, as another customer walked through the door. As I turned to leave, she called after me. "Be sure to enjoy the other almond tart. They're my favourite."

I looked down at the perfect, deliciously sweet tart sitting like a prize in my hand. The golden crust crumbled against my fingertips as the flaky almonds sank into the creamy, thick filling. It might have been my only meal that day, but it didn't matter. Mrs Lovell was busy packing bread and various cakes into a bag whilst the customer complained about the unpredictable weather. I slipped into a corner, ever watchful of the women behind me, and placed the tart on a table. Removing a dagger from my coat, I sliced into the pastry, and cut it in half. After hiding the dagger, I bit into my half of the tart, and placed the other upon the counter.

"For you, Mrs Lovell. Don't tell your husband," I said.

Taken aback, Mrs Lovell stuttered, "Thank you."

Without turning back, I waved and upon opening the door, a gust of wind caught me by surprise.

Outside, a newspaper vendor hollered at the top of his voice. His ramblings were undiscernible, but I almost choked on my last morsel of pastry as I read the headline on the front page: Murderer on the Rampage: Auldwyrd's Throat Slit. I walked over to the vendor, and, sighing, accepted a copy of the Daily Alba.

"Shocking that, innit?" the vendor said, with a heavy Cockney accent. "You sure you want to read that, Miss?"

Ignoring him, I quickly skimmed through the story.

"Not even a suspect," the vendor continued. "What do you make of it? I hope you're keepin' safe."

"Hmm," I replied, whilst reading about "poor" Councillor Bothwell, who found the body and thought it was his duty to inform the innocent citizens of Loch Fala. Of course he did; he wanted me to know how easily he could expose me.

"Come on sweetheart, are you takin' that or what?" the vendor grumbled. "Tell you what, give us threepence and I'll throw in a Phantasma for ya."

I looked up at the unkempt fifty-year-old man, wearing a navy flat cap, fingerless gloves with holes, a ragged ruby scarf, and a patched-up frock coat. "I don't have any money," I said.

"None?" he replied.

"No."

"You sure?"

"Aye!"

"What are you 'ere for, then?"

"I'm reading."

"This ain't a library."

"I'll be done in a minute."

"I've got a livin' to make."

"Then do it. There's people everywhere," I said, waving my finger at potential customers.

The man grabbed the newspaper out of my hand. "If you read it, you buy it!"

Rolling my eyes, I snatched the newspaper back. "Fine! Would you consider taking my scarf?"

"What?"

"You seem to need a new scarf. Would you take mine as payment?"

The man thought for a moment, before nodding his head. "All right, that'll do."

"I'll be naked at this rate, if this continues," I whispered to myself.

"What?"

"Nothing," I said. Glad at the thought of getting rid of him, I handed over the scarf and accepted the purchases.

"Enjoy Little Girl of the Ashes." he said.

Startled, I said, "Why… Why did you call me that? What have I got to do with ashes?"

With a blank stare he replied, "It's a story in the Phantasma."

Making apologies, I clutched the Daily Alba and the Phantasma to my chest and scrambled to make my way back into the bustle of the street. As I stepped into the middle of a puddle, I caught the reflection of the vendor, eyeing me with suspicion. As the crowd huddled around the market stalls, he disappeared.

In the distance, the clock tower bell struck one. It was now or never for getting the belladonna. It seemed that Mhayree was right. I had to go back to my family.

***

After walking the length of town, I arrived – for the first time in over a year – at the de Volonté manor. The grey stonework was dilapidated and weary against the imposing three storeys. Warts of moss nestled along the walls and sprigs of dead weeds tormented the corners of the windows. The house looked grief-stricken for hopes that had been lost. The rusted iron gate groaned as it opened.

I entered the house, but only silence welcomed me. The musky scent of its antique furnishings filled the air. The green and gold wallpaper was peeling from the walls, and the oak floorboards were scratched and scuffed. Portraits of past generations hung in the hallway; but not one image of me. The fire had been allowed to go out; ashes and soot dirtied the Persian rug. The photo frames had been smashed and the portraits torn, layers of dust covered each surface, and the windows looked as if someone had attempted to blacken them. From the corner, the mahogany grandfather clock chimed two o'clock. My father would still be at work, my sister, Amelie, would be in school, and my brother, Étienne – well, I didn't care where he was.

As I wandered through the parlour, a woman's sad and lonely voice called out, "Nobody is here."

"It's me, mother."

No reply.

"Kitty! Fran! Are you there?" I shouted, walking into the dining room. "Mother, where are the maids?"

Sitting at the table, my mother stared at the ceiling. "Not here. Nobody is here."

I stood behind the chair, and wrapped my arms around her. She didn't respond, even when I moved to sit opposite her and hold her hand.

"Why are you so warm?" I said. "Look, your fingers are turning scarlet."

Again, no response.

Underneath her dishevelled, white-blonde hair, tearstains covered her pale face, and her bottom lip quivered. Her ivory-laced corset and snow-white petticoat drowned her skinny, fragile body.

45

"Why didn't you dress today, mother?"

For the third time, she gave no reply.

"I brought a Phantasma for Amelie and Étienne," I said, throwing it onto the table, alongside the newspaper.

The noise jolted my mother out of her daydream. "Elise?"

"Yes, mother," I said, continuing to read about Viktor Auldwyrd's murder. "Don't worry, I'll be gone before father arrives home."

She patted my hand and sobbed. "Elise, my little girl, how did this happen? I'll make it better, you'll see."

"Have you seen Mhayree, lately?"

She hesitated, before answering, "Why?"

Before I could reply, she caught a glimpse of the Daily Alba and snatched it from me.

"Mother!"

"I won't believe any of it!" she cried, tearing up the newspaper and throwing it out the window.

"What did you do that for?" I said, jumping out of my seat.

My mother composed herself and brushed the strands of hair from her face before turning to me. "My goodness, you still have your coat and boots on."

"What about the newspaper?"

"If you wear them indoors, you won't feel the benefit when you go outside."

"I'm sure I'll be fine."

"It's winter, you know."

I laughed, and shook my head, knowing there was no use trying to make sense of her. "You're right. I'll go and take them off."

"No, just put your boots in the usual place and I'll take your coat."

"No, really, I can do it," I said, feeling the weight of the daggers inside my pockets.

As I walked into the hallway, I turned back to see her staring into thin air and fidgeting with her petticoat. "I'll be back in a minute, mother," I lied, heading around the corner towards my father's study.

The door, as usual, was locked. However, I had long since learned that my father was as lazy as he was stupid, and hid the key in a vase outside the room. I let myself inside and was taken aback by the putrid stench of stale alcohol and tobacco. Finding the belladonna was easy, as he kept samples amongst jars of eyeballs, tongues, and vials of bodily fluid. I rummaged through drawers, searching for his medical instruments to extract the poison from the plant. Each one was filled to the brim with sketches of his experiments on patients: dissections, mutilations, and lobotomies. Of course, despite the countless men, women, and children who died at my father's hands, the Councillors hailed him as a genius.

"Forget it!" I hissed, looking at the room which lay in disarray. "Back to basics."

Amongst a pile of empty port bottles, sat a bundle of old, tattered books. Standing at the desk, I removed the belladonna's berries, placed them in an ashtray, and squashed them with a hardback copy of *Gray's Anatomy*.

It would be easy; all I had to do was show up at Mhayree's house, feign a few "damsel in distress" tears, offer a heartfelt apology, ask if we could sit down to tea, and slip the belladonna into her cup.

Once finished with the berries, I poured the juice into an empty vial, and – with meticulous care and attention – cleaned up, leaving the room exactly as I had found it.

As I locked the door behind me, I caught my mother placing an envelope on a side cabinet, before she sneaked back to the dining room. Walking past, I noticed my name scribbled on the front.

"What's this?" I called out.

No reply.

Back in the dining room, I found my mother, standing with her back against the wall, gazing into the empty distance. Knowing there was no point talking to her, I placed the envelope in my pocket and left. As I opened the front door, I heard my mother sigh, "Goodbye dear."

When I reached the street corner, I opened the envelope to find ten pounds. Part of me wanted to go back and throw it in my mother's face, but another part – the more sensible one – remembered the costs of rent and food. Damn.

The clock tower bell struck three. Father would be home soon. My footsteps quickened.

Heading back into town, I stopped by the linen shop to buy a pile of fresh bedsheets. I was convinced that the owner, Mrs Ruthyard, thought I had a black-market business, whereby I resold the new sheets for a tidy profit, or some sort of fetish, the evidence of which could not be easily cleaned away.

As usual, Mrs Ruthyard was waiting behind the counter, peering over her glasses.

"The usual young lady?" she said, with a haughty tone.

"Aye, thank you," I replied.

Without taking her eyes from me, she pointed to a pile of sheets folded on the counter and held out her hand for payment. I removed the envelope from my pocket, and handed over three shillings.

"Until next week," Mrs Ruthyard said, sniffing.

Before I could answer, the air grew thick and hot, causing the room to spin. As I dropped the sheets, and steadied myself against the counter, Mrs Ruthyard ran towards the storeroom.

"You better not have scarlet fever!" she shrieked.

Then, standing behind her, he appeared. Jacque. Black hair, tied at the back. Random strands around his face. Blue eyes staring right through me. Ripped clothes hanging off his body. Blood pouring down his face, throat, and wrists.

I lifted the top slate of the counter and edged towards him, with my hand outstretched. Head tilted to the side, he watched, willing me to reach him. He held out his arms and smiled. The blood pouring from his mouth dripped onto the floor, spelling out the word "Elise". The room turned black until there was nothing left but him and me. As I stood inches away from him, the blood pooled around me, creeped up my legs until it covered my entire body. Jacque frowned and turned his back to me.

Suddenly, in the distance, I heard Mrs Ruthyard's voice. "Insubordinate little urchin! What do you suppose you are doing? Customers stay behind the counter at all times – at all times behind the counter!"

Within seconds, the blackness faded, and I found myself, once again, standing outside the storeroom. Mrs Ruthyard was pressed against the wall, looking flabbergasted and turning a sickly shade of rosy pink.

Jacque disappeared.

"I'm so sorry," I said, fighting back the tears. "I don't know what… I… I… I have to go."

Slamming the coins onto the counter, I grabbed the sheets, ran from the shop, down the road and around the corner into an alleyway. Alone and tired, I collapsed onto the cobbles, trying to catch my breath. It wasn't real, I told myself, over and over. None of it was real.

Unaware of how long I remained there, the streets fell silent as the market vendors packed up for the night, and the customers moseyed back to their houses. The sun was setting as the clock tower bells struck five.

Across the road, men and women sauntered into Danté's to sample his infamous watered-down whisky and questionable mutton pie. Within minutes, I joined them, if only to spend a few hours in the cocoon of music, food, and other people's laughter, where I could forget about killing Mhayree, about seeing Jacque and about the Inservium.

***

As night descended, I left the inn – stomach full of pie – and headed towards Mhayree's house. Every few steps, I checked my pocket to ensure the vial of belladonna was safe. I knew she would be suspicious of me, but how dangerous could a girl be – in particular, one laden with bedsheets, offering an apology, and craving a spot of tea?

Retracing my steps from the night before, I carried on, hiding between the shadows of hazy streetlights towards her front door, only to find it ajar.

"Hello?" I said, edging into the hallway.

No answer. A lamp sitting on an oak table shone onto a wooden box, alongside a note addressed to me.

"Mhayree, are you there?" I shouted, reading the inscription.

Dear Elise, take this box to the Inservium. Do not open beforehand.

"Now isn't this interesting?" I mused, searching room to room for any signs of life. All around, furniture was smashed and scattered across the house as though a struggle had taken place. Dagger at the ready, I walked along the hallway with shards of china vases crunching beneath my footsteps. A large portrait knocked from the wall blocked my way upstairs. Negotiating my way past the frame, I reached the first floor and found the nursery intact, but the drawers and wardrobe lay open and empty.

"Mhayree? I'm here to help you," I called out whilst crossing the landing to open another door. As soon as I stepped over the threshold into the master bedroom, I was welcomed by blood splattered walls and a pile of blood-soaked sheets. But no body. Uncertain as to whether Mhayree was the victim or perpetrator, I closed the door, only too glad I wouldn't have to share another pot of tea with her.

Preparing to leave, and standing in the hallway, curiosity got the better of me. I tried to open the lid of the box, only to have it snap shut on me.

Take the box.

Don't take the box.

Take the box.

Don't take the box.

How to save Jacque if Mhayree isn't dead?

Take the box.

Don't take the box.

Lie to Bothwell. Tell him she's dead.

Take the box.

Don't take the box.

Bothwell would never know any different.

Take the box.

Don't take the box.

But what if he did?

Take the box.

Laden down with the box and bedsheets, I stumbled onto the street, and whistled for a carriage. Within seconds, the skeleton driver arrived and jumped down from his seat, to open the door.

Startled, I fell back upon the gate. "So, it wasn't a dream."

He shook his head.

"How can this be happening?" I said, edging towards him and moving my hand up to touch his skull. "What are you?"

He grunted and turned away to avoid my touch.

"I won't come with you. Not after last time."

The skeleton didn't move. I whistled again. And again. And again. But no other carriage appeared.

"You can't take me to the Inservium. What if people see you?"

The skeleton clapped his hands, and a mass of fog engulfed him. Suddenly, a layer of skin, curly black hair, fingernails, a nose, mouth and a pair of brown eyes materialised upon his body – complete with top hat and tails.

"None of this is real, is it?" I said.

The skeleton smiled, took my arm, and led me into the carriage, placing the box and bedsheets beside me. After shutting the door, he climbed onto his seat, and with a crack of a whip we were off.

When we arrived at the Inservium, the building was lit with candles and organ music filled the air. No sooner had I stepped onto the pavement, the driver whisked off into the distance, leaving me standing at the gate, weighed down with the linen and box. I walked along the path of the graveyard and through the large, arched door, to find the Councillors kneeling in front of a fire pit, next to their Idol's statue. I paid no attention to their prayers and instead strode down the aisle and stood behind Bothwell.

"What is she doing here?" said the fat, decrepit Councillor Holt.

Bothwell's eyes bore into me. He rose to his feet, poked me in the chest, and growled, "How dare you disturb our prayers! That de Loire woman had better be dead, or so help me, I'll kill the boy for this."

"This is for you," I said, pushing the box towards him.

"What is it?"

"A surprise."

Placing it on the floor, he opened the lid and grimaced. "A little theatrical. We don't actually need to see evidence of your evil," he said, pulling out a clump of red hair attached to a severed head. Mhayree.

"Well, I-"

"I believe she had a daughter," Bothwell continued, throwing the head into the fire. "Was she there at the time?"

None of the Councillors reacted – or seemed to notice the bloodstained face melting in the flames.

"I believe not," I replied.

"Kill her too. Oh, and remember to put the weapons back," Bothwell said, patting my head. "The boy will remain safe. See what happens when you behave?"

Kneeling, he returned to his prayers.

Chapter Six

Knock, knock, knock.

"Go away," I groaned, pulling the pillow around my ears.

Knock, knock, knock.

"You answer it," I said to the spider, who had made itself quite comfortable crouching on my cheek.

Knock, knock, knock.

The spider turned towards the door, gave me a quick glance, then retreated up a thread and onto a beam.

Knock, knock, knock.

"Wait a minute!" I shouted, climbing out of bed.

A few arduous steps later, I reached the door, and with two hands, turned the handle to prise it open.

"Mother?"

"Yes," she said, peeling back a green hood to reveal her waif-like face, and red eyes.

Wrapping her arms around me, she held me tight. I didn't return the gesture.

"What are you doing here, mother?"

"I was just passing," she replied, releasing me. Her whole body shivered, as though her bones may shatter, as she pushed past me into the room.

"By all means, come in," I muttered under my breath.

Standing against a wall, she couldn't disguise her pain and remorse.

"It's lovely," she said, biting her lip.

"You don't have to lie."

She bowed her head and stared at the floor.

"We liked it, though," I continued. "Jacque and me.

That's his name, in case you are wondering."

"Is he good to you?" my mother said, peering up at me through her strands of hair.

"Better than you and father!"

As I walked past her, she reached for my arm. "You look tired."

"I am tired," I said, pulling away.

"But your nightgown. Your hair. Your hands. You look as though you haven't washed in weeks."

I caught my reflection in the mirror. She was right. With dark circles under my eyes, hollow cheeks, greasy curls, and sweat patches staining my nightgown, I resembled something that had crawled out of a grave.

"I do wash," I said, throwing my coat over the mirror. "I just didn't sleep well."

"And do you eat?"

"When I can."

Taken aback, her eyes welled up, and she collapsed on the end of my bed. "I'm sorry," she whispered.

"Well, it's too late for that now," I said, handing her Jacque's handkerchief.

As she dabbed her eyes, I noticed patches of scorch marks appearing from beneath the duvet.

"Jacque? French, I take it?"

"His great-grandfather was French," I replied, sneaking round the bed, to cover the marks. "They came here during the Revolution."

"Don't mention the Revolution," my mother said, holding up her hand.

"Why not?"

"It was a sad time," she sighed, gazing into the distance. "Where is Jacque, Elise?"

"He's... He's... Working."

"You can do better than that," my mother replied, giving me a sideways glance.

Refusing to answer, I turned away and looked out the

window at the grey skies overhead. "I think it's going to rain."

"Why don't you come for dinner?" my mother said, ignoring me.

"Absolutely not," I said, laughing.

"Please?" she pleaded, leaning towards me. "I will speak to your father. Come for me. For Amelie. She misses you so badly."

The thought of my father banging his fist on the table, demanding to be served, Étienne sniggering and leering at the maids as they presented the meal, and my mother's incomprehensible babblings, less than thrilled me. But Amelie would be different. She would sing, giggle, and no doubt end up hiding under the table, pretending her knife and fork were dolls.

"We can have rabbit stew, with creamed potatoes and vegetables," my mother continued.

"I do miss Amelie," I whispered.

"And cheese and biscuits afterwards," she continued, sweat appearing across her brow, and her hands turning scarlet.

"Are you all right, mother?" I said, reaching out to feel her forehead.

"Oh, it's nothing," she said, waving me away. "The room is very hot, that's-"

The spider appeared in front of us, dangling from the end of its thread.

"It can't be," my mother mumbled, as it descended past her nose and landed on my bed.

"What?" I replied.

The spider crawled along the duvet and under the pillow.

"No, no, no!" my mother said, leaping to draw back the bedding.

"Don't!" I screeched, reaching out to grab her.

Too late. The bedsheets were exposed – burned, torn to shreds, and singed through.

"*Ma petite fille*," my mother sobbed, drawing back her hand, as though not daring to touch the marks.

"It's nothing," I snapped, trying to strip the sheets from the bed. "It happens when you buy second-hand."

"They go on fire?" my mother scoffed, lying on the mattress. "Or you bought them like that?"

"Could you move, please, so I can dispose of them?" I said.

"Elise!" she replied, frowning.

"I had some trouble with candles."

"You have to tell me the truth!" she cried, tears rolling down her cheeks.

Feeling the panic rise in my chest, I threw the sheets at her and stormed across the room. "What else do you think happened?" I said, taking a deep breath. "Do you think I'm some sort of demon? What exactly are you saying, mother?"

She gave a blank stare. "Perhaps you were too warm." Her eyes fell to the floor, and she nodded, whilst murmuring to herself, "Yes, that's it."

"I've had enough of this," I said, opening the door, and pointing towards the hallway. "I'll be at the manor for five."

"What about the sheets?"

"I'll be there for five," I replied, through gritted teeth.

My mother stood up to leave. Walking past the mirror, her cloak caught the edge of my coat, causing it to fall. As she knelt to pick it up, she spotted a bloodstain on the sleeve.

"That's just-"

"Don't worry, we will fix this! We will fix this, my little girl!" she interrupted, dropping the coat and running towards me.

"I cut my hand, that's all," I said, unable to look her in the eyes. "There was a lot of blood."

She wrapped her arms around me, kissed my cheek, and whispered, "There always is."

***

56

When I arrived at the manor, the gate was chained and padlocked, and my mother watched me from behind a twitching curtain. A shadow of a man crept up behind her and dragged her from the window.

Then came the shouting.

I rattled the gate, trying to unpick the lock and untangle the chains. My mother ran out of the house in her bare feet, wearing her best paisley gown.

The shadow slammed the front door shut.

"Elise!" my mother smiled, reaching the gate. Her frail fingers unchained the gate, and guided me towards the manor. She never took her eyes off me.

As we entered the hallway, she searched for the shadow, visibly trembling as she did so. He had gone.

"Wait in the parlour," my mother said, taking my coat, making particular effort to ignore the bloodstain as she hung it on the coat stand. "I'll be in the kitchen, finishing dinner."

"Do the maids have the day off again?"

"Yes," she said, after a slight hesitation.

I lost hope for an edible meal.

"Actually," my mother continued, "we had to let them go. There was an incident with your father."

"Again?" I said.

My mother sighed, whilst nodding, and left me standing alone. Heading towards the parlour, I passed the dining room and my stomach sank. The table was set for six people, meaning only one thing – my father's mother would be joining us.

The pitter-patter of footsteps ran up behind me, and two arms wrapped around my waist. As I looked down, a mass of honey curls, two dark blue eyes, and a cheeky little smile greeted me. Amelie.

"Are you here now forever?" she asked, exposing two missing front teeth.

"Just for a little while."

"Oh… Do you have time to tell me a story?"

"I could try."

"Good!" she said.

Hand in hand, we went upstairs, where I noticed strips of wallpaper lying on the floor, and water dripping from the ceiling. As we reached the landing, Amelie turned to me and asked, "Elise, are you still my sister?"

"Of course, I am."

"I'll still be your sister then."

"Well, I'm very glad about that," I laughed.

"You should be. I'm a very good sister," Amelie replied, as we entered her room. As soon as she opened the door, memories came flooding back of make-believe tea parties, toy theatres, and hours spent pretending to chase Amelie on her rocking horse. She jumped onto her bed, and snuggled into a stuffed white rabbit. "Would you like to cuddle Pippy?"

"You keep him for now," I replied, climbing onto the bed beside her.

She rubbed his nose, and sat him between us. "We'll share!"

"That'll be nice," I said, stroking Pippy's ears.

"Elise… Where have you been?"

"I just had to go away for a little while."

Amelie's eyes widened. "On an adventure? Is that why you wear trousers?"

"What do you mean?"

"All the adventurers in my stories wear trousers," she said, pointing to two books sitting beside a broken doll's house. "Étienne said you met a boy."

I folded my arms and leaned back against a pillow. "Did he?"

"Did you meet him on your adventure?" Amelie said, springing up to stand over me. "Was he a knight? What was his name?"

"Jacque… His name is Jacque."

Amelie giggled, twirling the frills of her dress. "What is he like?"

"He's my best friend."

Amelie stared at me, frowning.

"Obviously, you're my bestest best friend!" I said.

"Tell me a story," she replied, dropping down to sit cross-legged beside me.

"About what?"

"The knight!"

"What knight?"

"Jacque!"

"Jacque wasn't a-"

"You said he was."

She rested her head on my shoulder and looked at me with such indignation it made me realise the stupidity of arguing, and so I settled down for the story. "Fine," I said. "Long ago, in a faraway land there lived a beautiful little Princess-"

"Are you the Princess?"

"No." I replied, pulling her to lie beside me. "Do you want a story, or not?"

Amelie patted my arm, and put her head against my shoulder. "Carry on!"

The Knight and the Maiden

Long ago, in a faraway land there lived a beautiful little Princess, and an ugly, older Prince. Both were taken care of by a young maiden who did not care for royal titles. All three were imprisoned inside the towers of a giant, grey castle. But this was no ordinary castle – it held dark enchantments. The walls were made of poisoned spears, the sun had cursed the windows, forbidding light to enter, smiles and laughter were eaten away by mirrors, and a ghost mother haunted the chambers. Guarding the castle was an all-seeing demon, who claimed authority and dominion over each of his prisoners. The maiden knew of a legend that said he had once been an angel, but after drinking the water inside the castle, he had become possessed like a rabid dog, and the evil had taken his soul. Some nights, the maiden heard the floorboards shaking, as the ghost mother wailed, lamenting the demon's very existence.

One afternoon, the demon and his captives sat by the fire after a large meal of animal carcass and gruel. He called the maiden to his side and took her hand in his. "You are to marry my brother's son."

The maiden pulled herself away and said she would never leave the royal children or the ghost mother alone with the demon. Grabbing the maiden, he struck her across the face. "You are my property, and so will obey me."

The maiden punched the demon and scratched her nails down his face. As punishment, she was locked inside a tower, forbidden to see another person.

Weeks passed, and nothing could persuade the maiden to change her mind. Each night, the demon pounded on her door, using bribery, blackmail, and guilt.

Finally, one night, on the stroke of midnight, the demon dragged the maiden from her bed whilst the ghost mother stood by watching and crying. He threw her into the street and the maiden stood there freezing in the middle of the damp winter, wearing nothing but her nightdress.

Hours went by, but the enchanted castle had cast charms against the maiden, stopping anyone from seeing or hearing her, as she pleaded from the street for help. Abandoning hope, she left her family behind and wandered the streets, in search of a home.

Cold and frightened, the maiden quickly learned that the streets were not kind to desperate girls. By day, she moved from corner to corner, head bowed to hide her shame, and palm outstretched, begging for food. At night, she slept in doorways, with only newspapers and litter to keep her safe from the world.

Women ushered their children away from her. Men made nasty jokes. Most of the time, though, she watched their boots walk by as people ignored her.

As the weeks went on, the maiden grew sick. Her bones protruded beneath her skin, her eyes sunk into their sockets, and she couldn't move without pain.

Everything in the world seemed lost, and death sat nearby, patiently waiting.

But then, just as the maiden was about to give up, the shadows began to lift. She had been watching a lady, who was posing like a muse for her passing admirers. The gas light was her spotlight, and her red dress a siren, luring all who saw her into falling with love at her feet. She pouted and grinned through wisps of chocolate hair.

The maiden knew she could be just like the Red Woman, and so rose up and mirrored her movements. A young knight passed by, but was not tempted by the maiden. She cried out as hunger gripped her and she collapsed to the ground. The knight ran to her side, taking her to the nearest tavern and bought her a hot meal and a bed for the night. He never left the maiden's side. She was safe, and, for the first time ever, believed in the goodness of strangers.

Days turned into weeks, and weeks turned into months. A new kind of enchantment was in the air. Memories of the demon and his castle were far behind, and happiness had finally found the maiden. She loved the knight. Nothing could have prepared her for what would happen next.

One morning, as dawn approached, five men wearing black hooded cloaks burst into their home. They dragged the knight out of bed and pushed the maiden aside. Fighting back, the knight kicked and punched free of the men. As he ran to protect the maiden, the five men grabbed him, and beat him until he lay bloodied and bruised. The maiden cried out for help, but nobody came. One of the men slapped her across the face; another pinned her to the floor. The knight, half-unconscious, pleaded for them to spare her, but they laughed instead.

As the maiden broke free of the men, a kick to her stomach and a punch to the face brought her to the floor. She watched the knight being taken away, knowing she had failed to save the man who had saved her.

The maiden had failed to save Jacque.

***

"You need better stories," said Amelie, yawning. "That one didn't even have a dragon in it."

"You can tell the story next time," I replied.

"I will," Amelie nodded, climbing off the bed, and heading towards the door. "Come on, let's go get dinner."

As my sister left the room, I wiped my eyes, and lifted my head to find the pillow damp with tears. Turning it over, I called out, "Just coming!" and left the room.

Walking downstairs, the sound of muffled voices rumbled down through the ceiling. My father and Étienne. Judging by their laughter, they were either sharing a joke or congratulating each other on one of their cruel antics – harassing beggars, making lewd remarks to barmaids, or torturing stray dogs.

Amelie skipped into the dining room leaving me alone in the hallway. From the kitchen, pots and pans clattered as the distinct smell of burning filled the air.

"*Bon sang, qu'est-ce que je fais?!*" I heard my mother groan.

As I paced between doorways, my father and Étienne pounded downstairs. Since seeing them last, the scratch I had left on my father's cheek had turned into a scar, and his beard and moustache had developed a slight grey tinge. Étienne was a foot taller – now towering over me. With their swaggers and dinner suits, they appeared like perfect gentlemen, but, as usual, their sweaty stench and dirty fingernails gave them away. Neither of them acknowledged me as they passed and headed into the dining room.

"Elise, are you coming?" Amelie said, poking her head around the corner.

"Of course," I replied, following her.

I entered the room with all eyes fixed upon me and took my place between Amelie and my grandmother. A rich, musky scent exuded from the old woman, and her large, pink gown cascaded over her chair, with the lace of the sleeves covering her bejewelled hands. As always, her hair was perfectly quaffed and coated with white powder, giving her the look of a shabby, aristocratic hag. She snatched her cane from under her petticoat, and rammed it beneath my chin.

"Elise – the disgraced child," she growled. "I no longer acknowledge you as a de Volonté!"

I narrowed my eyes and stared at her.

"*Putain!*" she spat out, before removing her cane.

My mother appeared with a tray of food. With trembling hands, she served each of us a plate of brown water poured over chunks of red meat, wilted mushed vegetables and curdled mash. Amelie's jaw dropped.

"Don't worry, I will make you something else later," I whispered in her ear.

She smiled with relief.

Grandmother pushed her plate aside, turned to my father and said, "Still no cook, I see!"

Examining a piece of meat dangling from his fork, he replied, "We do what we can."

"Do more," grandmother said, pointing her nose in the air.

My father glared at my mother and continued, "I thought she might have her uses."

Grandmother snorted, and he smiled in agreement.

My mother, sat opposite my brother, gazed into mid-air. Étienne, for his part, wolfed into his food. Locks of his wavy blond hair fell into his gravy, and lumps of mash escaped from his open mouth as he chewed.

"What is this?" Amelie said, poking at the meat.

"It's rabbit," I said.

Amelie gasped and slid under the table. "We're eating Pippy!?"

"No. No, we're not. Look!" I said, rearranging her food into the shape of a deformed face. She reappeared and squealed in delight as the blood from the meat mixed with the gravy, and dripped into the carrot mouth.

"Just try to eat a little. For mother's sake," I said.

She frowned, and held her nose whilst chomping on a piece of rabbit. As she gulped it down, her face turned green.

My father had long since given up on the meal. He shoved his plate across the table with such force that it collided with my mother's wine glass. She didn't react. Beads of sweat formed along her forehead, and the colour drained from her.

My father left the table, staggered towards the drinks cabinet, and poured himself a glass of port. He leaned against the wall, one leg crossed over the other, and stared at me.

"Mother, are you feeling all right?" I said.

"*J'irai bien*," she replied, eyes glazed and brow furrowed.

"Why are you asking?" Étienne said, with spinach leaves hanging from his mouth. "She's always like this."

"*Laisse-moi tranquille*," she mumbled, as her breathing grew shallow.

"Perhaps we should've been more concerned," I said, approaching her and placing my hand on her cheek. "She's terribly hot. We need to get her into bed."

Nobody moved but Amelie, who hid under the table.

"Which we would that be, Elise?" my father said, taking a swig of port. "Us, or that mongrel you've been sharing a bed with?"

My brother, laughing, almost chocked on a piece of meat.

"Oh yes, I know all about him," my father continued,

pouring another drink. "And now you come back... and sit at my table... eat my food. And expect me to accept it!"

My mother reached out to squeeze my hand.

"This is what happens when the daughters are the first born," my Grandmother interrupted, banging her cane on the floor.

"Thank the Idol for sons!" Étienne said, as his muddy brown eyes looked me up and down. "She was always an embarrassment – a girl wearing trousers? Those dark smudges around her eyes? Her hair! Is it any wonder she ran off with the first boy who offered?"

"I didn't run off; I was thrown out! Out onto the streets!" I replied.

"Well, that is not how I recall it," my father sneered, sucking his teeth.

"With the amount of alcohol, you drink, it's a wonder you remember anything at all!" I shouted.

The room fell silent as my father skulked towards me. My grandmother turned to get a better view. It reminded me of the stories she told me, about how her family witnessed the terror of the guillotine during the Revolution. Behind her sombre face, the slight glint in her eye always gave away her sadistic joy.

"You are my property, so whatever I decide to do with you is ordained by the Idol," said my father, bearing down on me. "I should have reported you to the Inservium the second I found out you were living out of wedlock with some boy! Do you have any idea what the Councillors would do to you?"

"Don't!" I said, leaning into him. "Or would you like a scar on the other side of your face?"

He grabbed my hand and snorted. "Thank the Idol that the Councillors haven't turned their back on the family. Bothwell visits at least once a week to ask if we have heard from you."

At the mention of Bothwell's name, my mother gripped

my hand tighter and groaned.

Father took no notice and continued. "He is so worried about our welfare. Not that you deserve such attention from the Councillors."

"Worried about your welfare?" I said, pointing around the room. "And yet he lets you live in filth."

"The Councillors do what they can. And now with all these murders, they've had to be even more of a sanctuary for the whole town. If they had the money, then they would gladly share it amongst their congregation."

"You know nothing about the Inservium," I yelled. "Your time would be better spent kneeling at the feet of a street walker than at the feet of a Councillor."

Grandmother banged her cane on the table. "Defiant *putain*!"

I turned to her and smirked. "The apple never falls far from the tree."

"How dare you!" she screamed. As her eyes narrowed, the veins bulged from her neck. She picked up her wine glass and threw it – missing me and my mother by inches.

"See what you have done?" my father said. "You've upset your grandmother."

"Get rid of her!" my grandmother added. "Deal with her like you did before."

My father moved towards her, and placed his hand on her shoulder. "Don't worry, mother, I'm not done with her. Why don't you go sit in the drawing room?"

With a grunt, she rose from the table, scowled at me, and left.

"What's a *putain*?" Étienne asked, scraping the last morsels of food from his plate.

"Obviously, all those years of education have been wasted on you," I replied, sitting down.

"At least I've never brought shame upon the family," Étienne said.

"This entire family is a shame!" I said, leaning back in

my chair.

A gasp came from under the table.

"I didn't mean you, Amelie."

My father drained his glass and returned to the decanter for a refill.

"How have you been, Elise?" my mother said, through shallow breaths.

"What?" I replied.

She burst into tears and rested her head on my shoulder.

"Yet another bout of hysterics," my father remarked.

"Let me take you up to bed," I said, feeling my mother's clammy cheek.

She closed her eyes and mumbled incoherent French.

"Is that what the boy said to you?" my father interupted, leering at me.

Picking up a knife, and twiddling it between my fingers, I considered tossing it into his skull. "Is that what you said to the maids?"

My father sat down and lit a cigarette. "They're just silly girls who can't take a joke."

Étienne sniggered and finished our mother's wine.

"Elise, *ma petite fille*," my mother whispered, clutching my arm.

"I'm taking you upstairs," I replied, prising her from the chair.

Étienne snorted and wine flew out his nostrils.

"Do you ever stop?" I said to him, guiding my mother out of the room.

As we climbed the stairs, my father's shadow pursued us.

"Who knows what you let that boy do to you!" he said. "I hope you didn't charge much. Then again, I doubt anyone would pay for a common little tart like you!"

"Marius!" my mother cried, clinging to the wall.

"Don't interfere!" he snapped.

My mother slid to the floor and covered her head with her hands.

"It's all right mother – I'm not afraid of him anymore," I said, turning towards my father. "He has no idea what I'm capable of."

He smirked and grabbed my hair. "You disgust me Elise. Your mother should have bled you into her chamber pot. I would have brewed the herbs myself to help it along."

"Walk away, Marius," I said.

"Then again, you probably know something about that," he continued, the reek of tobacco and alcohol on his breath. "Or do you have a little bastard waiting at home?"

"Leave her, Marius," my mother whimpered, avoiding looking at us.

My father ignored her, and placed his hand over my stomach. "Or perhaps it's wriggling inside you?"

"I'd love nothing more than to kill you right now," I said, pushing him away.

He laughed. "Don't worry Elise, there are plenty of men traipsing the streets, looking for whores."

"Maybe we could make money out of her," Étienne said, arriving at the top of the stairs. As he handed our father a glass of port, Amelie appeared behind him, untangling a red yo-yo.

"No," my father replied, taking a drink. "I'm not taking the blame for any diseases she might spread."

"You've suddenly grown a conscience?" I scoffed, and knelt beside my mother. "Let's get you to bed."

"I should hand you over to Councillor Bothwell," my father said. "Then hopefully they'll kill the boy!"

The blood gushed from my father's nose, as I pounded my fist into his face. "Say it again!" I yelled, dragging my fingernails down his cheek. "Go on, say it!"

Étienne hauled me away, and slammed me against a wall. My mother turned and sobbed into her dress.

"Ring-a-ring-o-roses," Amelie sang, grappling with the yo-yo. "A pocket full of posies."

Étienne wrapped his fingers round my throat, pinning

me into a corner.

"Get out of my house, you evil little tart!" my father spat, throwing the port in my face.

"Don't worry, I'm leaving," I replied, "and I'm taking Amelie with me."

My cheek stung as my father slapped me. "Stupid as well as reckless," he said. "Do you really think a loving father like me would allow his daughter to live in squalor?"

"I won't let you do to her what you did to me," I croaked, feeling Étienne's grip getting tighter.

"Even so," my father laughed. "…she is my property and she'll do as I say. And, unlike you, she will be compliant."

"In every way," Étienne added, digging his fingernails into my neck.

"Look!" my father said, forcing my head round to watch Amelie, skipping around in circles. "Look at how she doesn't react to any of this."

My mother turned to her youngest daughter and lowered her eyes, as though frightened and ashamed.

"Do you still want to kill me, Elise?" my father whispered, leaning into me, until his moustache scratched against my ear. "Do it! Let Amelie see you do it."

Watching my sister, I fought back tears, knowing he was right; I could not take care of her and would never let her witness a murder. "I'll come back for her," I said, giving my father a sideways glance.

As I bent his fingers back, Étienne's knuckles cracked. "Argh!" he squealed, releasing me.

"Stop whinging, boy," my father said.

Stained with port, and with my pride in tatters, I walked downstairs.

"Bye, Elise," Amelie called out.

Not taking my eyes off my father, I turned back and kissed my sister on the forehead. "Just wait a little while longer. We're going on a big adventure."

Arriving home, I found Miss Agatha lurking in the hallway, outside my door.

"How are you not freezing?" she said.

"What?" I replied.

"You're not wearing a coat – in the middle of winter."

I looked down, and found myself wearing only a pair of trousers and an oversized shirt. "Oh, I must have left it behind."

"And you didn't feel the cold?"

"Well I…" Without giving me a chance to answer, she thrust a letter into my chest, before walking away, mumbling. "I still want my money, Elise. Don't care if he has left you."

"Wait," I called out, entering my room.

"If this is more excuses, I'm not interested," Miss Agatha said, following me inside.

I walked over to the desk, and lifted the envelope full of money that my mother had given me. "Your rent money," I said, handing it over.

"What are those?" she yelled, pointing to the tally marks on the wall.

"Oh, those. Those were here when we moved in."

"No, no, that's not right."

"Look, you have your money," I said. "Please, just leave."

As Miss Agatha removed the coins from the envelope, her eyes widened. "There's almost ten pounds here!"

"Minus a few shillings," I said, ushering her out the door.

"But you don't owe this much," Miss Agatha replied, wriggling from my grasp.

"Just take it all. I don't care."

As I closed the door in her face, she shouted from the other side, "You're an odd child!"

"Thank you!" I yelled back.

Looking at the letter, I didn't recognise the penmanship, or its red seal, shaped like a bird. After I ripped it open, the spider crawled out from under the bed. "I still haven't forgiven you for before, you know," I said, reading.

Dear Elise,
There will be a carriage waiting outside before midnight. Pack all your belongings, for the Inservium must think you have disappeared.
Yours faithfully,
A Phoenix.

"Not another bloody mystery," I said to the spider, as I threw the letter on my bed. "I don't have time for this."

The spider didn't respond.

"You know I lost my coat?" I said, sliding my hand under the mattress, in search of the dagger I had intentionally forgotten to give back to the Councillors. One never knows when it might be necessary to slit someone's – or Bothwell's – throat. "I'll get it back, though."

After sliding the dagger into my boot, I filled the copper basin with cold water. "I just forgot it, that's all. It's not as though I'm turning into my mother."

The spider still didn't respond.

"And I'm sure the stress stopped me feeling the cold. That's all. And that's the least of my problems."

As I undressed and washed the port stains from my hair and face, I thought of my sister, and how much I regretted leaving her behind. "Jacque would have saved her," I said to the spider. "I should have saved her."

Grabbing a fresh set of clothes, I sat on the floor and watched the spider crawl up the leg of a table to sit amongst the wax of a candle. "There is the problem of Freya," I said as I wrestled to put on a pair of Jacque's trousers. "How can I possibly kill a child?"

The spider climbed up the candle. "Now, I know what you're thinking, but there are some things even I won't do – not even for Jacque."

The spider descended from a thread, back down the candle.

"Jacque! That's the only answer," I said. "He has to come home."

I stood up and placed the letter in a desk drawer, deciding to deal with it later. Taking one of Jacque's coats from the wardrobe, the faint smell of aftershave lingered on the collar. The thick woollen fabric drowned me as I put it on and headed towards the door. As I turned the handle, I looked back at the spider and smiled.

"Jacque is coming home tonight."

CHAPTER SEVEN

By the time I left my apartment, two men were lighting the streetlamps and whistling as they walked on by. Overhead, the moon cast its cold light upon the thick fog rising from the cobbled stones.

As I headed towards the Inservium, the rustling of newspapers caught my attention.

"Any spare change?" croaked a young man sitting on a street corner. He slipped into a dark alley and his voice – along with his phony English accent – grew louder. "I'd make it worth your while, Miss. Do anything you like. I'm a good boy that way."

"Pfft!" I scoffed walking away.

Within a few footsteps, the dim lamps of Poska's Inn glowed through a broken window. The pounding rattle of a piano swept into the street accompanied by the hearty bellows of the customers. Between renditions of old bawdy folk songs, a brown-haired woman wearing a tattered red dress stumbled out the door. Giggling to herself, she pirouetted into the middle of the pavement, with the ends of her skirt wrapped over one arm. Upon seeing me, she curtseyed, and gave a wide smile. Even with her dark curls shading her eyes, I would recognise her anywhere. The Red Woman.

"Any spare change?" the young man said again.

As the piano thundered into song, the Red Woman offered her hand to me. Just seeing her made me think of Jacque. I shook my head, and a sad expression appeared on her face. A man approached, and whispered in her ear. She laughed, took his arm, and went back inside the inn.

"Would you do anything *we* like?" a man's voice slurred. I turned around and saw two drunken men staggering along the street, bouncing off walls until they disappeared into the alley.

"You did promise to be good," whispered the second man.

Hiding in the shadows, I edged my way towards the sound of the young man whimpering.

"Maybe you could teach my missus a thing or two?" the first man sneered, prompting the second to laugh.

Then came the sound of a thud against the wall and the ripping of clothes.

Two gas lamps glowed upon the figure of a woman in a second storey room of the inn. The light revealed the two men, unbuckling their belts, and running their hands over the boy's body.

"If only they were all this handsome," the second man said to the first.

They both sniggered.

Their laughter didn't last long.

I grabbed the first by his greasy blond hair and pulled him away from the young man. As I slammed his head into the cobble stones and kicked his spine, his bones snapped, and he fell unconscious.

The second, turning pale, attempted to crawl against the wall and hide behind some crates of empty ale bottles. I jumped over the pile of rubbish, landed on him, and punched his face until blood burst from his eye.

Amidst his snivelling and cries, I wrapped my hands around his throat and squeezed. As he struggled, a medallion fell from around his neck. There, glittering in the darkness, was the image of their Idol, engraved within a bronze hexagon.

The symbol of the Inservium's first initiation stage.

"You're training to be a Councillor?" I said.

He didn't answer – or, rather, couldn't, from the amount of blood filling his mouth.

When sheer anger overtook me, I rose to stand over him. Without a second thought, I took a dagger out my boot, and thrust it between his legs. Of course, like his friend, he passed out.

From inside the inn, a woman was singing a rendition of a quaint Scottish ballad and encouraging her comrades to join in. Behind me, the young man sat sobbing in the corner of the alley. As I crouched beside the curled-up ball of skin and bone, he flinched.

"I don't think they had any spare change," I said, wrapping my arm around his shoulder.

The young man trembled. He couldn't have been more than sixteen years old. His heavy eyes refused to look at me as he buried his scraggy, blistered face into his knees.

"What do you want from me?" he muttered.

"Nothing," I said. "I know men like them all too well."

The young man sniffed and wiped his eyes. "Thank you."

"Take this," I replied, handing him the key to my apartment, "and follow me."

"Are you going to kill me like you did them?"

"No. Now are you coming or not?" I asked, with my hands on my hips.

After several reassurances that I wasn't going to drive a knife through him, the young man followed me. The inn's back door creaked open, prompting us to run.

We emerged from the alley to see that a crowd of revellers had gathered on the street. In the middle, the Red Woman danced around three men who were all vying for her attention.

"Now listen carefully," I said to the boy. "Do you see the house over there, three rows down, with an overgrown hedge and broken balcony?"

The young man nodded.

"Go to the top apartment and let yourself in," I continued. "You'll find food and a bed for the night. Take anything you please, sell it, pawn it, whatever you choose."

The young man tossed the key in the air and frowned. "That's very kind," he stuttered.

"But ignore the burnt sheets – I've had a few accidents with candles," I said, forcing a laugh. "And leave the books. Understand?"

"Everything but the books," he said, emphasising each word.

Before he turned to walk away, I grabbed him by the collar and whispered in his ear, "Tell no one what you saw tonight."

His cheeks rose into a mischievous smile. "Jacque would be proud of you," he said, before running away.

As I moved to chase after him, a pair of warm arms wrapped themselves around my shoulders and held glasses of red wine and vodka in front of me.

"Be careful, *kulta*," a woman's voice muttered. "Secrets never remain secrets around here."

She pressed the glass of vodka to my lips and poured the alcohol down my throat. Coughing and spluttering, I turned around to face the young blonde woman with a white powdered face, red-stained lips, and gentle kohl-rimmed hazel eyes. She glanced towards the alleyway and took a swig from the wine glass. Then another and another, until the contents – too thick to be the watered-down concoction served in Poska's – disappeared.

"My name is Saara," she smiled. "Did you like my song?"

She placed the two glasses – and the grey parasol perched over her elbow – onto the pavement, as her eyes darted between the Red Woman and me.

"What? Look, I don't care who you are, I have to go," I said.

She lifted my arms and began examining me – spinning me round and patting down my back and stomach.

"What are you doing?" I snapped.

"Are you injured?"

Shoving her, I said, "From what?"

"Hmmm… You seem fine. Did you like my song?" she asked, tilting her head.

At a loss for words, I sighed, before managing to reply, "Aye, it was very lovely."

"*Kiitos.* It's the first song I learnt when I got here."

"Is that right?" I said, edging away.

"Yes, I'm from Helsinki. So, you enjoyed the song?" she said, moving towards me.

"Absolutely! You should be on stage," I replied, quickening my pace. The blonde followed relentlessly.

"I didn't see you in the inn."

"No?"

"Perhaps you were outside?"

"Aye."

"In the alleyway," she said, slowing her pace. "Where you killed two men."

I froze.

Soon, Saara was by my side, pointing up to the second storey of Poska's. "I was standing by the window in the back room."

Two thoughts crossed my mind.

First, if she informed the Councillors, then they would harm Jacque to punish me for my foolishness.

Second, she may be an Inservium spy, setting a trap.

She linked our arms together. "Listen to me; I am going to help you. Nobody else has seen the bodies but it is only a matter of time before they are found. I am going to take you to a safe place."

"You are right," I lied, knowing I had to get away. "But before we leave, let me make sure my friend is safe."

I smiled and patted her arm to offer reassurance.

She thought for a moment. "Very well," she said. "I will meet you back at the inn in fifteen minutes. I trust you, don't let me down."

With her parasol once again perched upon her shoulder,

she walked away. Shining like a dark angel, with a tight black corset and crinoline skirt, she re-joined the revellers. The Red Woman turned to stare at me before disappearing inside the inn.

Standing alone, everything seemed clear. Not so far away, a boy who knew Jacque was ransacking my apartment. There wasn't time for me to go searching for answers. The only way to save Jacque was to kill as many people as the Councillors felt necessary. I looked through the windows of the inn to ensure Saara and the Red Woman were distracted, and saw them both drinking and dancing by the piano.

I ran straight to the Inservium.

**

By the time I reached the old wooden building, it was impossible to see beyond the dense fog. As I opened the Inservium's gate, the trees and hedges shuddered in the breeze, and I could hear organ music drifting through the cracks in the windows. A Councillor stepped out of the building and grunted as we passed one another. Inside was a group of ten or so townspeople, kneeling and praying to their Idol. I walked down the centre aisle, and not one person – including the secret mistress of Bothwell – raised their head.

Standing behind the pulpit, I knelt and pulled on the lever. The wall containing a secret compartment opened, and I wandered over and raided the box of weapons. I shoved two daggers down into my boots (one encrusted with opals, the other engraved with runes), wrapped a whip around my waist, and I tied two iron chains through my belt.

As I looked out over the rows of bowed heads, I felt disdain and pity for the men and women, mumbling their prayers. They sat, lips moving in silence, staring at the ground as though divine intervention would rise through the floorboards. Rich townspeople to the left, and the poor to the right, but it didn't matter to the Councillors so long as they filled the Inservium donation basket to its brim.

I removed three serrated knives from the box and stepped back out to the altar.

To play, or not to play? If Saara was going to tell the Councillors that she'd caught me in the act of murder, then I had very little to lose by exposing the Inservium's corruption. Perhaps a little scene would persuade them to reconsider their threats towards Jacque – after all, an angry girl who knows too much is not one to be underestimated.

Someone in the congregation coughed. A child fidgeted in his seat; his mother reprimanded the behaviour and told him to kneel and pray. A man blew his nose as two elderly women tutted. But, no matter the distraction, it seemed as though nothing could dissuade them from their devotion to their Idol. I decided to put them to the test.

I held the three knives in front of me, took a deep breath and started juggling. Tossing, twisting and catching each blade, higher and higher – and nobody noticed.

Part one of test complete.

With the knives resting between my fingers like claws, I swayed my hips and arms like the Red Woman. The little boy looked up, wide-eyed and giggling. As he shook his mother's coat and pointed at me, she grabbed his arm and pulled him to the floor.

"I told you to pray," she hissed. "You've been so naughty this week. If you don't behave, the Idol will send you to the bad place."

The little boy's lip quivered as he turned to me. I winked at him and shook my head, to assure him his mother was lying. Nevertheless, he bowed his head, closed his eyes, and started praying.

Part two of test complete.

A hand seized my arm and pulled me down behind the altar. As the knives fell towards the floor, I stretched to catch each one before they had the chance to land.

"Amused, Elise?" Bothwell smirked.

"Relax; apparently nothing can distract them from their Idol."

"Their Idol? I see that you've completely lost faith, Elise," Bothwell said. "I'm concerned that if the other Councillors were to find out, it may jeopardise Jacque's safety."

"That's if he's still alive," I replied.

"Would you like his body delivered to your door to relieve your uncertainty?"

"I want names," I said, staring straight into his cruel, vindictive eyes.

"Of?"

"People you want me to get rid of. As many as you like."

Bothwell arched an eyebrow. "Have you killed the girl?"

"No. She's barely six if she's a day." I said, narrowing my eyes. "Even I have my limits."

"Poor Jacque. I'll be sure to let him know."

"She's just a little girl!"

"And little girls grow up to be... Dangerous," he said, looking me up and down.

"It's probably just as well you were never blessed with fatherhood."

Bothwell scoffed, stroking my face. "No, being a father was not meant for me."

"Let's call this a trade," I said, snatching his wrist. "I'll murder everyone on the list, and, in exchange, you spare the girl's life."

Bothwell, pursing his lips, considered the proposition.

"And I want Jacque returned to me, tonight."

Bothwell laughed.

"Give me as many names as it takes to get him back," I said.

"You do not have the privilege of making demands," Bothwell replied. "Murder is an abomination. Do you know what we do to girls like you?"

I leaned forward and whispered, "You use us, and sit

back and enjoy the performance."

Bothwell stared as I stood up. I hid two of the knives in my coat, and the third, I kept hold of, folding my arms to conceal the blade.

"You never know who I might kill instead," I said, glancing towards the congregation.

As I made my way along the centre aisle, I heard the strained groan of Bothwell rising to his feet.

"My dear child," he called after me.

I turned around and the heads of the townspeople shot upwards to worship his every word. Embracing the attention, he stood centre stage in front of the altar and held out his arms to me.

"The Inservium will always be your home. Always. Let me find the list of prayers you so desperately need," he said.

"Thank you," I said, with a smirk.

As Bothwell made his way to the vestry, I sat down, and a ruddy-faced woman with yellowing teeth leaned over to me. "He is such a gent, isn't he?" she said.

"I prefer to use another four-letter word," I replied, smiling through gritted teeth.

The woman ignored me.

"Is it safe for you to be out all alone?" she continued. "What with these murders going on?"

I wrapped my coat tight around my chest and took a deep breath. "Don't you worry about me. I'm tougher than you think."

"That's what I'm praying for. To be kept safe by the Idol."

"I would expect nothing less."

"He's protected me for the past ten months." the woman said with a look of adoration. "I don't know what I've done to deserve his graces."

Slouching down into the pew, I replied, "You must be paying the donation box well."

The woman furrowed her brows, confused. I patted her hand and she went back to praying.

A short while later, Bothwell returned and motioned me towards him. He slapped a folded piece of paper into my hand. "Three names to start off with," he growled.

Before I had the chance to reply, he stormed off, snapping his fingers for his mistress to follow.

***

I turned into Mitchell Lane and a thick mass of fog eclipsed the detached two storey white wooden house belonging to the Kreeks. With no light radiating from the square panelled windows, it appeared that the family must have already gone to bed. I searched the row of houses up and down for any signs of passers-by. All but two of the nearby houses looked to be in darkness, with the only noise coming from the whistling of a worn chimney. I climbed the steps onto the porch and peered through the glass door, looking for any indications of movement. Finding no signs of life, I unclipped a pin from my hair and unpicked the lock.

The door slid open. As I entered the hallway and climbed the stairwell, the grandfather clock chimed eleven times.

Before leaving the Inservium, I read the names written on the paper that Bothwell had given me. I knew full well that three lives would not be enough to save Jacque. Two of the names I did not recognise, however the third, Rasmus Kreek, was the son of our family lawyer. At twenty years old, he was only a few years older than my brother, and, in recent months, had gotten engaged to the daughter of a blacksmith. Her photo sat on the cabinet beside Rasmus's bed. As I stabbed her fiancé through the heart, her angelic face was spoiled by a spattering of blood. Perhaps she would find comfort knowing hers was the last face he looked upon before he died. There was a time when my mother hoped he would take an interest in me. He was a handsome man however, looking down at his dead body, I felt satisfied that his death brought me closer to Jacque.

***

Less than twenty minutes later, I was making my way towards the address of my next victim, Katja Ustov. The sound of hooves resonated in the distance as four black stallions and a carriage materialised from within the fog. The crack of a whip pierced the air as two of the horses reared upwards. As they galloped towards me, the carriage – made from human femurs, tibias and spines – rattled and pounded the cobbles. Each horse loomed ten feet over me; the satin of their manes glistened in the moonlight, and their noses pointed towards the sky in unison. Translucent skin exposed the outline of their skulls, hollow sockets replaced their eyes, and blood foamed from their mouths. The skeletal driver – much like the one I encountered outside Mhayree de Loire's house – jumped down from his seat. Whip in hand, he walked towards me, blue flames flickering where his eyes should have been. With one flick, the braided leather wrapped around the door handle, and opened the carriage. He grabbed me, covering my mouth, and pushed me inside. As he climbed into his seat, he cracked his whip, and despite my kicking and screaming, charged into the night.

For miles, I tried to escape – rattling the handle, banging the doors and roof, yelling, cursing, and ripping the upholstery. Outside the window, the moon and stars were held captive behind a mass of clouds, and, as the gas lights from the town faded into the distance, we travelled onwards.

"Let me out," I shouted.

The faint scent of violets filled the air. As I inhaled, my breaths grew shallow.

"Let me…" my voice croaked.

With the smell becoming overpowering, my eyelids fought to stay open. It was no use; I collapsed onto the floor and drifted into the darkness.

Within seconds, I opened my eyes to find the carriage shining with a silver hue. Forcing myself to sit up, I saw a girl reflected in the window. Me. Shadows dripped from her mouth like blood. The girl smiled, her face chiselled and radiant. She teased me, blew kisses, batted her eyelashes, and laughed at me. Her eyes glistened with a thousand constellations; her thick, black curls dominated her petite features, and her ruby red lips pouted, waiting to be kissed. She raised a finger and waved it as though chastising me, and winked. Then, placing her razor-like fingernail against a raised vein on her neck, she sliced through the skin. As the blood dribbled down her collarbone, she wiped a drop with her finger and offered me a taste. For a second – and I swear, it was only a second – I leaned in.

As I drew back, she smiled again.

The dream ended.

Upon waking, two skeletal arms dragged me from the carriage and tossed me onto gravel. As the driver stood over me, he grabbed my waist and rolled me onto my back, I began hitting him until fracturing and breaking his bony fingers.

"Get off of me!" I yelled.

After I kicked and punched him hard enough to dislocate his shoulder and jaw, he gave up and walked away.

"What the hell was that?" I said.

The driver turned around and pointed at me. I looked down and saw patches of my clothes singed, smouldering, and reeking of smoke.

"Great," I muttered, patting the ashes from my trousers. "It's not just bedsheets that are getting ruined."

Dusting myself off, I stood up and saw an old castle, with vast towers reaching high above the trees. Buttresses protruded from the walls, lined with latticed stained-glass windows, and piles of stone and ash were scattered along the ground – some still clinging to the ruins.

"Where are we?" I asked, and turned to find the carriage

engulfed in flames. Smoke billowed into the sky, as the fire spread, ravaging everything it touched.

Three of the horses had managed to escape and stood side by side on the road. The fourth, however, was being burned alive. I ran, trying to untether it from the carriage, but the driver restrained me.

Hair and bone amassed in piles of ash, fragments of tail floated like sparks in the air, entrails melted into the road, and bloody foam seeped into the stone.

The other stallions collapsed to the ground, lying on their sides, bucking their heads as though mourning.

"Did I do that?" I mumbled.

The driver nodded and let me go. He wandered over to inspect the charred carriage and kicked a dismantled wheel.

"I'm sorry. I didn't-"

A gargoyle swooped down from the castle, flapped his wings around my hair and growled into my face. Waving my arms, I swiped him away. In the distance, the driver was searching for his missing fingers and screwing them back into place. Needless to say, he ignored my cries for help.

My ankle caught the edge of a rock, causing me to fall. The gargoyle perched on my head, and his razor-like claws dug into my scalp. He bent over, snarled, and sniffed my scent. After letting out a gut-wrenching screech, he dismounted, and landed on all fours on the ground. He narrowed his eyes and bowed before flying onto a watchtower, where he paused and solidified.

"This is a dream, it's just a dream," I whispered, lying in a dishevelled heap.

The castle door opened, releasing a dusty gust of wind with a musky aroma. The driver approached and threw me towards the darkened entrance, where I landed on a hard-wooden floor.

As the door began to close, I caught a glimpse of the horse's ashes on the roadside. The ground grumbled, and a cloud of smoke burst from the remains. Out sprang an emaciated, blood-breathing muzzle, four sturdy front and hind legs, black shoulders and body, and a flowing tail.

With a strange mix of fear and amazement, I lay there unable to move. The door slammed shut. In the darkness, I heard debris falling from the crumbling brickwork, and the howling wind resonating through the walls. I crawled towards the door and tried the handle. Locked.

"I think I was safer with the undead driver and horses," I found myself saying, out loud.

As I stood and slowly made my way through the dark, a row of wall-mounted candelabras ignited on their own accord and shimmered against the grandiose sumptuousness of a Great Hall. Vast ivy-patterned pillars soared towards the domed ceiling where carved moons and stars gazed down on me. Luscious tapestries in silver and gold spread across the walls, showcasing tales of mythic heroes and heroines battling serpents, hydras, and dark knights. Bronze statues, roaring fires, and drapes of black velvet, crimson silk, and plum organza lured guests to be bewitched by that which would never be theirs. But all this was eclipsed by the imposing, winding mahogany staircase, which commanded the centre of the room.

At the top stood a familiar red-haired woman, holding a decapitated head of her own likeness.

Mhayree de Loire.

CHAPTER EIGHT

"**W**elcome to Castle Árnyék," Mhayree said, raising an eyebrow at me as she tossed the head into the air. It bounced and rolled across the floor, stopping at my feet. Its ice blue eyes pierced into mine and strands of red hair clung to the serrated neck wound. I bent down to pick it up, and the half-shut eyelids slid open, exposing the gateway between life and death.

"Uncanny, isn't it?" Mhayree said. "Just a little trick I learnt from an old friend."

I couldn't read the expression on her face. She turned away from me and removed a three-armed candelabrum from the wall.

"Come with me," she said.

I followed, still holding the waxwork head.

She led me down a darkened hallway, which felt never ending. A mouse squeaked as it scurried along the floor and a low hum reverberated within the walls. The faint candlelight shone upon rows of suits of armour. As we passed them, I heard the sound of moving rusty metal. Looking back, I saw that each one of the helmets had turned its head to follow Mhayree and me. She appeared nonchalant and continued to walk.

"What kind of person fakes their own death?" I said.

"One who's on a hit-list," Mhayree replied.

"You could have run away."

Mhayree shook her head. "They would have sent you to find me."

"Why you?" I said. "Why would they want you dead?"

Mhayree whipped round and glared at me. The flame from the candle flickered, exposing the anger in her eyes.

"Never mind," I said, deciding it best not to push the subject.

Mhayree turned and ushered me to continue walking. "Did they believe I was dead?" She said.

"The Councillors?"

"No, the Undertakers."

"Well, I don't-"

"Aye, the Councillors, Elise."

"I believe... they did," I stuttered. "We all did. Bothwell, in particular. He tossed your head in the fire."

"How oddly appropriate. Did they give you any instructions?"

I stayed silent, hesitant to recall Bothwell's last words to me. Mhayree stopped to face me. She said nothing, but her stoic serenity unnerved me.

"They told me to kill your daughter," I mumbled.

A gust of wind extinguished one of the candles. Mhayree's eyes narrowed and she gave me a sideways glance. "That won't be happening. You do understand, Elise?"

"I wasn't planning on trying," I said, lowering my eyes.

She smirked, walked ahead a few paces, and led me around a corner, into a gallery. Within the darkness, a row of large gilded frames hung on the walls, featuring portraits of men, women and children through the centuries. Some appeared to be families, others were depicted alone. On the frames, gold plaques displayed the names of the subjects, alongside their dates of birth and death. As we passed them, the flames from the candelabra shone upon their faces – each one felt familiar.

Mhayree turned around and caught me slowing down to study one or two of the portraits. She stood beside me and looked up towards a rosy-cheeked brunette woman who appeared joyous and full of life. Her bright, brown eyes sparkled against the candlelight and seemed to be following Mhayree and me as we walked away.

"Do you recognise any of the people?" Mhayree said.

"Perhaps," I replied.

Mhayree stopped to face me. "You killed them, dear."

Taken aback, I paused beside the figure of a woman dressed in an opulent blue dress with hooped skirt. Then I remembered. Her round, petite face appeared calm and radiant – unlike the night I drove a dagger through her heart and left her at the bottom of a winding stairwell. Street gossip said she lay there for five days before a neighbour found her. Unable to recall her name, I read the plaque: Joselyn Warcaster – March 15th 1653 – September 3rd 1897.

The date must have been wrong. She couldn't have been 244 years old when I ended her life. Brushing it off as a mistake, I moved on and stood in front of Nicholas Bacchus.

Just before slitting his throat, I found myself thinking about his lovely big blue eyes. He was in the bathtub, smoking a cigarette. The scent of it reminded me of Jacque. Trying to maintain his dignity, he didn't put up much of a struggle. To date, it was still one of my easier kills. It was also the first time I tried a cigarette. I didn't care for it much. Again, I examined the plaque under the portrait: November 23rd 1702 – October 5th 1897.

Impossible – 194 years old.

One by one, the memories of each murder came rushing back. I didn't know what was more confusing – re-living the deaths, or the supposed ages of my victims.

"Over here," said Mhayree, holding the candelabrum up towards a tall, feisty-looking woman, with an aquiline nose, and dark sensual eyes. "Did you know that you orphaned five children when you killed her?"

I moved closer to the portrait: Eleanor Dubois: February 29th 1716 – October 9th 1897.

Strangulation by whip, I recalled, and one that took longer than necessary. In the end, I had to sever her jugular just to end her suffering. She lived and died in a small garret filled with canvasses of unfinished paintings. They say after an artist dies, their work increases in value and their families profit. This did not happen to Miss Dubois. Instead, the Inservium confiscated her artwork to sell and kept the profits for themselves.

"No, I did not," I replied, hastily walking away.

A stone fell from the ceiling, causing me to trip over it. As I looked up from the floor, the imposing countenance of Fredrick Rowanson stared down at me.

Mhayree appeared beside me. "Wasn't that one a bit messy?"

"That's an understatement," I said, closing my eyes. "It took five daggers and two swords to inflict thirty-seven wounds."

"You counted?"

"He was one of my first kills and I was testing different methods. The counting helped me to focus."

"Do you remember anything else about him?"

"No," I said. "Bothwell told me that no amount of cleaning would take the blood off the walls. I hear the house has been abandoned ever since."

Mhayree helped me to my feet, and I pointed to the plaque.

"What?" she said.

"How is that possible? 1705 to 1897?" I replied. "That makes him 192 years old."

Mhayree didn't answer, and stepped in front of Olivia Hathor: January 25th 1703 – August 12th 1897.

Miss Hathor put up a good fight! I came out, battered and bruised, with a bloody nose and burst lip. Despite Jacque training me to fight, each one of the techniques had been put to the test. Unluckily for Olivia, I carried enough chains to tie her up before driving a sword through her heart. One of the Councillors offered me her diamond necklace as payment. I declined and asked for Jacque instead.

"She was 194, Mhayree," I said. "That doesn't make any sense."

No reply.

"And why are their portraits here? How did they all know each other?"

"All in good time," Mhayree said, before walking away.

"For now, just reflect on the fact that you murdered them."

Amongst others, I thought.

Looking up at my victims, I felt ashamed. Not for murdering them, but for not giving a damn about their lives. Once they were dead, that was my job done. Their deaths were a means to an end. Jacque was all that mattered. It never occurred to me that somebody, somewhere, might grieve for these people.

Mhayree stopped in front of an arched doorway engraved with an etching of the moon. She turned the handle and opened the door. "Go in."

I stepped inside without taking my eyes off her. The room was sparse, with bare floorboards, crumbling paintwork, and a leaky ceiling. Two chairs and a couch surrounded a fireplace. The glow of the fire within shone upon two figures – my mother, with Amelie perched upon her knee.

"Elise!" my mother exclaimed, putting my sister down. She ran, arms outstretched, and grabbed me, holding me close. "I was so worried about you."

"No need," I said, pulling away.

Beads of sweat appeared across her forehead as she dabbed a tear from her eye. "No matter," she said, attempting to smile, "you're here now."

Amelie wandered towards us.

"Hello," she whispered, tilting her head.

I knelt down to hug her. "Thank goodness you're all right. I've missed you so much."

"A big fire brought us. And it went phtzzzz... Phtzzzz... Phtzzzz..." Amelie said, stifling a yawn.

"Fire?" I asked.

"Aye, well enough of that for now," Mhayree interrupted. "I think it's time for this young lady to join the others in the nursery."

She took my sister from me, gave her to our mother for an obligatory good night kiss, and left the room.

An awkward silence filled the room as my mother and I avoided looking at each other. She sat on a black, high-backed chair in front of the fire, and I paced the room. In the corner hung a portrait, bearing down upon us both. This one was impossible to forget – my first victim – Rebeka Toulouse: 7th February 1652 – 18th May 1897. Her eyes reminded me of my mother; even more so than when I drove a machete through her abdomen. In the portrait, she stood next to a man, and two children – a boy and a girl.

"Elise," my mother muttered, beckoning me to sit next to her. I sat down and placed the wax work head upon a table.

"Where are father and Étienne?" I asked.

She lowered her head. "At home. I could not let Amelie suffer as you did. As soon as you left-"

"I was thrown out of the house."

"Yes. I knew I had no choice. I escaped with her in the middle of the night. Marius can't find her here. She will be safe now. You too – you'll never have to leave. That's why Mhayree sent you that letter."

I leaned back in the chair as my mother braided the hair on the wax work head. "You mean the one signed from a Phoenix?"

"Yes," my mother said, smiling to herself.

I folded my arms and watched her become lost in her own little world. She turned misty-eyed and appeared deep in thought, as though gazing at a far-off land. "Is 'Phoenix' some sort of code word?"

"No," my mother said, frowning, and avoiding eye-contact. She leaned forward and stoked the fire with a rusty iron poker.

I slouched down and waited for her to elaborate. She didn't. "So, are you actually claiming Mhayree is a Phoenix?"

"One of many," Mhayree said, walking through the door, carrying a handful of laundry. "You included, Elise."

"Me?" I said, unsettled by her sudden appearance.

"Let's not get into this now, Mhayree," my mother said, tutting and shaking her head. "We've said far too much already."

"No, I think we should get into this now," I said, standing up. "You've invited me to a creepy, haunted castle…"

"Haunted?" my mother said, with a nervous laugh. "You have such an imagination, my love."

With my hands on my hips, I tapped the floor with my foot impatiently. "What about the portraits, mother? Have you not seen the plaques?" I pointed towards Rebeka Toulouse. "How can that woman over there have been 245 years old when she died?"

My mother looked at Mhayree, worried.

"And what about the others in the gallery?" I continued. "None of them were under 100. That doesn't make any sense."

Mhayree pursed her lips and started to fold the laundry on the table. My mother moved to stand in front of the window.

"Are either of you going to say anything?" I said. Both of them remained silent. "No? Fine. What about the letter? Who delivered it?"

"I did," Mhayree answered, grappling with the puff sleeves of a rather large blouse.

"How?" I replied. "When I went back to your house, you'd already gone."

"I was in hiding, not gone."

"Where?"

"None of your business," Mhayree said, eyeing me with suspicion.

"And you couldn't have waited for me?" I said, walking towards her. "You didn't even try to help save me."

Mhayree raised her head and glared at me. "What do you take me for? I-"

"And what about Étienne?" I interrupted.

My mother turned around and joined Mhayree and me. "Beyond saving. He is to join the Inservium. His father and Bothwell were very persistent."

"He is his father's son!" Mhayree snorted.

"Yes," my mother whispered, stroking my face. "But I'm doing everything to ensure that you don't end up your father's daughter."

Mhayree widened her eyes, as if mocking the sentiment. The women sat down beside each other. Mhayree lifted the wax head and twirled its hair. "Talking of sons and daughters," she said, "the Councillors are now ordering the killing of children... Starting with my Freya."

My mother glanced up at me.

"I'd hate to be the idiot who tried to harm her," Mhayree continued.

"Your daughter is safe," I replied, rolling my eyes.

"Oh, I know she is!" she said, giving me a death-stare.

Neither she nor my mother took their eyes off me.

Mhayree continued to play with the wax head. "Who taught you how to make those?" I asked, trying to divert her attention.

"Madame Marie Tussaud," she smiled. "She went to London to sell her paintings. We met at one of her exhibitions at the Lyceum Theatre. Luckily, she left behind that no-good, lazy husband of hers in France."

"Does this have a point, dearest?" my mother said, with almost a tinge of jealousy in her voice.

Mhayree took no notice and continued. "And the stories she could tell of Marie Antoinette and Louis. Just shocking. *And then*, she showed me their death masks she created after they'd been guillotined during the Revolution..."

History was not my strongest subject, but even I knew that the dates didn't match up. "Correct me if I'm wrong, but, the French Revolution was in 1789-"

"Lasted ten years," my mother interrupted. "Worst decade of my life!" Her cheeks flushed and her neck shone with sweat. I ignored her and assumed that she was rambling.

"And was Marie Tussaud a Phoenix, too?" I sniped, turning my attention to Mhayree. "I'm not sweeping that under the carpet."

"I always had my suspicions, but no," Mhayree said.

"And you supposedly met her in?" I said, pacing up and

down.

"1803." Mhayree said, stuffing her hand down the side of the chair to retrieve a packet of biscuits.

I leaned against a wall, and looked up at the ceiling, exasperated. "That was 94 years ago. Mhayree, you can't be any more than 40."

"What's the matter, Elise? You look like you've seen a ghost," she said, nibbling a digestive.

"Is that what you are?"

"Oh, no my dear. The only ghosts around here are the ones you created," she said, narrowing her eyes. "You see, your auntie Mhayree here, is in her 150s. And your mother? Well she's still a baby, in her 120s."

I looked to my mother for reassurance. None came. Instead, she dabbed herself with a handkerchief, and blew a sweaty strand of hair from her eyes.

So, this is the asylum, I thought. Here, delusions run free and madness reigns over the castle. Queen Mhayree thought she was immortal and my mother – her lady in waiting – bowed to Her Majesty's whims. Perhaps there was also a princess hidden in a tower somewhere, waiting to be rescued.

"Mhayree, this may not all be necessary," my mother cried.

"Mirella, she's displaying every sign of transitioning. You can't hide from it any longer."

My mother nodded reluctantly and stood in front of Rebeka Toulouse's portrait. Gazing up, she sighed, before turning to face me.

"What I am about to tell you will sound strange, but you have nothing to be afraid of."

"Go on," I said, wandering over to her.

"We are not like other women, Elise," she continued. "You, Mhayree, and I were born cursed…"

"Some of us prefer to consider it a gift," Mhayree added.

"That depends on perspective," my mother replied, before wrapping her arm around my shoulder. "Hundreds of years ago, a Hungarian noble woman called Erzsébet Báthory was imprisoned for the mutilation and murder of over six hundred and fifty young women. She believed that the secret of eternal youth was held within the blood of virgins, and so took to bathing in and drinking the blood of her victims."

"Bearing in mind that the evidence against her was tenuous at best. Too many political enemies against one powerful woman," Mhayree said, standing up.

My mother shook her head in disbelief. "She murdered hundreds of innocents, Mhayree."

"I'm just saying, read some alternative books about the history," Mhayree said, smiling. "And, if you're pointing the finger about murdering innocent people, let's not forget…" she added, pointing at me.

My mother's eyes widened, offended. "Anyway, this earned Báthory the nickname 'The Blood Countess'. One night, October 31st 1604, thirteen young peasant girls were summoned to the Countess's castle on the pretence of becoming handmaidens. Instead, what awaited the young girls was a night of being whipped, impaled, and having the flesh bitten from their bodies."

Nice to know that there are worse people than me in the world, I thought. My mother kept watching me, as though waiting for a reaction. The worried expression on her face suggested I was disappointing her.

"The story goes," she continued, "that one of the girls, Gizella Havasi, lay in a pool of her own blood and witnessed the Countess lapping up the drops as they seeped into the floor. At that moment, she made a blood vow that for every drop that spilled from her veins she would take back a thousand times over."

Mhayree nodded, smirking, and I wondered if it was Báthory's bloodlust, or Gizella's gutsiness that impressed her. Still, my mother didn't relent.

"As the life began to drain from the girls, the Countess soaked them in freezing cold water before tossing them out onto the snow. If it had been any other night, then the young girls surely would have died. However, unbeknownst to Báthory and her servants, the girls were followers of the Old Ways – they were witches."

"If either of you two bring out wands…" I said. My mother ignored me and carried on.

"They cried out to the Moon Goddess to save them. On the stroke of midnight, the Goddess came to each one with a proposition. They could either succumb to their wounds and die, or become vampires and live forever – which of course would come at a price."

Her hands trembled, and I guided her towards a chair. Mhayree kissed my mother's cheek, and held her close to offer comfort.

"You should not encourage her fairy tales, Mhayree," I said.

"Still not a believer?" she replied.

"I'm too old for ghost stories," I added, before wiping my mother's forehead with a handkerchief. "Perhaps you should concentrate on getting better."

"I agree. The history lesson can continue at some other point," Mhayree said, turning from my mother to look me in the eyes. "The bottom line is, Elise … You're a vampire. A Phoenix vampire, to be exact. Congratulations!" She then returned to my mother.

I burst out laughing. Between the Councillors forcing me to become a murderer, my father thinking me a whore, and my mother and scary Mhayree drinking too much laudanum, I considered my own madness to be closer to sanity than most. Watching the two women, I came to pity them. Inservium law was not kind to females. We were afforded no right to own property, our children legally belonged to their fathers, and a mere hint of sexual or imaginative expression could land us a lobotomy. Perhaps Mhayree and mother were prime examples of a bored mind.

"You've been reading that book that just came out, haven't you? The one by that Stoker fellow," I said.

"Dracula? Aye. Why?" Mhayree replied.

"Have you, Elise? I'm not sure I approve of you reading

97

such stories!" my mother gasped.

"But her killing people you're all right with?"

My mother shot Mhayree a look of horror. "Obviously not! But I think we can agree, Mhayree, that those blood transfusion scenes were clearly euphemisms," she whispered.

Her eyes twinkling, Mhayree muttered, "Indeed. And we know all about that."

With that, I was done. For all I knew, Jacque was already dead. If not, me staying in the castle wasn't going to save him. I would continue my murdering rampage until he came back to me. Erzsébet Báthory would look like an amateur next to me.

As I left the room, I heard Mhayree whisper, "She will come back. We are the only ones who can save the boy."

"Pardon?" I said, turning back.

"That didn't take much time," she said.

"What do you mean you are the only ones who can save Jacque?" I replied, prowling towards her.

"Who?" Mhayree grinned.

I threw a sharp right hook to her face.

She stopped grinning.

Then, grabbing her by the hair, I dragged her across the floor, and pinned her down onto the desk. From our previous fight, I learned not to underestimate her. So, I climbed on top of her back, wound one leg around her neck and under her chin, whilst my other leg stabilized my own weight. She began choking and banging on the table with her palms. My mother rushed towards us and tried to pull me away from Mhayree.

"Elise, she's going to die!"

"Yes, mother, I'm familiar with people's expressions when they are dying," I said, pressing more of my weight between Mhayree's shoulder blades, and pushing her windpipe deeper into the desk. "Tell me what you meant Mhayree!" She let out a few gurgles whilst losing the battle to dislodge me from her back. "What do you know about Jacque?"

"Elise!" my mother screamed. "I'll tell you. I'll tell you

about Jacque."

I stopped, and the room fell silent. My mother held my arm, prising me from Mhayree. "Elise," she whispered.

Keeping an eye on Mhayree's every move, I released her and stood on the desk. She stared at me and rubbed her throat.

"I've got to hand it to you, you're good. Even without your fancy weapons," she laughed. "A promise is a promise. Come with me and you'll find out about your boy."

Without hesitation, I leapt down from the desk.

"This had better not be a trick," I said, as Mhayree wrapped her arm around my shoulder. She shook her head and guided me out the room.

"No," my mother said, grabbing my hand. She looked up at the portrait of Rebeka Toulouse. "We start with her."

"This isn't more vampire nonsense, is it?" I sighed.

My mother gave a sad smile. "Humour me, if you will."

I rolled my eyes, leaned against the desk, and drummed my fingers on the surface.

"Her maiden name was Havasi," my mother said. "She was born in Marcali, Hungary. And this is her husband, Matheo Toulouse. He died during the French Revolution."

My mother paused to face me.

"And?" I said, shrugging my shoulders.

"And," she continued, pointing towards the boy in the portrait, "this is Pierre, who died at the age of seventy-nine. And the young girl – their daughter – is me, aged five and a half."

As she stood under the figure of Rebeka, the family resemblance was impossible to deny. With a sick feeling in my stomach, I walked over to join my mother as the realisation of what was happening hit me. "All dead, except me. But, of course, you already know that, Elise," she said.

At that moment, neither of us could look at each other. We both knew that I'd murdered my own grandmother.

CHAPTER NINE

"How could you possibly not have known?" Mhayree replied.

"In my experience, it is best not to know too many details about my victims."

Mhayree scoffed and leaned against a chair. "You didn't read about it in newspapers, or pay attention to town gossip?"

"I didn't recognise her name," I said. "It's not like I've ever met her before. And whose fault is that, mother?"

"It's all very complicated," my mother stuttered, pacing up and down in front of the portrait.

Mhayree stood up, looking like a governess about to impart a history lesson. "None of that matters. This is a Second Cleansing, Elise," she said. "The Inservium have been hunting the descendants of the original Thirteen Phoenixes and exterminating us like rats in a sewer."

My mother reached out her hand towards Rebeka's portrait. She smiled as though remembering happier times. As her fingers touched the oil paint, she stopped herself and pulled them away. "In 1667 during the First Cleansing, your grandmother and Gizella – your great-grandmother – travelled from France when they heard the Inservium were killing our kind. Your grandmother was in the heart of the battle. At only fifteen years old, she was the youngest warrior of the coven. Luckily, the inexperience of youth didn't dampen her ability to kill."

"How many?" I asked.

"Enough. You've killed more, I believe," Mhayree said,

under her breath.

"Mhayree!" said my mother.

"Sorry," Mhayree replied, taking a seat. "But you have to admit it's a family trait."

She returned my sideways glance with a smirk.

My mother, oblivious to the catfight brewing between Mhayree and me, continued babbling. "Every night the Councillors hunted the families of the original Phoenixes. Men were beheaded, their severed skulls sent in boxes to their wives or mothers. Women were raped, paraded around for the Councillors' pleasure and finally murdered. Their bones were buried within the walls of the Inservium. And the children – who your grandmother tried to keep safe underground – were kidnapped, rounded up and burned alive in a mass pyre."

For several minutes, I remained silent, unable to find the right words. My mother and Mhayree watched me – scrutinising – and waited for me to say something. Anything.

"They don't teach that in history," I blurted. Those weren't the right words. The two women frowned at me.

"No, they don't," Mhayree said, her voice slow and deliberate.

I looked up to study the portrait of Rebeka Toulouse. "Am I like her?" I said.

My mother nodded. "You do look alike."

"I didn't mean that. I'm talking about the kill-"

"Let's not discuss that," my mother interrupted, closing her eyes.

I stepped forward, and examined the fine features of my grandmother's face. The cold, blue eyes, striking cheekbones, and elegant, heart-shaped mouth. Not a woman to be messed with, I thought.

"How cruel and ingenious of the Councillors to force her granddaughter to murder her," I mumbled.

"We will not talk of this," my mother said, pointing a finger in my face.

"And now they come after you again. What possible threat could *you* pose?" I said, looking her up and down.

She didn't answer. Instead, she continued to stare at the portrait as though lost in her own world.

Mhayree, watching my mother, reached out to hold her hand. "We are different from the humans. Which, to the Inservium means we are unpredictable. We are the unknowable and the misunderstood. The uncontrollable. They use their religion and laws to justify their crimes. They think their Idol is worth more than our Goddess and God. Our customs are not their customs. Our beliefs, history, and existence are inconceivable to them. And the ultimate insult is… we refuse to worship them," Mhayree said.

"No. We just hide from them," my mother muttered, releasing Mhayree's hand.

Mhayree lowered her head and crossed her legs. The Councillors would have accused her of promiscuity for baring her ankles; but for me, at that moment, the small rebellious act made her a heroine.

"Well they don't permit drinking blood in the streets – only wine, water and the occasional sherry," Mhayree said.

"Do not pretend that's why we hide, Mhayree," my mother said.

"You drink *blood*?" I asked, disgusted.

My mother ran her hand along the gold plaque bearing her name, a hint of a melancholic smile appearing on her face. As her hand fell, she sighed. Walking past, she patted my shoulder and drifted like a dandelion seed out of the room.

"Don't you think you've kept enough secrets from me?" I shouted at her. "Bothwell wouldn't have had power over me if you'd been honest."

"Behave!" Mhayree said, standing up.

"Does this mean the Councillors never had any intention of returning Jacque to me?"

Mhayree's face fell, and she looked at me with pity. "I

don't know." She picked up a candelabrum, and ushered me to follow her.

The hallway was chilled, with a fusty dampness lingering in the air. My wisps of breath lost themselves within the darkness as I looked up and down the narrow corridor, but found no sign of my mother. Mhayree remained silent and walked along the floor with the grace of a lily floating on a pond. Her skin was frosted opal, her lips drained to milkyness, and the whites of her eyes drowned in blood. The rise and fall of her girded mulberry bodice ceased. She was an animated corpse.

Pressing myself against the wall, I feared one day I would transform into a beautiful monstrosity like her.

Mhayree linked her arm through mine to guide me. "Do not be afraid of what you will become," she whispered.

"My mother said she would tell me about Jacque. Was that another lie?"

"Do not make assumptions about your mother. You have no idea what she has done for you."

"I know she brought Amelie here… and not me," I replied.

"Oh, she came for you. You were out murdering our kind." Mhayree hauled me from the wall. "Now, come with me."

Seeing her elongated incisors slice through the words like a guillotine, I had no desire to disobey.

We climbed a rotten oak staircase to the third floor – the moonlight shining through the large gaps of missing stone exposed the buttresses outside. As we reached the landing, I sensed the presence of three beings watching us. A flash of dark hair darted across the corridor and crouched behind a balcony. As she settled, the woman snarled and bared her pointed teeth at me. She lunged forward, and a young man wearing a top hat and cravat held out his arm to stop her. A third woman – leather clad with snow white curls cascading to the floor – laughed whilst shaking her head, heckling me. Mhayree loosened my fingers from her arm as my nails dug into her elbow.

"Not everyone will welcome you here. You would be wise to remember that," she whispered.

We stood beside a wall guarded by a bronze statue of a masked woman. Mhayree clasped her hand around its outstretched palm and pulled it downwards. A gust of wind and mass of dust swept over us as the wall opened to reveal a secret passageway concealing a stone staircase.

"This way," Mhayree said.

As we climbed the winding steps, a pair of flapping bat wings skimmed past my cheek, causing me to stumble backwards. Within the darkness, Mhayree's voice echoed, "Stay with me." Regaining my footing, I counted the one hundred and ninety-nine steps leading to the top of the turreted tower, where an arched doorway greeted us. Mhayree laid the candelabrum on the stone floor and dusted down her muslin skirt before inviting me in.

We entered a domed room draped in scarlet, silver, and violet rags; silk and velvet cushions were scattered across the dusty surfaces, grey and green furs spilled over a misshapen, wrought-iron bed, a cracked gold filigreed mirror hung upon the mouldy brickwork, and the musky scent of books entwined with the dusting of jasmine perfume. In the midst of these exotic surroundings, a young man knelt with his eyes half closed, staring down at a blank piece of parchment resting on his knees. His head was tilted to the side and held in place by a female's hand clenching his slicked-back, dark brown hair. Behind him sat a young woman in a cobweb-covered wheelchair, with her lips pressed deep into his exposed neck, causing two drops of blood to slither down his collarbone. When he glimpsed the two of us standing before them, he nudged the legs of the female. Her rapturous gaze darted towards us and her mouth, dripping with blood, broke into a dirty chuckle. She swiped her wavy veil of blonde hair from her face and whispered into the man's ear. Her stained tongue swiped the edges of her red coated fangs with every syllable.

The man shot his head back and let out a hearty, "Ha!" With that, the female unravelled her arm from around his chest and placed her wrist against his lips, inviting him to bite down and suck the vein.

"Mhayree, always good to see you!" the woman said with a Russian accent. "I take it this is Elise, the-" she made a stabbing motion with her hand and gave a slight grimace.

"Aye, and the little madam just tried to kill me!" Mhayree replied.

"Again? Please don't try to kill me, or I will be forced to retaliate." The woman held out her free arm. "My name is Natashka Mikhailov."

I leaned over, trying to avoid eye contact with the man, and shook Natashka's hand. She caught me glancing at her guest, and asked, "Are you hungry? He has plenty to go around."

The man ceased feeding and faced Natashka. He gave her an incredulous look before shaking his head in amusement and returning to the vein.

"She's not at that stage yet," Mhayree said.

The blonde gave me a look full of pity, and peered over the man's shoulder to examine the blank parchment. Frowning, she said, "Surely you have drunk enough of me to find inspiration."

He released her wrist and gave a knowing smile. "Oh please, you enjoy it!"

Natashka raised an eyebrow at him.

With a cheeky tilt of his head, he continued, "Who knows you better than I do?"

She rolled her eyes and groaned in defeat. "Go with Mhayree. I have to speak with Elise for a little while."

The two began conversing in a strange language. Each time his hand gesticulated, her eyes would follow as though anticipating her next meal. She reached for a grey linen shirt piled on top of a wooden trunk. "Here," she said, "I made you this. It should replace that blood stained one."

Standing, he took the shirt and embraced her.

Mhayree lifted the candelabrum from the floor, and, with her finger, wiped away the blood from the young man's throat. Not once did she look at me as they walked out the door.

I bowed my head and stood with my hands behind my back whilst Natashka licked the remaining red stains from her mouth.

"Elise," she whispered with a half chuckle. I looked up and saw her impish smile and eyelashes flutter. "Maybe you should sit down, and take off your coat, which appears to be swallowing you."

I gritted my teeth and grinned. Strolling over to the bed, I sprawled across the edge of the blankets, hoping my bohemian performance was fooling the blood thirsty Russian. As I took off Jacque's coat, and placed it on the bed, I thought, for a brief second, a low growl came from under the green furs. Natashka wheeled herself in front of the cracked mirror, grabbed a pot of black kohl, and began swiping dark rings around her eyes.

"Am I the first person that you have seen like this?" she enquired.

"No, no I have seen people in wheelchairs before..." I reassured her.

"I meant a vampire who is feeding."

I could feel my cheeks blushing as I cleared my throat. "Oh! I mean aye."

"I see..." Natashka said. "And you have not seen people in wheelchairs, Elise. They keep us hidden away or locked in institutions." She peered at me through the cracks in her reflection and gave an enigmatic smile before applying crimson lipstick to her lips. "I hear you killed my horse!"

"What?" I said.

"The black stallion you set fire to – Veritas – he is mine."

"I... I... it's... funny story..."

Natashka brushed away my desperation with a wave of

her hand.

"He is fine. We fed him some graveyard soil and he was back to his old self – before the cremation obviously!" She puckered her lips, blowing a kiss into the mirror whilst sprucing her hair and readjusting the black, mesh sleeves on her dress.

I'm going to wake up in an asylum, I thought.

As I looked down at a spider crawling along the floor, two rickety wheels and a pair of bare feet approached. Natashka laid her hand upon mine and said in her Russian coolness, "Do not worry Little Girl of the Ashes. In 1837, when I was in transition, I set fire to the Winter Palace of Saint Petersburg. The blaze lasted three days, killing thirty men, and believe me, they did not come back to life. That is a true reason for guilt!" She patted my hand as sadness teased away her smile.

"1837?"

"Yes. I remember quite vividly hearing the screams and smelling the burning flesh. Oddly enough, the royal ministers considered the imperial throne more important to be saved."

"How old are you exactly?"

"Less than four-score... My grandfather devised a plan to tell Emperor Nicholas the fire happened because of smoke blowing into a vent and setting light to Peter the Great Hall."

"I murdered four people tonight," I confessed.

"You have murdered many more before. Why should those four be any different?"

"Because tonight, I enjoyed it."

Natashka looked into my eyes, as though searching for a glimmer of a soul, and gave a sad smile. She manoeuvred herself to sit in front of a colossal stack of books, removed one scribbled with disjointed symbols, and left the towering hoard to wobble.

"Little Girl of the Ashes?" I said.

Natashka didn't answer.

"You wrote the poem in the Phantasma, didn't you?" I continued.

107

A slight smirk teased at the corners of her mouth. She called me to join her and opened the dusty relic to a page written in unfamiliar script.

"Do you read Bavossian?" Natashka asked.

I shook my head.

"Hmm… you will need to learn," she said. "It is the language of the Phoenixes, first created by one of our founders, Juliska Bavos, so that others could not decipher our secrets. Have you never heard your mother or Mhayree speak it?"

I thought back to when Mhayree had spoken to the skeleton driver outside her house, and the whispers of the three vampires from the hallway of the castle. A vision came to mind of my mother sitting on a rocking chair, singing to me when I was a child. She would stay with me in the nursery – located far away from my father's study – and wait until I fell asleep. She told me the songs were a secret, and that she would teach me one day. She never did. Night after night, I drifted to sleep to the sound of her sweet, safe voice, and would no longer be afraid of my father.

Mina da voina hakkan troita.

Soista na dollna.

Sipna kriina voikka.

I could not translate the lyrics, but they brought back lost memories, of a language hidden within me.

"I will teach you." Natashka said. "Do you know how our families became vampires?"

"To be honest, I've been told a lot," I said, folding my arms and tapping my foot on the floor. "Apparently, I murdered my grandmother, my mother is over a century old, and then the word 'vampire' gets thrown around. Can you guess at which point it all became a little bit farfetched?"

Natashka threw her head back and laughed. "Just wait," she said. "What part of the origin story did your mother and Mhayree tell you?"

"They told me about Erzsébet Báthory. How she mutilated

the original Thirteen and left them for dead," I said. "Then some goddess appeared and offered them a deal."

"It's not the most poetic version of the story I've heard," Natashka said. "But you understand the basics."

"Thank you," I said, shrugging.

The Blood Vow

"Now we get to the good part," Natashka said, flicking through the pages of the book. She raised her arms as though conducting an orchestra. The flames of the candles flared giving a spotlight to the wall opposite. Shadows crept along the wall, twisting and writhing into the silhouettes of dying maids. "To the thirteen girls the choice seemed simple – do whatever they had to do to survive. Now, the Old Ways tell us that on the night of October 31st the Moon Goddess visits the Underworld to mourn at the tomb of her dead lover, the Sun God."

The silhouettes contorted into a melting moon whose tears formed the shape of a woman crying beside the sun. From the depths of the shadows a skeleton hand loomed towards the consorts. I faced Natashka and found her slumped forward with her head down and her fingers tracing the words in the book. "Each year, the God sacrifices himself to the King of the Reapers to allow Death to take dominion over the Earth. As the Circle of Seasons revolves, the Sun God returns."

I tilted Natashka's head upwards to face me. My hand recoiled as, looking back at me, two black, hollow sockets replaced her green eyes. Natashka's chin dropped to her chest. Caught between curiosity and stupidity, I couldn't persuade myself to leave.

Without pausing, Natashka continued. "The Moon Goddess, upon hearing her thirteen daughters crying, abandoned her lover in the Underworld. With the waning moon suspended over the Báthory castle, the Goddess appeared to the girls and offered each one a choice." From the ether, my mother's voice filled the room, repeating what she had told me mere hours ago, "succumb to their wounds and die or become vampires and live forever – which of course would come at a price."

The shadowy figures turned red, as crimson fluid oozed from the wall and slinked towards my feet. Logic and reason finally convinced me to move, as I edged my way to the door and reached for the handle. It snapped from my hand. The lock clicked and I found myself imprisoned. Natashka's voice echoed through the room.

"In return for the gift, the Goddess demanded the blood vow crafted by Gizella be honoured by each girl as a forfeit for their humanity. One by one, the thirteen agreed and so surrendered to their long sleep in the tomb of the Sun God."

Battering the door, I called for help. No one answered. I banged my fist against the wall and rattled the handle. The door remained fixed to its wooden frame. The crimson fluid pooled round my feet and receded into the floorboards. Again, I tried the handle, and screamed, pleading for someone to help.

"As the months passed, winter yielded to the blossoming buds of spring and the Sun God awoke in the tomb to reclaim his kingdom. The Goddess, standing by his side, rejoiced in presenting their thirteen daughters, who remained in slumber," Natashka said.

"Day and night," she continued, as the shadows on the wall contorted into a young maid under a pair of narrowed eyes, "the God and Goddess waited for the girls to reawaken. Summer green turned to autumn gold but none of the thirteen stirred. Once again, the King of the Reapers took rule over the earth and the Sun God prepared for his journey into the Underworld. The Goddess, fearing the lonely darkness without her lover and her daughters, vowed, before the God's sacrifice, the thirteen would be resurrected."

"That night," she continued, lowering her voice as the silhouette of a red moon rose on the wall. "The Blood Moon hung on a thread of a spider's web high above the barren earth plain. The Goddess took a sword and sliced the moon into a crescent, collecting its blood in a cauldron." A pair of pointed teeth emerged from the moon. "Descending into the Underworld, she knelt at the side of each girl and sank her teeth into their bare necks. As their blood drained into the tomb, she poured the moon's blood from the cauldron into their mouths, giving them the gifts of night. Retrieving a piece of the moon's web from the sky, the Goddess sealed the girls' wounds with the silver thread."

"The Sun God, although weakening, embalmed the girls in his waning rays of fiery sunlight. In doing so he gave his last sacrifice and finally succumbed to his yearly slumber, yet again leaving the Goddess." The shadows shuddered, wrapping around the figure of a maid. Natashka's body convulsed as her arms rose higher and higher.

"The flames, raging and untameable, ravaged the thirteen bodies but never burning through flesh. On the third night, the Goddess sat on the snowy hillside where she had once found the mutilated girls. Beneath the ice, the earth shook as the snow charred and melted."

A silhouette of a Phoenix glowed in the centre of the wall, wings outstretched, emblazoned, its head bowing to the moon. Scarlet droplets dripped from its feathers, burst into flames and dissolved into the ether. Natashka fell limp, and her arms collapsed onto her lap. "One by one, the thirteen rose from the ground and stood before their Goddess. Resurrected from the flames and thirsty for blood, the Phoenixes were reborn."

The shadows scattered. The blood disappeared. The door unlocked, offering me a chance of escape.

But I stayed anyway. Curiosity and stupidity win every time.

CHAPTER TEN

The book slammed shut, snapping Natashka out of her trance. "Interesting, isn't it?" she beamed. "Why are you standing at the door?"

I paused for several seconds before managing to stutter, "I like it over here."

Natashka raised her eyebrow, unconvinced. "Were you scared?"

"No, I don't get scared," I said, walking towards her, and hiding my trembling hands inside my trouser pockets. A drop of blood dribbled into the corner of my mouth where I had chewed my bottom lip a little too hard.

Natashka laughed and said, "You should not do that in front of a vampire!"

Unsure if she was attempting humour or issuing a serious warning, I frowned and shuffled a few steps away from her.

I licked a drop of blood, and a sharp pain shot through my gums. As I held my mouth and groaned, Natashka pulled me towards her and yanked my lips apart. "Finally, your fangs are preparing to grow! You do not enjoy blood, no?"

"No!"

Natashka pondered for a moment, her eyes, sparkling with curiosity. Grinning, she concluded, "Well, you will enjoy plenty now." She spun her chair and heaved another book onto her lap. "Come, there is more."

"I'm not sure I can take much more," I said.

"Oh, but it's fun," Natashka replied. "I never get to impart my wealth of knowledge. People just aren't interested in the Old Stories anymore."

"Well… Now, this is just a thought… Have you considered not scaring them half to death?"

Natashka, taken aback, stared at me.

"No? Never mind," I said. With my gums pulsing, I collapsed into an oversized armchair.

Natashka settled beside me and threw a cushion onto my chest. "Here, bite down on this. It helps to break them through."

As I sank my teeth into the soft velvet, my mouth throbbed with a dull pain – a good pain – the kind of pain that means relief is on its way.

"How much of your family history do you know?" Natashka asked.

Muffling my mouth against the cushion, I answered, "My mother is an oddity, and my father is a complete fu-"

"We start with the original Phoenixes," Natashka interrupted. She unclasped the silver moon shaped buckle which bound the leather book. Rifling through the worn corners of the pages, she stopped and showed me the sketched portraits of the thirteen women.

"This is Gizella Havasi, a direct ancestor of yours. After marrying a Hungarian artist, she moved to France and began a French line of vampires. They had three daughters – including your grandmother, Rebeka. Your family settled in a little town outside Paris until your mother was instructed by her Aunt Colette to come to Loch Fala."

"Instructed? She told me she came here to be a nanny a year after meeting my father."

"No, she arrived twenty-five years ago and married your father the same year you were born. As your paternal grandparents were also French it made for an easy match."

"Has everything about that woman been a lie?"

Natashka grimaced, and replied, "It's uncertain. She and Mhayree are very secretive."

She held out her hand to halt any further interruptions and continued. "These women here are Lena Vadas, Lilianna

Dali, Frida Katona, Nikolett Fodor, and Renata Vida. Nobody knows what has happened to their lines. The Inservium killed many of their descendants and most of whom survived went into hiding. Juliska Bavos, as you already know created our language and wrote many of the books you see here. Her line remained in Loch Fala and fought the Inservium during the First Cleansing. Juliska died in 1703 trying to save her son, Viktor Auldwyrd, from the Councillors."

"Viktor?" I said, flinching.

"Yes Elise, we all know you killed him," Natashka sighed.

"Honestly, he didn't put up much of a fight!"

"He and his wife had been infiltrating the Inservium for decades. After you killed her, perhaps he thought he didn't have any more reason to live," she said, raising her voice. She pointed to a picture of a round faced woman and continued, "This is Ilona Samsa. She stayed in Scotland and gave birth to four daughters who continued the Scottish, Irish, English, and Welsh lines of vampires. Mhayree is a direct descendant. There is a rumour that Ilona is still alive somewhere but nobody has seen her in seventy years-"

"I don't mean to be rude," I interrupted.

"Go on."

"This is a little overwhelming. There's too much to take in all at once. The Cleansing. The blood drinking. The mythology."

"History, not mythology," Natashka scowled.

"History… Not mythology…" I replied. "And now you want me to memorise the entire family tree?"

"I struggle to see the problem."

"My head is pounding," I said, massaging my temples. "I think I'm getting a migraine."

"And yet, you are still here. It would seem your need for the truth is greater than a slight headache."

I said nothing. She was right. Damn.

"Everything you need to know is right here in this book," Natashka said. "Remember what you need to know at this moment, and, if need be, you can return to read again. The pages will remain the same... Perhaps a slice of *pirog* would help?"

"I don't know what that is."

"Oh, it is delightful! It is a round – sometimes oblong – piece of dough filled with berries, nuts, or if you prefer a more savoury variety, cottage cheese. Let me check if I have a piece lying around."

"I am honestly fine," I said, holding up my hand.

"No, no. I have a craving now. You keep reading," Natashka said, manoeuvring herself to sit beside an apothecary table.

I continued looking through the book and found the portraits of two waif-like women. Noemi and Emilia Bokori. The sisters travelled from Hungary to Italy to start a range of vineyards to produce their own red wine.

"Well, they claimed it was red wine..." Natashka muttered.

Between them, they raised fifteen sons and daughters, most of who kept to Western Europe. A couple travelled to the United States and New Zealand, but they preferred hiding from civilisation.

Natashka squealed with excitement as I turned the page to find a portrait of a blonde, round faced woman with a regal countenance. "Kamilla Nemes, my great-grandmother. Mhayree tells me you've been using her weapons."

"When?"

"When you tried to kill her."

"Oh!" I said, trying to focus on the book.

"What were they like?" Natashka said.

I gave her a sideways glance and smiled. "They were very good daggers."

Natashka squealed again. "Excellent! Anyway," she continued, "Kamilla moved to Russia where she married into the Dvoryanstvo – our nobility – and became a Grand Duchess. My family and I spent our summers with the Tsar and his family in the Alexander Palace-"

"How do you know what pages I'm reading?" I said.

"I just do. Remember, our founders were witches as well as vampires," she said, winking.

She turned to face me, and I narrowed my eyes at her. "You're so suspicious," she laughed.

"True," I said. "So, are you a Russian Princess?"

"I'm a Duchess! I could have had you executed for not curtsying when you came in, but..." she shrugged.

"Mhayree didn't curtsy either..." I said.

"Yes, but she already owns a severed head," she replied. "Keep reading."

I flicked over the page and found Dorika Jonas – the oldest member of the coven.

"After the coven parted ways," Natashka said, "she left Loch Fala and established the Scandinavian line of Phoenixes. You'll also see pictures of her children – twin boys who died of Tuberculosis, and a daughter."

"Died? Aren't vampires immune to illness?"

"The boys weren't vampires. When a female is born into a Phoenix family, she usually transitions naturally into a vampire – not always of course. My sister, for instance, was not destined to become a Phoenix. The males, however, have to be bitten by a female to induce the transformation."

"And their mother didn't bite them to save them?" I said.

"It was too late." Natashka manoeuvred herself once again to sit beside me. "I do not have any leftover *pirog*," she huffed. "My profound apologies."

"Shame. Perhaps some other time," I replied, without looking up from the book.

A spider crawled over Natashka's hand. Instead of swiping it away, she let it wander onto the arm of her chair, dangle from its web until it reached the floor, and scurry behind the fireplace. She lifted the book from my lap and continued.

"And finally, we come to Katalin Arany. The dark-haired

beauty who weaves destruction wherever she goes. During the First Cleansing, there arose a rivalry between Katalin and Gizella as to who should lead the coven into war. Gizella wanted a humane method whereby the Councillors would be held accountable for their crimes. Katalin had other ideas. When the Councillors murdered her husband and three of her four children, she retaliated by slaughtering innocent townspeople. And so, the other Phoenixes had no choice but to exile her, along with her son and unborn child."

Natashka took my hand, traced a finger along an invisible line connecting Katalin and Gizella, and continued. "Before leaving, Katalin captured Gizella and sliced open a vein from both their wrists. As the blood merged on the floor, Katalin cursed the descendants of her rival and vowed that if Havasi and Arany bloodlines united, misfortune would follow the lovers for all time."

Natashka stared, prompting me to react.

"What?" I said.

She rolled her eyes and flicked through the pages of the Arany family tree. "Katalin's offspring," she indicated. "Two sons, one died at the age of nineteen with smallpox. The other was transformed into a Phoenix and married a Comtesse at the French court. They have one surviving son who secretly married a peasant girl and joined the Revolution. They too have a son who has married twice. His second wife is a Phoenix on the Emilia Bokori side. In 1878, they had their first son. Jacque."

Chapter Eleven

Eleven Months Previously

"If your father could see you now, he would have a fit!" Jacque laughed, watching me doing pull-ups on a timber beam. "How are you doing up there?"

"Are you still keeping count?" I said, sweat dripping down my face. "My arms are burning."

"You're either at twenty-six or twenty-seven."

"Jacque, you should be concentrating!"

"Indeed. But there is something rather distracting about a lady exercising in her corset and *my* trousers."

"Remember, dearest, this was your idea," I said, lowering and thickening my voice into a French accent. I attempted my best Jacque impersonation and added, "There are many hidden dangers in the world, Elise. There may come a time when you must defend yourself."

Jacque took a cigarette from behind his ear and began searching for matches. The floor became a mess of scrap paper and books as he emptied drawers, pillows were scattered from one end of the bed to the other, trouser and coat pockets were turned inside out, and the armchair sides he scraped out offered no more than a few crumbs. I couldn't help but enjoy watching the furrowed lines on his forehead deepen.

"Right, where have you hidden them?" he asked, at last.

"You'll have to come find them."

"My love!"

"I'm sorry but I'm very busy right now doing pull-ups in

my corset," I groaned, pulling my chin towards the beam.

"Have you hidden the matches down your corset?" Jacque laughed.

"There is a distinct possibility that's what happened," I said.

Jacque's smile widened, and the room filled with his hearty, boyish cackle. He lowered his head, and a shadow cast from the beam covered his face. Despite hanging fifteen feet from the floor, I sensed his shy blue eyes glancing up at me. He strolled over to our writing desk, removed a black band from one of the drawers, and tied up his wavy hair. By this point, as my muscles seized, and my already aching arms started to cramp, all I wanted to do was give up. But I didn't.

"You're doing well," Jacque said.

"For my first time?"

"For any time."

Two hours had passed with Jacque helping me climb up and down the timber posts. Each time I hung from the beam, completing a set of five pull ups, until I was strong enough to attempt thirty. I must have looked a wreck with my hair clinging to my head, eyeliner running down my cheeks and sweat dripping off my nose.

Jacque ran towards one of the posts, threw his arms and legs around the timber, scaled upwards, and bounced onto the beam. His acrobatics used to baffle me; however, over the past few months I had grown accustomed to his peculiar movements around our home.

"So, are we going to play?" he asked, dropping his legs and hanging by his hands.

"Always!" I replied, managing a sly grin through the pain. "As you failed to accurately keep count, I have decided to start from scratch."

Jacque raised an eyebrow, impressed. "Just like we discussed – make sure your hands are shoulder width apart and facing away from you."

"Uh huh."

"Now ease your full body downwards until your arms are completely stretched."

"You do know you've already told me this?" I said.

Jacque smiled. "And pull yourself up till your chin is over the beam."

Although exhausted, I pushed through the agony it took to tense my upper arms. Fingers clenched until the knuckles turned white, face straining, teeth gritted, I was determined not to be beaten.

"Just a few more, Elise," Jacque promised.

"One... Two... Three..." I counted, hoping each pull up brought me to the last. "Four... Five... Six..."

The extra sting came when I turned to Jacque and noticed he wasn't breaking a sweat.

"Can you take any more?" he said.

"Oh, definitely!" I lied, blowing a strand of hair out of my eyes.

I could hear him laughing whilst studying me. "Up to ten."

Bastard.

It took whole-hearted defiance to complete the final set. Tears rolled down my face, disguising themselves as sweat. Nothing would break me.

"Eight… Nine… Ten," I puffed, dragging myself upwards for the last time. The relief of resting my chin on the beam did nothing to ease the pain.

"Now, to get down," Jacque said. I hadn't factored this into the situation. "I know it hurts, but I need you to listen. Watch what I'm about to do."

He swung his legs backwards, forwards, then over his head, let go of the beam, somersaulted into the air, and landed in a squat on the floor.

"Your turn," he encouraged.

My first instinct was to shut my eyes and pretend the challenge didn't exist. I had trusted Jacque this far, and at least to his knowledge, this was my first time. Little did he know that his *sweetheart*, after watching him scale the rooftop of our house while training, decided to test her own limits. I would be better, I told myself. I would be stronger.

All through the bruises and lashes from learning combat whilst testing my balance on tree branches, the afternoons of sprinting in the pouring rain, skidding through puddles and spraining both my ankles, the bouts of stomach cramps and hallucinations trying to build an immunity against poisonous plants. Jacque never found out.

"What if I do it wrong?" I said.

"Then I'll get you a cold compress."

"And you know where I'd tell you to shove it."

I looked down to the floor and scrutinised the drop. Jacque was watching me and drumming the floorboards with his fingers. It wasn't too far, and a broken leg can always heal.

My hands, slippery with sweat, started sliding from the timber. I can do this, I thought, just swing your legs. So, I did.

"Bend your knees," Jacque called.

I complied. Feeling brave, I took a deep breath and released my fingers, letting go of the beam. The nerves in my stomach fluttered like moths attracted to a hungry, all-consuming flame.

Something was wrong. A blur of tattoo-covered limbs, unruly hair and naked torso ran across the room, and tossed a mattress onto the floor. A thud. Then pain. Then there was darkness.

***

"Elise… Elise, are you alright?" I heard Natashka shout, patting my hand.

"Hmm? Oh aye," I said, gripping the ancient book of family trees which sat on my lap. "What happened?"

"You seemed to go into a little daydream," Natashka replied. "I've been sitting here for ages waiting on you to snap out of it."

"Sorry," I said. "I was just thinking back."

"To Jacque?"

"And me."

Natashka frowned. "Perhaps it was too soon to let you see the book."

Part of me regretted opening it. As I flicked through the pages, I knew I was reading family histories of which I was not a part, and yet, they defined me. It was impossible to deny the sketched portrait was of Jacque; the scrunched dark hair, the kohl eyeliner, the protruding cheekbones - it was him for certain. Scrawled beneath his name – Jacque Angou – lay his date and place of birth, and his parentage. As he had said, his family had been part of the French aristocracy, residing in Paris. His great-grandfather had been given the title of Comte to compensate for his wife being a mistress of the king. This little snippet of ancestral history, I noted, did not feature in the pages of the family tree.

With each page of the Angou family tree, I came to know his mother, Sabine, his father, Roux and his paternal grandparents, Claudette and Georges. Beside Jacque there was a picture of a young man, Rémy.

"I know him!" I blurted out.

"Who?" said Natashka.

"Him," I replied, pointing at the picture. "I saved him last night."

"You must be mistaken. The family rarely leave France – except for Jacque, apparently."

"No, I can guarantee you that man is on the streets of Loch Fala," I said. "Or he might be in my apartment."

Natashka stared at me. "You let a stranger into your apartment?"

"I felt sorry for him," I replied. "I show kindness – sometimes."

"This can't be a coincidence," Natashka said. "Money is no object to the Angous. Why would he need to be homeless? There must be some discord within the family."

I frowned, thinking of the frightened, urchin who sat on the street, offering to exchange his body for mere pennies. "He's been sleeping rough for a long time."

"How do you know?" Natashka asked.

"I just do."

In the picture, Rémy's matted dark hair was transformed into thick shoulder length curls and his hollow cheekbones appeared plump and rosy. His eyes were wide with youthful expectation.

"What did you save him from?"

I didn't answer.

"Jacque has a brother?" I whispered to myself.

"He never told you?" Natashka answered.

"No... No, he didn't," I said, saddened by yet another secret. As I ran my fingers over the image of Jacque's face, I wondered whether I'd truly known the young man who, out of nowhere, had entered my life. Little inconsistencies to which I had once been blind started to reveal themselves. For instance, the reluctance to discuss his childhood in any detailed manner. Then there was his vehement revulsion of the Councillor's practices, despite claiming to have had no dealings with the Inservium. I don't believe in organised religion, he claimed. It also occurred to me that for a man who grew up in France, he knew little of its language. My family kept to themselves. I was home-schooled. I didn't see other children. We moved around from place to place. On the few occasions that I pressed for information he diverted my attention with self-deprecating jokes or suggested a spontaneous trip to the artisan café where we'd end up sipping absinthe into the early hours of the morning.

"Does Jacque know what he is?"

"Who he is, would be a better term. And yes, I believe he does," Natashka said.

"Does he know who I am? Does he know about the curse?" I asked with a slight shrill to my voice.

"That, I am uncertain of."

The thoughts of mine and Jacque's last training session lingered in the back of my mind. "There are many hidden dangers in the world... There may come a time when you must defend yourself." How very prophetic of him. Or perhaps, like an excellent chess master, he planned how to

123

manoeuvre and sacrifice his pawn to make way for his all-powerful Queen Katalin.

I scraped my fingernails across the picture of the Arany matriarch, Katalin, Comtesse d'Angou. A faded image of her husband lingered below her own. As I stared into her face it was easy to imagine her as vindictive, with sulphur running in her veins. I hated her with a deep guttural revulsion. We existed in the same world, but like two positively charged magnets, my blood inherently repelled hers.

Most of all I despised her for being a part of Jacque.

Natashka's voice trickled into my head, "You do not need permission to be angry."

"This isn't anger," I mumbled.

"Then what is it?" Natashka asked, peering beneath my bowed head. She cupped her hand under my chin and brought it up till we faced each other. "You need to say the words, Elise."

I couldn't answer.

Natashka frowned before releasing me. As I brought my hands up to cover my face, I felt the heavy weight of the book being slid off my lap.

"I will only ever tell you this once, Elise. You can cry, you can scream, and you can be angry. But you never... ever... let anyone defeat you!"

Now I was angry.

"I am not defeated," I snapped.

Natashka raised an eyebrow and reached for a silver gilded vanity mirror siting on a table. Turning it towards me, she said, "You look defeated."

Such a polite understatement. In the mirror was a scraggy little lamb with doe eyes and early signs of wrinkles around her mouth. Not the Elise I remembered.

I shoved the mirror into Natashka's lap and straightened my back and shoulders in defiance. "Beauty isn't everything! And what is the point of keeping up appearances if I am alone?"

Natashka shook her head and narrowed her eyes. She wheeled herself in front of a large trunk sitting beside her bed. As she removed piles of books, and what looked to be various whips and blindfolds, she threw them onto a pile of furs lying on her bed. The ominous growl which I'd heard earlier sounded again.

"What is that?" I asked as Natashka opened the lid.

"Oh, nothing for you to worry about," she replied, with her arms buried deep inside the trunk. "*Ura!* Here it is!"

Out came a mass of purple velvet with familiar lilac ivy embroidered throughout. As Natashka gathered the material, two ruffled sleeves escaped her clutches and flopped over her knees.

"My coat," I said.

Natashka sat beside me and gently placed the coat onto my lap. "Your mother brought it with her. She tried everything to get the blood stain out, but in the end, she replaced the fabric."

Unfolding the soft material, I found a small patch a shade or two darker than the original velvet stitched into the coat's sleeve. The edging was laced with silver thread merged with the embroidered outline of a crescent moon cast behind two interlocking initials – M for Mirella and E for Elise. My mother and I forever entwined.

"I'll leave you alone for a while, let you gather your thoughts," Natashka said, moving to the door. "Come downstairs when you are ready. Oh, and if you do decide to change… perhaps consider a wash at least… then be sure to do so behind the screen."

I glanced around the room, checking the walls, ceiling, and stacks of books for signs of anyone she thought would see or smell me.

"There's no need to look so confused," Natashka laughed. "In this room you can never be sure who may be watching."

"What do you mean?"

"You know, people hiding."

"Who?"

She didn't reply.

"Tell me who you meant."

"Do you want me to make some *pirog*?"

"No," I said, huffing as I realised it was pointless trying to make sense of her. "How will you get downstairs?"

"One strange thing at a time, I think. You can't imagine what surprises are lurking round the corner. That reminds me, when you are done, go to the ground floor, take the second passage to the left and turn the corner. You will find me waiting in one of the parlours." As her words faded, she left the room, closing the door behind her.

It only took a few moments of solitude to make me miss the Russian ice maiden. Her presence made the room feel less vast and cold. She brought normality to being a Phoenix – a vampire – a blood drinker. She gave hope to me surviving the transition. Looking around the empty tower and remembering the vagueness of her directions, it occurred to me that I still didn't know where I was to meet her.

I draped the coat over my arm, sighed at the absurdity of wishful thinking, and walked behind the screen. A copper basin and jug filled with water sat waiting on top of a stool. Behind it, propped against the wall, was a cracked, full-length mirror. I hung up the coat, and, tracing the lines of ivy with my fingertips, thought of Jacque. As the old phrase goes, there's a fine line between love and hate. A very fine line indeed. Despite his lies and secrets, I couldn't help but miss him. I rolled up my sleeves and poured the freezing water. My hands turned raw against the bitterness.

Doubt is such an odd thing. Reading one page of an old book had made me question everything I knew about Jacque. A few untold secrets and I was no longer his. A few lines on a family tree had tried to erase every memory, every bit of laughter and every piece of happiness. But he had lied to me.

Untying my hair, the pins scattered across the floor as my dark locks unfurled to my waist. As I washed my face, my cheeks stung from the severe scrubbing. Jacque's shirt drowned my shoulders, making me look like a wilted flower. My trousers sagged and my fingernails were encrusted with dirt and blood. I looked into the mirror and compared myself to the girl I used to be. She would dance on top of a table at the slightest opportunity and strut down the street wearing only an overgrown coat over her undergarments. If anyone dared call her a degenerate lunatic, she drew them dirty looks and laughed at their stupidity. Now she was gone. Perhaps she was never coming back.

"Pull yourself together woman," I said to myself, readjusting my shirt. Taking one last glance into the mirror, I shook my head and smiled.

The purple fabric of my coat reflected in the glass with the embroidered initials shining in the candlelight. Almost without thinking, I grabbed it, put it on and stepped out from behind the screen. Walking towards the door, I heard a low growl again. I tried to ignore it, but as the noise grew more ferocious, so did my curiosity. The floorboards creaked with every creeping step I took towards the bed. The growl softened. Edging closer I held out my hand to pull back one of the green furs. To my surprise, what I found was not some poor dog or nightmarish creature, but instead a young naked man with fangs, granite wings and horns, bound to the bedposts by his wrists.

"Excuse me," he said. His plummy English accent was a far cry from the guttural snarl. "Could you put that back please? Miss Natashka won't be happy if I'm uncovered when she returns."

"The Russian did this to you?"

"Of course. All the time."

"I see. Did you hear our conversation?"

"Oh no," the man replied, frowning. "Miss Natashka instructed me to go to sleep."

"Well I'm sorry to have disturbed you. Do you need anything?"

"A drink would be nice, if I may?"

Taking a glass of water from a table, I put it to his lips and tucked a strand of hair behind one of his horns.

"Thank you, Miss," he said.

I offered a polite smile before returning the blanket over his head.

"Night night," I whispered with a wink, before going out the room, down the winding stairwell, and through the secret passageway into yet another hallway.

Trying to remember the directions Natashka had given me, I found myself in a dusty corridor echoing with the clicking of death-watch beetles. With every corner I turned, the whistling wind welcomed me into abandoned rooms adorned with family portraits. The period styles may have varied – Napoleonic, Renaissance, Edwardian – but one trait remained common throughout. Each face belonged to a person whom I had murdered.

Room by room, I opened the doors to find yet more relics of the past, until finally reaching an old music room with a rusty grandfather clock, long stopped, a creaky rotting crib, and a lopsided piano. As I turned to walk away a sticky coating of cobweb covered my face. Almost immediately after I removed the silky residue from my face, a tune rose from the piano. Haunting notes reverberated round the room, high mixing with low, ecstasy subdued by sadness. I turned around and saw the ivory and ebony keys rising and falling by themselves.

As disconnected rhythms vibrated into booming song, the splintered floorboards rose, and clusters of wrangled fingers, contorted arms and writhing heads emerged to answer the call of music.

The bodies climbed out, dragging their fellow wraiths from the depths of darkness. Decaying flesh dangled from their limbs. Eyeballs hung from sockets. Blood dripped from wounds across their throats and chests. Stabbings. Decapitation. Strangulation. I knew their causes of death, but not their names. I just called them my victims. They formed two lines at either side of me and faced each other. The women in their busty bodices, fishnet stockings and lace knickers posed like derelict beauties, with feathers in their hair. The men in kilts, top hats and bare torsos stood to attention awaiting the ladies demands.

They looked right through me. I was invisible to their eyes. In perfect synchronicity they bowed to their partners. Boots stomped with the intensity of pounding notes, legs kicked the air, and arms spiralled around heads. Burling faster and faster, a haze of bodies merged into one. The room started spinning with swarms of dust. I ducked to avoid the flailing limbs, fell to the floor, and edged towards the wall. Smoke rose from under the floorboards, the broken grandfather clock toppled over, and the crib wobbled to the music. In the hive of madness time stood still, stone walls melted to blackness and the wails of the wraiths numbed my ears until the piano lid collapsed, silencing the room.

"They cannot see you, you know," Natashka informed me. "They are part of our world but we will never be part of theirs."

Taken aback, I turned to see Natashka and Mhayree at the doorway. "What are they?" I asked.

"Restless souls," replied Mhayree. "Unfortunately, they did not receive the correct burial rites and so they are damned to roam here for eternity. Of course, you provided a helping hand in that."

"What is it you want Mhayree?" I snapped, standing up and walking towards her.

"Oh, did I hit a nerve, dear?"

I narrowed my eyes and focused my attention on Natashka. "Who the hell was under your blankets?"

"You met Sebastian?"

"Natashka! Really, that poor Gargoyle," replied Mhayree.

"As he does not spout water from his mouth, he is a Grotesque and not a Gargoyle," Natashka replied.

"Fascinating," Mhayree said, feigning a smile.

Natashka rolled her eyes. "We have a job for you Elise."

Mhayree, leaning against the wall with her arms folded, said, in an all too casual manner, "We need you to kill another Phoenix."

Chapter Twelve

Mhayree and Natashka waited for my response. I remained silent, shocked by their blasé request for me to kill someone. Instead, I turned around and found the ghosts descending into the floorboards and disappearing. A faint tick-tock, tick-tock disturbed the stillness of the music room. Attempting to decipher the source of the noise, I wandered over to the grandfather clock, with its charred wood and rusted metal, lying broken on the floor.

As I knelt down to take a closer look, the first chime rang out.

Second chime.

Entombed in a shattered glass casing, its long, brass hands pointed towards four and seven.

"Elise, did you hear us?" Natashka asked.

Fifth chime.

"We want you to kill for us," Mhayree said.

Sixth chime.

Turning my attention from the clock, I squared up to the redhead and stared straight into her icy blue eyes. "What makes you think I'm the resident assassin for hire?" I said.

"For hire? Don't be silly, Elise, we're not paying you," Mhayree replied, with a smile teasing the corners of her mouth.

Ninth chime.

"You mustn't consider it a murder. It is a service. A mercy," said Natashka, twirling her fingers to pluck a cobweb from her hair.

"I only murdered to save Jacque," I replied.

Eleventh chime.

"No, you murder on the command of the Councillors," Mhayree said. "We don't have time for this. Come with us." As she placed her hand behind my back and guided me from the room, the clock struck midnight. The colour drained from the two women's lips and cheeks, leaving them deathly and hollow. Their breathing ceased as a set of fangs emerged from their gums. The corpses led me into the darkness as all signs of mortality abandoned them as they transformed into their vampiric selves.

Removing a match from her sleeve, Mhayree struck it against the boning of her corset, producing a flame which flickered against her terrifying corpse. As we passed a series of floor candelabrum, she held out her arm like a Pre-Raphaelite painting and lit the tapered candles.

"We're heading to the kitchen," said Natashka. "I hope you are hungry."

"Famished. I can't remember the last time I ate," I replied.

"Hmm, I can't remember the last time I fed," said Mhayree, biting her bottom lip.

"Of course, there is a difference between eating and feeding," Natashka laughed.

"Which is?" I asked, unsure whether or not the answer would bring comfort.

"To eat is to consume that which nourishes. To feed is to receive what nourishes. For example, humans eat food – potatoes, grains, meat. We feed from a blood source – animals and humans," said Natashka. "Obviously, one has to make their own decision as to their preference between beast or man. Would you agree, Mhayree?"

Lighting the final candle, Mhayree formed her thumb and finger into a pincer. "I have never fed from a man," she said, extinguishing the match in her hand.

As we stood at the top of a staircase, Natashka placed herself on the edge of a step.

"Do you need some help?" I asked, stepping forward to

take hold of the wheelchair handles.

Smiling and fluttering her eyelashes, Natashka replied, "That would be wonderful, thank you. Would you mind shoving the chair forward, so as to make me somersault down the stairs?"

"What?" I said.

"Mhayree, tell her it's fine. We do it all the time and I've only broken my neck once."

I turned to Mhayree, who was leaning against the wall with her head resting upon her forefinger. When I opened my mouth to speak, she held up her hand to silence me.

"Are you sure about this?" I asked Natashka.

"Of course," she replied. She arched her back, stretching her arms above her head, and a rip appeared down one of her sleeves.

I moved forward and, trembling, wrapped my fingers around the handles. At the slightest push, the creaking chair rolled forward and the two front wheels shuddered as they tumbled onto the step below.

"I don't believe this," murmured Mhayree.

"Shh!" Natashka replied.

As I pushed a little harder, the chair slid further towards the steep drop. Natashka fastened her hands around the back wheels, anchoring them to the floor.

"You were playing with me, weren't you?" I said, sighing with relief.

She turned, straining her neck to face me. "I just wanted to see what you would do, *Zaya*."

"I don't find it funny!" I said.

"I do." Mhayree wrapped her arm around my shoulder. "That should ease the shock – or at least prevent you from soiling yourself when you see how she really gets downstairs."

I edged away, feeling no desire to underestimate Natashka's tricky nature. Mhayree caught me trying to sneak behind her. "Come out from behind my skirt and brace yourself, dearie."

"Please, I need to concentrate," Natashka announced, circling one of her arms above her head.

"It's transmogrification, not a performance of Swan Lake," Mhayree said.

"Jealousy is an ugly shade on you, Mhayree. Now move."

Mhayree complied with Natashka's command and ushered me out of the way. Natashka, still holding the wheelchair steady, bowed her head as her arm collapsed to her side. Her shoulders twitched and her head jolted. Tendrils of fog emanated from beneath her feet, the smoke growing dense until they covered the chair and her body. Black ink seeped from the roots of her blonde tresses, gliding through the strands until they moulded to her skull and ears, which transformed into a pair of fuzzy protruding points.

"Wonderful, isn't it?" Mhayree whispered to me.

I felt the corners of my mouth rise into an unexpected smile. I didn't know if it was awe, bewilderment or an overwhelming willingness to suspend belief, but neither terror nor horror soured the delights.

"How does she do it?" I asked.

"Nobody knows. Natashka has her secrets."

As Natashka released her fingers from the wheels, her two arms shuddered amongst the fog, causing the rickety chair to topple onto the next step. I lunged forward to grab the handles, but Mhayree pulled me backwards. All my attempts to wriggle free proved fruitless, as her tight grip held me to her chest, making it impossible to breathe.

The chair proceeded to tumble down the stairs. The black mesh and satin of Natashka's dress unravelled and reformed into a leather lining, spanning over elongated, skeletal claws to create wings. As the fog consumed the chair's entire wooden frame, a fully-formed bat emerged from the dense cloud. Flapping her wings, Natashka soared to the ceiling and looked down her nose at the mere non-shapeshifters standing beneath her, before flying into the darkness. When the fog disappeared, Mhayree released me, and I began choking on a deep breath, full of dust. Mhayree slapped my back, but it only made the coughing and spluttering worse.

"You know my dear, for someone whose demeanour suggests a soulless villain, your heartbeat exposes your fear too often," she said.

"You cannot possibly feel my heart through these," I wheezed, clutching my coat and bodice.

After a final spine-rattling slap, Mhayree walked down the stairs. "I don't have to feel it... I can hear it."

"Is nothing private around here?" I said.

"Careful. Your heart rate is going up again," Mhayree replied, laughing.

"I resent that violation, Mhayree."

"If you've nothing to hide, then you've nothing to fear," she said.

I've plenty to hide, I thought, and even more I'd like to forget. To distract me from such thoughts, I asked, "Mhayree, what is a *Zaya*?"

"It means 'bunny'. Natashka must like you," replied Mhayree, turning round and holding out her hand. "Come on, she'll be waiting downstairs for us."

She held my hand, and guided me down the steep, narrow steps.

"Are there no more candles?" I said, looking into the pit of darkness below.

"No," Mhayree replied. "You will get used to it."

As we ventured into the stairwell, I placed one foot in front of the other, fumbling to detect the safest path. Mhayree grabbed me as I tripped on the loose stones. To keep myself steady, I trailed my hand along the wall's rough serrated stonework, catching my nails on the damp moss and leaves invading the cracks. In the distance, footsteps came rushing up the steps. As they drew closer, an icy draught brushed against my cheek. Then it happened. Voices invaded my head. A chorus line of tormented men and women vying for attention. Screams, laughter, and the taunting of shrieking ghosts. They knew my name. They told me to kill. They told me to die and be like them.

I clutched Mhayree's hand, refusing to let go. Through the gloom, she hummed an old folk tune, so familiar to me, from when my mother used to invite her to afternoon teas. Her sweet, dulcet tones swirled in my head, mingling with the cruel taunts of the ghosts, and cursed them to silence. Without losing her grace and dignity, Mhayree fought and claimed victory with a song – and here I was, a murderer, afraid of the dark.

By the time we reached the bottom stair, Natashka was in vampire form once more, straightening the creases in her skirt and tucking the edges round her feet. She acknowledged us with a nod before manoeuvring the wheelchair down the hallway.

"We are almost there," said Mhayree, as we followed Natashka. "Keep hold of my hand, it's darkness all the way in this part of the castle."

"Remind me to buy you a stockpile of candles," I replied.

"No need. I can see perfectly well without them, thank you. As will you, soon enough. The candelabrum is only needed for human visitors."

"Do you get many humans stumbling across the threshold?"

"Well, there's you," Natashka said, stopping outside a lopsided wooden door.

"She's not human, she's a vampire," Mhayree said, opening the door.

Natashka's voice resonated through the room as she entered. "Compared to this rabble, she is human."

Mhayree and I followed Natashka into the kitchen, where a gaggling ensemble of vampires gathered round a large oak dining table. Pots and pans rattled; the stove crackled, kettles whistled, and a cauldron overflowed with a bubbling red liquid. A feast spread across the table, with blood being poured over sponges, mashed into potatoes, soaked into black pudding, and piped along the edges of iced cakes.

They turned around to stare at me. In the midst of the sneers, growls, and baring of fangs, I recognised the familiar faces of the three creatures who had accosted me in one of the castle's passageways. Rising to her feet, the white-haired woman slinked towards me, her curly tresses dragging along the matted leather of her skirt's train. She stood before me, and her scent of rosewood and lavender oil perfumed the air, enticing me to move closer. As she wrapped her hand around my throat, the sharpness of one of her fingernails traced my skin, forcing me to gasp against the strange sensation. Tears rolled down the chiselled contours of her face. She drew back her colourless lips, and a pair of fangs approached my neck. Powerless to resist her, my head rolled back, and I saw the crumbling stonework float from the walls and merge into a whirlpool of greys and black. Feeling her mouth against my chin, I closed my eyes and groaned against the squeeze of her hand choking the breath from me. Nothing in that moment could force me to move. The only people in existence were her and me. Her smell. Her voice. Her touch. Anything she wanted; I would have given to her. All she had to do was take it. A bite. A taste. My death. She could have it. I needed her to have it. As the room grew darker and the blood rushed to my head, the scream of a woman broke the hypnosis.

One by one, the stones settled into their original formation, and the silhouettes of the vampires came into focus. Above me, suspended in mid-air, was a listless body with white curls and a snarling, hungry mouth. Natashka sat beside me – her outstretched hand, upturned like a vulture's claw, was pointed towards the white-haired one. As the helpless vampire thrashed in agony, the remaining coven members sought safety under the large wooden table; all except Mhayree, who was perched on top of a worktop with her skirt hiked up to her knees.

"I think she has learnt her lesson," said a familiar-sounding voice hiding under the table.

"Very well," Natashka replied. She snapped her fingers, and the white-haired vampire crashed to the floor. Whimpering in frustration, she crawled into a corner and curled up in submission.

"That was unnecessary, Natashka," exclaimed the voice from under the table. She emerged, tall and elegant, to examine the damage.

"Wait, why do I know you?" I said, unable to place her name.

"Oh good, you've come round," Natashka said, patting my hand.

"We've met before," said the tall woman. "I was drinking outside Poska's Inn. Saara."

"Wine?" said Natashka. "You mean blo-"

"Enough!" Saara yelled, and pointed to the white-haired vampire. "You went too far with her, Natashka."

"Well, I, for one, enjoy a good show before dinner," announced another woman, as she too appeared from under the table to join Saara. Her red, ragged dress swept along the floor and flowed around her hourglass figure as she stood up. The Red Woman. By this point, I wasn't surprised. Everyone I met seemed to be a vampire.

"She was going to kill Elise," Natashka argued.

"And how many of us has she killed?" said a female vampire with a Caribbean accent, intense, brown eyes, silver jewellery draped around her swan-like neck, and red lips, sipping from a goblet. The coven aimed a round of jeers in my direction.

"It's an old argument, Mia," Mhayree dismissed, climbing down from the stove. Out the corner of my eye, I glimpsed the white-haired vampire being comforted by her two companions. The gangly, dark-haired female crouched to whisper into her ear as the male kept his face hidden. The four of us stared at each other with a silent understanding that a conspiracy was underway.

"How can you be so flippant, Mhayree? After all, she slaughtered one of your nieces," Mia fumed, smashing the goblet against the wall.

"There isn't a person here who hasn't had a family member killed by her hands," a man yelled as I kept watch of the three conspirators.

"She also unknowingly murdered her own grandmother, so I think we are even on the family annihilation score," Mhayree replied.

The wooden door creaked behind me. A hush fell over the room as my mother entered, looking bedraggled and restless. Mhayree walked towards her, pulled out a chair from the table and gestured for her to sit. My mother stood before me, and, with a melancholy smile, stroked my face and sat down. She leaned over and massaged her temples, as Mhayree took a seat beside her. All eyes in the room glared at my mother.

"Out of all your failures, Mirella, that treacherous beast is the worst of all!" cried a petite, pixie-like female, who was parading as a velvet-clad aristocrat. As she narrowed her eyes, and scratched her nails along the wooden surface, Mhayree grabbed a goblet of wine and threw it in the upstart's face. In retaliation, the pixie vampire bellowed like a banshee and crawled over the table to take a swipe at Mhayree. In turn, a ruckus ensued throughout the room as the rest of the vampires began shouting and attempted to break up the fight. Rising to her feet, despondent and weary, my mother steered me against the pantry cupboard, away from the brawl.

"Do not move," she warned. "Today is not your fight." Abandoning me, she staggered, as if disorientated, towards Mhayree, who was struggling to fight off two male vampires.

As my mother attempted to prise away one of Mhayree's assailants, Mia leapt over the table and threw her across the floor. I ran and knelt beside her to help, but, amidst the commotion, forgot about the three vampires in the corner.

A hand grabbed me by the hair, ripped it out by the roots, and whipped my head round. In front of me, a mass of curls lunged forward. The white-haired one.

She growled.

"I don't have the patience for you right now," I said.

Swiping her ankles, I knocked her to the floor and catapulted myself on top of her chest. She let out a piercing cry and I stood and forced the heel of my boot into her throat.

I bent down and whispered, "This was far too easy."

As I dug my boot buckle into her chin, her two comrades pounced on me from behind. The man pinned me to the floor as the raven beauty – instructed by the white-haired one – kicked me in the ribs. Their pathetic efforts did nothing but make me laugh. For a few more seconds, I allowed the three amateurs their moment of fun. Of course, whilst attempting to stifle my amusement, I offered the mandatory fake groans as they beat me. If I had to endure an identity crisis, losing faith in Jacque, being tormented by ghosts, and being hypnotised, then a moment of entertainment was owed to me.

As I raised my head to blow the hair from my eyes, my mother crouched beside me, and presented me with a carving knife. I grabbed the handle, propelled myself from the floor – knocking my assailants sideways – and stood, ready to attack.

Grinning at my opponents, two retreated back to their corner, leaving the white-haired one to stand alone.

"Guileless ragamuffins!" she yelled. "She killed my brother. Have you no honour?"

Seeing her companions huddled like frightened children, she turned her attention to me. We stared at each other, goading one another to make the first move.

The white-haired one stepped forward.

I remained still, watching as she approached.

She laughed.

As she circled me, I turned to follow, keeping my eyes fixed upon her.

She stalked the ground, hands on hips, and her leather skirt curled along the stone floor.

For no other reason than to toy with her, I inserted the knife into my hair as though pinning it up and held my empty, open palms in front of me.

She bared her fangs at me.

I raised an eyebrow, and offering temptation, took a step towards her.

It worked.

She lunged at me, and I back flipped onto the table, crouching into position. The room fell silent as the coven desisted squabbling to watch us. Mhayree shoved Mia and sat beside Natashka, who was preoccupied with dipping bread into a goblet of blood. My mother, looking weary and with ragged breath, stood in front of the crowd, with her arms wrapped around her chest.

The white-haired one slashed at my ankles with her claw-like fingers and attempted to climb atop the table. I leapt into the air, spun around to somersault off the wall and landed tip-toe on to the ground.

My opponent turned to face me. She grabbed me by the throat and squeezed, forcing the veins in my neck to throb. To relieve her grip, I ran my nails down her wrist, causing blood to ooze from the scratches. She yelped, slapped me across the face, and jumped down.

I booted her in the kneecap, and heard a crunch as a bone snapped. She collapsed, crying and pounding the stone floor in agony.

I walked away.

Leaning against the remains of a mouldy wooden cabinet, I took a few deep breaths, and tried to resist inflicting more cruelty upon the poor creature. I only kill to save Jacque, I lied to myself.

I only kill to save Jacque.

I only kill to save Jacque.

I only kill to save Jacque.

In the buckled rim of a copper pan, my eye caught the white-haired one's snarling reflection stalking my mother.

"Mirella," the white-haired one hissed. "Help me."

Her hostile plea persuaded me to turn and face them both. My mother's once gentle eyes now looked cold as she crouched beside the wretched vampire writhing on the floor. Wrapping the long white curls around her wrist, my mother clenched her hand, and pulled the vampire's head back, to expose her neck, and held it in place. My mother held out her hand, inviting me to sit beside her. I hesitated, suspicious of her expectations. Both she and the white-haired one stared at me – my mother in desperation and the vampire with contempt.

"She's too weak," said the white-haired one. "Just like you, Mirella." She sneered and turned to sink her fangs into my mother's shoulder.

"Elise!" my mother called, wincing and reaching for me.

Without hesitation, I ran, prised away the blood-sucking parasite, and beat her into submission.

As I punched the vampire's ribs, my mother removed the knife from my hair and placed it in my hand. She held the vampire's head to the floor and wrapped her fingers around the neck. With a nod, she granted her approval.

One swipe across the throat and the white-haired one was dead.

I dropped the knife, ashamed that my mother had witnessed me kill. As it landed, she smiled and drew me towards her – safe and protected.

Chapter Thirteen

"**G**ood morning, *Zaya*."

"*Zaya*? That's not my name," I mumbled, straining to open my eyes. When the room came into focus, I found myself lying in a creaky four-post bed, swaddled under woollen blankets. A hand patted my cheek until I roused. Natashka. She smiled, as though innocent of the part she played in Mhayree and my mother's conspiracy.

"No, your name is Elise de Volonté," said Natashka. "Do you remember now?"

Swatting her hand away, I rolled over and turned my back to her. "Get out," I hissed.

"Now, *Zaya*, I know-"

"Get. Out."

Natashka sighed. After a few moments, the door groaned as it closed. A murder of crows cawed outside the window, and I thought back to the events of the previous night.

***

The white-haired one's body lay at my feet. As I lifted the bloodstained knife from the floor, my mother took it from me, pinching it between two fingers, and threw it onto the table.

"See? I told you she would kill for us," Mhayree announced.

I looked to the tearful Natashka. Mhayree sat at the table and devoured a slice of blood-soaked Eve's pudding.

I stood to leave, mortified that they had manipulated me.

My mother grasped my hand, trying to appease me, but I pushed her away and left the kitchen.

The coven of onlookers recoiled as I passed.

It was settled; I no longer only killed to save Jacque.

I staggered down the darkened hallway, and heard footsteps rushing to catch me. I ran, scratching my hands and face on rogue twigs sticking out of the stone walls.

"Elise, stop!" my mother cried out, through the darkness.

"*Zaya*, wait! You must hear what we have to say!" shouted Natashka.

"Listen to your mother," said Mhayree.

Their voices hunted me down the hallway as I continued running. Like an animal caught in a trap, I struggled against the confines of the ever-narrowing, pulsating walls as they closed in around me, crushing my body. No amount of pushing or shoving halted them squeezing my lungs, suffocating me.

"*Zaya!*"

My arms and legs contorted and jolted out their sockets. My fingers dislocated from their knuckles and twisted towards my deformed wrists; the strain wracked my neck and rattled my spine.

"Stupid girl!" screamed Mhayree.

Bile rose in my mouth and forced my jaw apart until it distended like a python about to devour its prey. A deep, tormented scream burst out from me.

A hand grabbed me, pulled my hair, and pinned me to the wall. A second hand grasped my face and held my mouth open. A third hand held a glass bottle against my lips, and poured a bitter citrus liquid down my throat.

"What do you think she saw?" my mother said.

"I don't know," said Mhayree.

"Take her to the upper floor of the east wing," Natashka instructed, her voice fading into the distance.

I slumped to the floor. Unconscious.

***

A knock at the door.

"Elise? I have brought you some breakfast," said my mother, as she opened the door uninvited.

"Leave me be."

I pulled the blankets over my head and nestled into the soft furs beneath me. The sound of crinoline swishing along the floor drew closer.

"Perhaps I have left you be for too long," my mother said, as she sat on the edge of the bed, turning down the blankets to look at me. She placed a tray over my lap and scooped a spoonful of runny boiled egg from its cracked, brown shell. "Eat this."

I turned my head away.

"You need to get your strength up," she said. "Amelie will want to see you today."

I propped myself up against the pillows and ate the egg from the spoon.

"I would expect an exhausting game of Blind Man's Bluff. And I believe she has found a skipping rope, tiddlywinks, and some skittles."

I smiled, thinking of my sister ransacking the castle during the night. "With any luck, she'll be too tired to run me ragged."

My mother fed me another spoonful of egg. "Hmm, not so. She doesn't sleep past midnight these days, and yet seems to have the never-ending steam to charge on like a train. Do you remember when I took you on the Express D'Orient?" she asked, hopeful.

I dismissed the question with a nod.

"Amelie reminds me so much of you at that age," she said, placing her hand upon mine.

I snatched my hand away and took the spoon from her. "And look how well I turned out."

She stood from the bed and wandered to the window. "We all have to make sacrifices, Elise. It may surprise you that the woman you killed last night offered to die for us."

I poured some tea into a chipped cup and dropped two sugar lumps into the caramel-coloured concoction. "I'm not a fool, mother, she begged you for help and you handed me the knife to finish her."

"Yes, because you denied her the dignity of a swift death. Instead you chose to toy with her like an alley cat teasing a mouse. You have turned cruel, Elise."

Sipping the tea, I said, "She attacked me."

My mother turned towards me, her blonde curls shading the disappointment in her eyes. "We have learnt that provocation is the most effective way of inspiring you to respond. I heard Natashka had to intervene when you failed to resist Katja's hypnosis. You weren't supposed to get all hot and bothered. It wasn't an invitation. Sometimes we forget just how young you are."

I slammed the cup down, causing it to smash against the saucer. My mother flinched, yet appeared undeterred as she strolled towards a wardrobe. "Of course, you recognise the name Katja? Katja Ustov?"

On hearing the name, I rummaged in my trouser pockets, searching for the list of names supplied by Bothwell. It was gone.

"It fell out your pocket when Revenik dragged you from the burning carriage," my mother said.

"The skeleton?" I asked.

"He is a Reaper. Though, I suppose he does look like a skeleton," mother replied. A flutter of moths escaped from the wardrobe as she opened its decaying doors. "Of course, he gave Mhayree the list as soon as he found it."

I shoved the tray off my lap, spilling the food. "You will return that list to me. It's the only way to save Jacque," I yelled.

"No, my dearest girl, you will not be murdering any more of your kind."

"Then you condemn him to die. I will not go back to you

and father, if that is what you hope for!"

My mother turned around and slapped me across the face. "Do you not understand? We are at war. Katja died to protect us all. She sacrificed herself to make the Inservium believe things are still as they ought to be. You kill, we die."

Beads of sweat began forming along her brow and neck as she turned to walk back to the wardrobe. I held my cheek, astonished that my mother had struck me. She was the one who nestled me to her chest and read aloud Grimm's Fairy Tales when my father was in a drunken rampage. She did not do discipline – that was his expertise. Rifling through the wardrobe, she retrieved a black woollen gown from a shelf and shook off the dust. The elongated sleeves dangled to the floor, forming the shape of a trumpet, and a silver and gold belt swung against the high-waisted girdle.

"You will wear this to Katja's funeral. We owe her the dignity of the proper burial rites," my mother said, draping the gown over the bed.

"I don't think I'd be welcome," I mumbled.

"The coven will think even less of you if you do not pay your respects," she replied, walking towards the door. Before she turned the handle, she looked at me and asked, "What happened to Rasmus Kreek?"

My silence told her everything. He was already dead.

"This war is more important than you and Jacque, Elise."

***

Ding… Dong…
The bell tolled.
Ding… Dong…
Ding… Dong…
I awoke from a restless sleep.
Jacque had slayed the white-haired one.
But only in my dream.

146

The pounding in my chest felt unbearable and a numbness tore through me. I opened my mouth to cry, and scream, and wail, but nothing came out. There was no-one to comfort me. Nobody would come to make me feel safe again. A painful, guttural noise broke from me. I finally cried. Alone.

"Elise!" Mhayree hissed, banging the door. "Come out this instant."

I awoke on a futon and rubbed my eyes, burning my fingers on the embers caught in my eyelashes. My bones stiff and achy, I groaned, finally managing to force myself to stand. The mourning gown, itchy and heavy, hung from my body. But at least this time I hadn't set myself on fire.

I opened the door to find Mhayree standing with her hands on her hips. A black veil shrouded her face, cascading like a waterfall down her waist and resting on a silver, moon-shaped buckle, which supported the weight of an exuberant black ball gown.

"I'm so glad the potion didn't kill you," she remarked in a sardonic tone.

"Potion?"

"Aye, the one I poured down your throat last night."

"You will never cease to exceed my expectations," I said, shaking my head.

"It was for your own good, your mother knew that. That's why she pinned you down. You were becoming hysterical."

I banged my fist against the door, eliciting no reaction from Mhayree. "This damn castle was trying to kill me!"

Mhayree lifted her veil and narrowed her eyes to scrutinise me. "Go on."

"The walls closed in to suffocate me… crushing until my body broke… it was agony. Didn't you hear me scream?"

"I heard you," Mhayree replied.

"Didn't you see? I thought you could see in the dark?"

Her expressionless face bore through me. "Let's discuss this after the funeral." Beckoning me to move from the threshold, she leaned over to close the door. She pointed towards the futon to draw my attention to a cluster of scorch marks charring the delicate roses embroidered along the yellow silk. "That was an antique."

"More expensive than almost a year's worth of bedsheets?"

"Significantly so," she replied.

***

The grey sky threatened rain as Mhayree led me through the courtyard and into the vast forest surrounding the castle. Leaves crunched beneath our feet. Branches snapped under the weight of some invisible entity. Crows and ravens flapped high above the treetops. Trickles of water weaved around us. The forest rustled and howled as we slinked through the maze of spruces, pines and rowans. Each tree guarded and escorted us deeper into the black undergrowth. A myriad of midges entwined amongst the gusts of wind twisting between the bark and rocks.

We reached a clearing, where stood a small, white granite mausoleum supported by pillars, hand-carved with sun and moon symbols. Mhayree knocked on the arched door three times and the panels opened of their own accord.

"This way," Mhayree whispered.

As I followed her, the speckles of sunlight creeping through the grey sky radiated over a line-up of four bodies, lying on stone slabs. Their faces looked bloated as their mouths and noses exuded blood, their decomposed skin clung taut against the protruding bones and their elongated fingernails curled at the ends.

"They are transitioning," said Mhayree, as she led me through the centre aisle.

"Vampires?" I asked. Mhayree nodded. Passing the slabs, I was certain an expulsion of breath came from one of the bodies.

At the other side of the room lay a trapdoor. Mhayree opened the latch, and inside the dark tunnel, a wooden stairway reached into the darkness. We climbed the narrow passage deep into the underground until we reached a vast cavern, lit by a succession of torches, mounted on the stone bricks. Rows upon rows of stacked coffins rested, interred within the walls. Mhayree and I passed the burial sites, the plaques bearing the names of my vampire ancestors flickered against the flames:

The Vadas Family – Béla, Ádám, Endre, Zoltán, Aniko, Catherine, and Albert – Husband and children of Lena Vadas.

The Katona Family – Eliza and Eleanor – Daughters of Frida Katona.

The Fodor Family – Louisa, Annabel, Franklin, and Charlotte – Children of Nikolett Fodor.

The Vida Family – Christoph, Kelvin, Philipp and Rosa – Husband and children of Renata Vida. Her body lay in the centre.

The Arany Family – Romain, Gustav, Xavier and Cosette – Husband and children of Katalin Arany.

All of whom were killed during the First Cleansing, 1667.

In the centre of the room, the coven was sat around the body of Katja Ustov. The mourners sobbed into their handkerchiefs as the melancholy song of a harp played in the corner. Joined together in their sorrow, the coven's midnight pallet of silk gowns, capes, leather coats and velvet gloves contrasted with the vibrant peacefulness of Katja. Her white curls covered the nakedness of her body, her stillness conjured the image of a tomb effigy, and the manner in which the corners of her mouth turned upwards made me believe her eternal sleep offered sweeter dreams.

In the midst of the gathering, Natashka held out her hand to me, beckoning me to sit beside her. I clasped our hands tight together and took my seat. As she dabbed her eyes, I saw streaks of black tears hiding behind a pair of tinted spectacles. We smiled at each other with a silent understanding of forgiveness.

Mia, who I remembered from the brawl in the kitchen, presided over the ceremony, speaking in a foreign language – Bavossian, no doubt. She lay two gold coins over Katja's eyes, and draped three ribbons of silver, red and white, over her chest. As she chanted, she traced the outlines of a sun and moon into Katja's limbs with a dagger. Raising her hand, she encouraged the gatherers to stand, and she removed one of the torches from the wall. The flame shimmered against the ebony of her arms as they trembled and lowered the torch to set Katja's body alight.

Mia stepped back, and four men gathered around the altar – posted at each corner. To my confusion, the skin and hair remained untouched as the flames engulfed the body. As the men lifted the stone slab and carried it towards its final resting place, Mhayree called out, "This wasn't the plan!" The coven snapped around to confront her. "The body has to be taken back to town."

"She was the descendant of Juliska Bavos. She deserves to be buried with her family," replied Mia.

"The Inservium must believe that Elise killed her," said Mhayree.

"She did kill her," I heard a man reply.

"For them," Mhayree said, exasperated.

"Have you no shame, Mhayree de Loire?" asked Mia.

A hand shot up in the front row, silencing the conversation. Standing, Saara faced the coven and removed her crepe veil. "Mhayree is right, we must carry on as though ignorant of the Inservium's intentions. Katja has received burial rites to ensure passage to the Underworld. It is now safe to move her body." She moved and stood behind the altar. "My mother supports the decision. And as you all know; she is one of the original Phoenixes."

"And did Dorika express this to you personally?" asked

Mia.

"*Joo,* she did," Saara confirmed.

No one dared look at Saara as she sat down.

"Who is to transport the body?" a woman enquired.

Everyone turned to look at each other, hesitant to volunteer. Amidst the silence, a voice echoed throughout the crypt. "I will take the body." Straining my neck, I turned around and saw my mother standing in the back row. The vampires muttered between themselves as she stared at me. "And Elise will go with me."

Sensing the eyes of the coven on me, I thought it best not to argue.

***

Dawn broke over the horizon as a shroud of orange, red, and magenta blossomed across the early morning sky. In the hours that passed, the coven debated… and debated… and debated as to whether or not my mother was the most suitable person to escort Katja's body back to town – after all, I might go psychotic and attack her. The vampires returned to their human guises as the sunlight rose, forcing the elders to go to bed, and the younger members to continue arguing. Mhayree threatened to impale anyone who insulted or implied my mother wasn't capable of carrying out the task. By the time morning arrived, my mother had won, and we stood in the middle of an empty, grassy plain.

"Thank you. You can place the body on the grass," said Natashka. As the four men carrying Katja laid the slab down, she continued, "You may leave us."

The men tipped their hats to the four of us and departed. Natashka fumbled inside a beaded purse and removed five quartz crystals. She handed them to Mhayree and instructed her to place them in a circle formation on the grass.

"What's that for?" I said.

"She's creating a pentacle," Natashka replied.

"Black magic?"

"No, *Zaya*. It is the craft of the Old Ways."

"If you're going to judge things about which you know nothing, we can transport you elsewhere, if you like," Mhayree interrupted. "Salem, perhaps?"

"North Berwick is closer. Or Pendle. Or East Anglia," Natashka added. "Our British neighbours executed many a so-called Witch."

"Another history lesson?" I groaned.

"This isn't the time," my mother said, pointing towards Katja. "Mhayree, help me with this." She and Mhayree lifted the body and heaved it into the middle of the circle. As Mhayree stepped back, my mother gestured for me to move and stand in the centre. I hesitated, imagining all sorts of demons and magical chaos which might be summoned if I stepped over the quartz threshold.

"The body won't be fresh for much longer, Elise," said Natashka.

My mother grimaced at the prospect. Natashka placed her hand on my back, nudging me towards the circle.

"At least you don't have to wear that itchy old gown anymore," Natashka said.

I nodded, shuffled forward, clutching my coat, and stood beside my mother. She took my face in her hands and kissed my cheek. Then she stood by my side and squeezed my hand, offering reassurance. She nodded to Mhayree, who was holding a match in her hand. She struck it against Natashka's wheelchair and a flame sparked on the tip. As she hurled the match at one of the quartz crystals, a line of flames erupted, connecting the five stones to form a star. I made to run; however, my mother wrapped her arms around me.

"Do not worry, *Zaya*, I will make you some *pirog* for when you return!" Natashka said, waving.

I closed my eyes.

"*Kownos*," whispered my mother.

The last thing I saw was a flash of light.

***

My mother freed me from her arms. Opening my eyes, I found myself standing in the middle of a smoke-damaged drawing room. The charred wallpaper tainted the air with its burnt aroma and the furniture sat in piles of ash upon the blackened fibres of a scorched carpet. My mother caught me surveying the room.

"Katja had a temper," she said, smiling.

"She set fire to the house?"

My mother paused. "No, not in the usual sense."

Katja's body, naked and exposed, lay between us.

"It wasn't the most graceful of ways they put out the fire," I said.

"Hmmm?" my mother replied, looking round the room.

"On her body. She's still smouldering."

"It's not like she's going to complain," my mother said. "And besides, we didn't have time."

"But…"

"I will fetch her a dress. You stay here," my mother said, walking towards the door. "And stay away from the windows. We don't want anybody to know you are here."

"That's why I kill people at night," I blurted out.

My mother froze, and I realised how chilling my words must have sounded. Neither of us acknowledged the statement. Instead, she walked away.

A dreadful silence filled the room as I walked around, trying to ignore the body on the floor. However, a strange guilt kept building, forcing me to crouch down, and take its hand in mine.

"You are much braver than I am," I whispered as a couple of tears rolled down my cheeks. "Foolish, but braver."

The room temperature rose to an unbearable heat. I unbuttoned my coat and loosened my shirt, but couldn't draw breath through the stifling, muggy air. My face and neck grew sticky with sweat and red, itchy blotches appeared on my hands.

Cramps gripped me and I bent over, shaking and whimpering to hold my stomach. Mother entered the room carrying a long white gown and a knife. I wiped the tears from my eyes and lowered my head so as not to alarm her.

She stepped around Katja's body and with gentle precision dressed it in the gown. Afterwards, she splayed the limbs in such a way as to suggest collapsing after a struggle.

"Listen to me, Elise," she said, slicing her hand with the knife and smearing the blood over the white dress. "When aiming to kill someone it is best to do it outright with the minimum amount of suffering. Do it with respect and dignity."

I moved my damp sweaty hair from my face and tried to draw breath through the heat. "What do you know about killing someone? About looking into their eyes as they are pleading to live?"

Ignoring me, she continued, "Aim for the jugular. Or, if that is not possible, there is an artery which runs down the inner thigh. Sever it."

Her voice faded and the room turned to a thick haze. My gums throbbed as fangs pierced through the flesh. Dizzy and disorientated, I heard myself slur, "Why didn't you tell me I was a vampire? That you were a vampire?"

"I'm not. I failed to – Elise!"

The room turned black.

Chapter Fourteen

I awoke, surrounded in darkness, lying with my arms crossed over my chest. Unfolding them to rest by my side, my hands brushed against ruffles of silk and a small cushion beneath me. My head banged against a lid and hard wooden panels trapped my arms and legs. Unable to see and breathe through the thin air, I felt as though my body had been bound, constricted, and submerged under water, with no way to escape.

Far away, I heard the sound of stifled male voices:

"*Et quod non prodest omnes in nomine Domini misericordia.*"

A crowd chanted the words, "*Nunc Idoli.*"

The Inservium funeral prayer.

It was then I realised I was buried alive.

The prayer continued:

"*Sed nunc dimittite eam ut huic mulieri peccata.*"

Again, the chanting, "*Nunc Idoli.*"

"*Fiat ei daemonium non peribit in nomine eius.*"

Punch after punch, I banged my fists against the coffin lid until my knuckles split. I kicked to smash open the panels and screamed until hoarse for someone – anyone – to help. My stomach and chest knotted as panic and anxiety surged through me. The moisture and blood from my palms and knuckles mingled with tears.

After several minutes of failed attempts, my body collapsed, exhausted. I stared into the darkness, cursing, begging, and bribing deities, before forcing myself – through sheer defiance – to kick and scream all over again. Searing heat rose through my arms and legs, as sweat trickled down my forehead. As the last remnants of air disappeared, I wheezed and choked, gasping for breath. I hammered the sides of the coffin, feeling the wood turn warm from the temperature of my hands. Behind my eyes, a pain ravaged as though a bonfire spread across my brain with no means of escape.

From my pupils, sparks sputtered and flared across the coffin, and charred the bloodstained wood. As they fizzled into the grain, the rising heat pulsing through my body erupted into flames. My hands tingled as electricity rushed through my limbs, reaching the crown of my head to the soles of my feet. My muscles contracted against the spasms and the intense heat forced me to draw breath before my lungs collapsed, dissolving like melted wax. The coffin's foundations shook – the fragments snapped and splintered. Paralysed, I bit down against the helplessness and the nausea rising in my throat. Boiling streaks of tears scalded my cheeks and I shut my eyes pretending none of it was real. Instead, I was home with Jacque. As always. Across my stomach spindly legs tickled my flesh, and crept into the flames. They crawled along my fingertips, up my arms, reaching my neck and settling between my collarbones. The sting of two punctures caused droplets of blood to ooze from my skin and slink towards my shoulders. The flames pounded, ebbed and flowed as though gravitating towards their mother. A woman's voice whispered inside my head;

"*Inna talla manto. Ceelid.*"

"I don't understand," I mumbled, covering my ears to drown out her voice.

She repeated her words as the flames consumed me. The dry earth bled between the crevices of the fractured wood and coated my body. Creatures of the underground infested me – beetles scurried over my face, worms squirmed between my fingers, and ants scuttled up my feet. With the lid of the coffin bowing more dirt seeped inwards. Wood and earth weighed me down.

The woman's voice grew louder;

"*Wamutak, ceelid.*"

The flames continued to burn. Beneath the embers my skin turned to ice. My vision and sense of smell intensified. I saw microscopic fibres fertilise the earth and could smell the soil laced with the oak odour of my coffin. I heard blood rushing through my veins, thrashing against my heartbeat. The rhythm waned until silent. There was no pulse, no breath, and no heartbeat. I was dead. Yet, I was alive.

Fighting against exhaustion, I kicked through the coffin, creating a hole big enough for me to slip through. Crumbling soil and mud flooded the opening, gathering in my mouth and eyes. I scrambled towards the gap and shovelled the tumbling dirt behind me. As I rose, the flames blazed through the earth, clearing a path. I planted my feet into the soil, stood, and used my hands to reach the surface and climb out of the grave. With all my strength, I pulled free and collapsed beside a gravestone.

All I wanted was blood.

A dark figure appeared over me, casting a shadow over the streaks of sunlight through the trees. Beneath a black cloak, a familiar face peered down upon me with a finger pressed against her lips, hushing me to silence.

"This way," whispered Mhayree, placing a cloak over me. "We mustn't be seen."

"Mhayree!" I said, grabbing onto her. "Where is she?"

"Who?"

"The woman in the coffin. I heard her," I said.

Mhayree smiled. "You will find out soon enough. Now move."

I tied the cloak's cord around my neck and strained to stand up. Lightheaded and adjusting to the brightness, I steadied myself against the gravestone.

Mhayree lifted the hood over my head. "Hide your face, nobody can see you," she said, ushering me towards a willow tree. Before moving any further, I looked back, examining the gravestone left behind: Elise de Volonté: 11th March 1879 – 7th November 1897. May She Rest in Peace.

"Am I dead, Mhayree?" I asked, glaring at the carved fleur de lis perched upon the headstone.

"You are transitioning," she replied, holding my hand. "You are becoming a Phoenix vampire."

"I was buried alive. I was afraid, Mhayree. Why would you do that? Why would my mother allow you to do that?"

Mhayree pulled me close and wrapped her arms around me. "You did wonderfully. But we must leave."

Holding me by the shoulders, Mhayree led me behind a tree.

"Why should I go back with you?" I snapped, "Back to people who hate me. To a mother who lies to me. To a castle that tries to kill me."

"This is just confusion. It is perfectly natural during transition."

"Do not pretend you would miss me, Mhayree. That you wouldn't feel better knowing your daughter was safe from me."

"Don't try to provoke me by threatening Freya," said Mhayree, pointing a finger in my face. After stepping back from me, she turned her head left and right, as though searching for something.

"What are you doing?"

"Checking for witnesses. Nobody can see you – especially like this," she replied, studying me, head to toe. "Your mother and I faked your death. The Councillors believe you died trying to murder the third person on your list. It means they don't know about you becoming a vampire. You are safe. And we are safe. For now."

Safe? I thought, unable to remember how that felt, as I looked through the tree branches at my grave. In one day, I had gone from being a human and assassin, to a vampire and disappearing into the shadows.

"This was your funeral," said Mhayree. "The Councillors

will be around somewhere. Your father and brother, also. We must go."

"What about Jacque?"

"If he is anything like his great-grandmother Katalin, he will survive," Mhayree said, laughing.

I turned and glared at her. She offered a smile, as if regretting her dismissal. "We will find a way to help him," she assured.

As she linked our arms together and prised me from the tree, two Councillors stood before us.

"Mhayree de Loire!" exclaimed the gaunt, leather-faced one.

"Councillor Reid. It has been a while. I haven't seen you since the Inservium decided to have me murdered," Mhayree replied.

"I'm sure I don't know what you're talking about, child. What say you, Councillor Garris?"

"Ravings of a mad woman," said the second man, adjusting his spectacles to better scrutinise Mhayree. "And what of this one?"

Councillor Garris pulled back my hood and recoiled in horror. "Demon!" he screamed, raising his Idol medallion as though warding off evil. My reflection emerged within the gold plating, – a grotesque face with bulging eyes, yellowing, bloated skin, with reddish-black patches scattered around my lips. My forehead protruded due to my thinning black hair and receding hairline.

Words failed me as I lifted my hands to shield my face and felt my sharp, pointed nails dig into my head. Mhayree stepped in front of me like a lioness protecting her cub and covered the hood over me. She turned to face Reid – who was cowering on his knees, chanting a Latin requiem – and punched him in the face. His nose turned bloody as he grunted lewd profanities at Mhayree and me, before collapsing.

Garris unveiled a bejewelled dagger from under his

cloak and aimed it towards Mhayree's throat. She ducked and swiped his kneecaps with her foot, causing him to fall. Out of her boots, she produced Scottish and French daggers – a sgian dubh and a laguiole. She turned and tossed the laguiole into my hand. As I caught it, Councillor Reid ripped off his medallion from around his neck, threw it into the distance and pleaded, "Don't hurt me. Please let me live. I will renounce the Idol and worship your devils."

"There are no devils in the Old Ways," replied Mhayree.

"Lies. There is only one Idol. You sold your souls to false gods," exclaimed Councillor Garris, as he thrust his dagger into Mhayree's leg. She fell, cried out in pain, dropping her weapon.

I moved forward, knelt beside Mhayree and pulled the dagger from her thigh. As the blood flowed through her petticoats and onto her skirt, its intoxicating scent caused my mouth to salivate. I felt both thirst and hunger, and knew neither one would be satisfied until I tasted the blood.

"Not yet, my dear," Mhayree whispered. "We do what we have to, to get out of here."

Garris turned to Reid and said, "I am disappointed in you, brother. You would be an abomination, like them?"

An abomination. Like them. No other words could have hurt me more in that moment. As a woman, I was mistreated. As a murderer, I was an outcast. As a Phoenix vampire, I was condemned. Judged and found wanting for being nothing other than what the world had made me. And the Councillors considered themselves blameless.

I did not.

I lunged towards Garris, pointing the bejewelled dagger and laguiole towards his jugular. He cursed me in Latin and called for Reid to help him. To his dismay, the Councillor crawled away, shaking like a coward. Without warning, my strength weakened and Garris managed to overpower and pin me to the ground. Mhayree stood, flinching against the pain in her leg, and limped towards us. She pushed Garris over, punching and stamping his ribs. As he yelped, he dug his fingers into her leg wound, causing her to drop to one knee.

"Elise!" Mhayree cried.

Attempting to move, I saw the sgian dubh lying beside me. I remembered my mother's advice on precise methods of killing and decided it an opportune moment to test her theory. Whilst Garris stood over Mhayree, I grabbed the blade and thrust it into his thigh, bursting an artery.

He collapsed and died, like a slaughtered animal, watching the vultures circling.

Mhayree lay on the ground, shaking. "Thank you," she croaked.

"My pleasure," I replied.

"If this had been night time, I would have been stronger. He would never have got the better of me."

A gruff male voice interrupted, "Stronger at night? Now that is something we did not know."

Mhayree and I looked at each other, knowing too well we had forgotten about Reid's presence. As she took a deep breath, Mhayree composed herself, ready for another round with the Councillor.

"You didn't fathom that out during the First Cleansing? We may have overestimated the Inservium's intelligence," she said.

Reid clambered to his feet and walked towards us. "You women always seem to have secrets."

Mhayree tried to suppress a wry smile. As Reid approached, his cloak brushed along the puddles of Garris's blood and wafted the salty, metallic scent into the air. I closed my eyes and the smell entered me, invading my nose and mouth, as though giving me life.

Feed or kill?

Feed or kill?

I felt Mhayree's hand reach for me. Her trembling fingers locked around mine as the two of us lay still, too exhausted to move.

When I opened my eyes, I saw Reid straddled over Mhayree, with his hand covering her mouth. He reached across and snatched the bejewelled dagger lying beside Garris's body and directed it over her heart. As the blade pierced her corset, I struggled to crawl across the grass, fighting against the bloodlust, and retrieved my laguiole. Before Reid could stab through Mhayree's heart, I plunged my blade into his throat.

Mhayree shoved Reid away from her. He and Garris lay side-by-side, dead.

Mhayree stumbled to her feet, gripping the leg wound and removing the dagger from her corset. Gritting her teeth against the pain, she staggered forward and helped me to stand. "Well done, my dear," she said, patting me on the shoulder. Again, she studied the streets in search of witnesses. She replaced the hood over my head and said, "We don't have much time. You must finish your transition."

"Finish?" I replied.

"Aye, you are still decomposing. You need to rest in the mausoleum for the transformation to be completed." Mhayree rifled through a pocket in her skirt, produced five quartz crystals, and formed a circle around the two bodies. "Step inside, Elise. We are going home."

"You're taking the bodies?"

"I'm hiding evidence. Now hurry, before anyone else finds us."

I stepped into the circle and Mhayree performed an incantation. A flash of light transported us into Castle Árnyék's Great Hall.

"Mhayree! *Zaya.*" exclaimed Natashka, peering over an old, dusty book, titled *Daemonologie.* "A little bit of frothy reading."

"We brought dinner," said Mhayree, pointing to Garris and Reid's bodies. "I will ask Mia, Ruben, and Lucille to drain them."

Natashka wrinkled her nose in disgust. "What about the

bodies?"

"I thought your horse might take an interest."

"Oh, Veritas does love a treat," Natashka grinned, before frowning at me. "*Zaya*, you seem unwell."

"Now is not the time for understatement, Natashka," said Mhayree. "I'm taking her to the mausoleum. We should talk after I return. Can you meet me in the undercroft?"

Natashka nodded and Mhayree escorted me from the room. As we left, a man and woman entered holding hands. Watching how happy they looked provoked a tinge of sadness and jealousy within me. She – petite and delicate – reminded me of the twirling ballerina hidden within the music box my mother gave me when I was a child. She nestled into his chest and he gazed down upon her with copper, cat-like eyes. He wrapped his arm around her shoulder, and his blond hair covered her face, making their bodies appear as one. It reminded me of the times Jacque and I walked through town, facing the crowds of onlookers gasping and tutting at our displays of affection.

The two lovers acknowledged Mhayree and me with smiles. I found it surprising neither one grimaced at my appearance. It almost made me feel guilty for hating them. To distract myself from thoughts of Jacque, I attempted to strike up a conversation with Mhayree.

"Undercroft?" I asked.

"Aye," Mhayree replied.

"What are you going to talk about?"

"Business."

"Anything I can help with?"

Mhayree remained quiet.

"Is it about Jacque?"

Still no answer.

"The Councillors?"

Nothing.

"Mhayree?"

My efforts to extract further information were answered

with staunch silence.

In the mausoleum, two of the four corpses had disappeared since our previous visit. The other two appeared to be at a similar stage of decomposition as me. Mhayree instructed me to lie on top one of the slabs between the female bodies.

"What happened to the other ones?" I asked.

"They transitioned three days ago. You passed them in the Great Hall."

"Three days? Mhayree, how long was I buried in the coffin?"

"Five days. Enough questions."

"But-"

"You need to rest. Only a few hours more."

Mhayree helped me onto the slab, removed my boots, crossed my arms, and closed my eyelids. "Mhayree, I am afraid."

"Then you are sure to succeed," she replied, kissing me on the forehead. "No one will disturb you here. Once you are awake, come back to the castle."

"What if-" the door banged shut and an icy draught swept over me. I opened my eyes and found myself, yet again, surrounded by darkness. This time, buried alive in a mausoleum.

Lying awake on the stone slab for what felt like an eternity, I was scared to shut my eyes in case I never woke up.

I'm not afraid of death, I assured myself.

But who would save Jacque if I died?

The existence, or lack thereof, of an afterlife did not concern me.

Ceasing to exist and my life amounting to nothing but murdered bodies and regrets did not make me uneasy.

Perhaps it did, a little.

In that case, who would save me?

Do vampires have souls? Was it worth condemning mine to save Jacque?

Of course it was, I reminded myself. He would do the same for me. Maybe.

Too late to change my mind.

To pass time, I decided to hum a tune. Not one I recollected hearing from music halls or Poska's Inn, but one which conjured faint memories of a time long ago. Out of the darkness, a raspy, American female spoke to me, "Please stop that incessant noise."

"Who's there?" I exclaimed.

"Clara Price, descendant of Lilianna Dali," she replied, as I heard her shuffling off a stone slab and stepping onto the floor. "When did you awaken?"

"I haven't yet finished."

"Then you had better get to it," she said, whilst yawning.

"I'm afraid," I stuttered.

"It will be worse for you if you fail." The mausoleum door opened, allowing sunlight to sweep over her. I watched her shadow walk away and close the door.

How can anything be worse than living as a decomposing corpse? I wondered. After pondering options – contracting bubonic plague, yellow fever, or marrying the man my father initially chose – I decided I had nothing left to lose, so I closed my eyes.

One sheep.

Two sheep.

Three sheep, I counted.

Moments later, I felt myself sinking into the black abyss. In the darkness, my body collapsed, dying, devoured by flames. A woman's voice called to me. A silver light materialised in the distance and she descended from it like a spider, emerging as a silhouette. Her outstretched arms and hair billowed like tendrils, extending into the void. Webs covered her eyes and her silver lips curled like a crescent moon. She spoke to me without moving her mouth.

"Inna vakat da channa, tios inna channa da vakat. Lukon inna olkkan. Ceelio."

Fear paralysed me, leaving me unable to speak. Silken threads trickled from the woman's fingers and crept towards me. They weaved inside my ears, eyes, and mouth, penetrating me, until a cocoon enveloped my body and extinguished the fire.

She threw me into the void, unspun the threads, and disappeared. I hung in mid-air, helpless as the fire reignited over my body.

A whip cracked and hacked across my torso. I remained stoic against the pain, and growled in defiance. When two whips slashed my back and face, the sharpness caused the corners of my mouth to flinch. Hands grabbed my hair, forcing my head back to expose my throat. A dagger suspended fifty feet hurtled downwards and sliced through my jugular. Blood spurted from the wound, filled my lungs, and seeped along my collarbone. Despite the agony, I refused to show weakness. A sword stabbed through my stomach, ripping muscle. It drove into my spine, snapping the bones. A set of iron chains twisted around me, and dragged me to the ground. As I lay, broken and dying, dozens of ghosts formed a circle around me. They displayed their wounds like macabre marionettes, dancing to the tune of their puppeteer and accusing me of their murders. Then it struck me – the purpose of the attacks was to re-enact how I had maimed and killed my victims.

Death won.

Collapsed in a pool of blood, I felt numb and defeated, with only the strength to mutter apologies to the ghosts.

With hands and feet trembling, and hair matted to my face, the pain of my mangled body was excruciating and relentless.

The woman reappeared and knelt beside me, her face inches from my own. She placed my head on her lap and stroked my cheek. She felt soft and warm, yet not formed of flesh. Instead, she was like smoke mixed with intuition – intangible, but undeniable.

The webs over her eyes retracted, thread by thread, revealing two sockets with white irises and flames for pupils. Her eyes filled with tears. "*Lukkon dalla matam*, Elise."

A tear fell, creating an icy streak down her face. It reached the edge of her chin, dropped onto the ground, and transformed the surface into mirrors. The woman lifted my head and raised it to show my reflection. Instead of wounds and a decomposing corpse, I saw scars form and fade.

"Elise, *da olkkan*," the woman whispered against my ear.

I turned to face her in search of answers or reassurance. None came. She opened her mouth and revealed two rows of fangs and a bright red tongue like a lizard. She shrieked in triumph and cradled me in her arms like a mother does her child.

As she catapulted me into the darkness, I awoke inside the mausoleum.

CHAPTER FIFTEEN

I survived.

The mausoleum doors opened to reveal the full moon dominating the night sky. The frosty air swept through the room, nipping at my toes and fingers. Something felt wrong – or right. I was still Elise de Volonté – daughter, sister, lover, and long-term murderer.

Vampire.

I stepped off the slab – as the cold, silver moonlight swept over me – put on my boots and left the mausoleum.

When I entered Castle Árnyék, a fire blazed in the fireplace, and the crackling embers pierced my ears as splinters from toasted logs succumbed to the searing heat.   Blended extracts of oak, birch, and pine drifted through dusty air, giving a distinctive smell to the Great Hall; leftover cakes and abandoned tea sets lay scattered across coffee tables and the laughter of children travelled from the nursery down the hallway.

"Elise!"

"Saara!" I replied. "I am looking for my mother."

Saara, holding a pile of tattered woollen blankets, walked towards me, her fangs displayed as she smiled. "Of course you are. I believe she is with Mhayree, in their bedchamber."

"Their bedchamber?"

Saara looked at me in disbelief. "Yes. Why would they not share a bed?"

"And where would their bedchamber be?" I said, confused.

"Up the staircase and seven doors to your left," Saara

pointed.

"Thank you," I replied, smiling, and felt my fangs graze my bottom lip.

Saara placed her hands around my shoulders, examined my mouth, and beamed. "Now, you are strong, like a Phoenix, *kulta*."

I nodded, not quite certain of her meaning.

"I must go and take care of the children. I will visit you and your mother soon. She will be very proud of you. It will put her mind at ease that you are safe. I'm only sorry I could not have helped you sooner," she murmured.

"It's not your fault I ran away from you," I laughed.

"No, but your mother gave me strict instructions to bring you here."

"My mother did?"

"She was livid when I arrived back without you. Mhayree had to restrain her. She's quite the fighter, your mother," Saara giggled.

"My mother, a fighter?" I said.

"Hmmm," Saara nodded. "Then, of course, she demanded Mhayree send Revenik with the carriage."

"No, my mother only saved Amelie."

Saara frowned, shaking her head. "You should speak to her," she said, turning to leave.

Watching Saara disappear under an archway into the parlour, I wondered which of my mother's guises was truest – the one I pitied or the one Mhayree and Saara respected.

I climbed the staircase, growing conscious of how the wooden steps bowed beneath the pressure of my feet, and reached the landing with four strides at most. Locating my mother's bedchamber, I knocked and, without waiting for a response, turned the doorknob. As I entered the room, a naked body clambered off the bed, as my mother untangled her legs from around its waist.

"My love," my mother exclaimed to me, panting and looking flushed. As she lay sprawled on top of the bed, with her white nightdress soaked in blood, she attempted to conceal herself with a blanket. Beside my mother, Mhayree stood behind one of the four poster curtains and pulled a chemise over her bare flesh. Despite having her back to me, I saw, in the mirror, the redhead licking blood stains from her mouth.

"Have you been feeding from my mother?" I spat at her.

She stared at me through the mirror, wiping her sweaty hair from her face.

As my mother crawled across the bed towards me, her nightdress and blanket rose to reveal deep, fresh bite marks along her inner thighs. A line of blood escaped from the wounds, drawing my mother's attention towards her exposure. She clutched the blanket around her body, lowering her head as if to shield the embarrassment. When she found herself able to confront me, she leaned forward. "Elise, it is nothing for you to worry about. I am perfectly well. Mhayree needed to heal her leg, and my blood helped to do that. Isn't that a good thing?" she said, stroking my face.

"It's nice to know that's all it meant to you!" Mhayree snapped and stormed out of the room.

As she left, my mother climbed off the bed, calling her name, but was interrupted when Saara entered the room, holding Amelie by the hand.

"Mama," Amelie yawned.

"*Anteeksi!* But she will not settle until she has seen you," said Saara.

"It is quite alright," my mother replied, before turning to Amelie and continuing, "one moment, my darling."

My mother walked behind a screen, and Amelie ran towards me, with a tatty ragdoll in her hand. I lifted her into my arms and she prodded my nose with her finger. "You look different. Why?" she asked.

"Don't be silly, nothing has happened to Elise," my mother said.

"Are you a vampire, now?" continued Amelie.

170

"What? Of course not! Where did you hear such things?" my mother called.

"Children talk," said Saara. "There's twelve of them downstairs."

"Can I be a vampire when I grow up?" said Amelie.

"What? Listen…" my mother stuttered.

"Why are you still awake, young lady?" I said, sitting on the edge of the bed and balancing Amelie on my lap.

She held out her doll and whispered. "Sugarplum won't go to sleep. She's very naughty. I told her she won't get any gingerbread, but she didn't listen."

"Poor Sugarplum," my mother said, as she reappeared, wearing a pale green, French-style dressing gown and stockings. She poured a glass of milk from a jug sitting on a nightstand, and handed it to my sister.

Poor Sugarplum, indeed, with her one eye, scruffy, yellow hair, ripped floral dress, and triangles drawn in crayon at her mouth.

"What are these?" I asked.

"Fangs. She's a vampire," Amelie shrugged, before taking a gulp of milk and continuing, "like you."

"Who told you Elise was a vampire?" asked Saara, sitting down beside Amelie.

"Freya," Amelie replied, handing me her glass.

"Amelie! You weren't supposed to tell!" whined a child's voice from behind the door. The handle turned, and in walked a little brunette girl holding Mhayree's hand.

"It would seem this one can't sleep, either," said Mhayree, following her daughter and standing against the wall, refusing to look at my mother.

Freya sat next to Amelie and the two broke into giggles. "This is my sister, Elise," Amelie said, patting my arm.

Freya pointed to me and yelled, "I told you she was a vampire!" The pair collapsed on the bed, in hysterics, and Amelie replied, "I know! You were completely right!"

"Freya, how do you know about vampires?" asked

Mhayree, concerned.

Amelie sat upright and said, "Suzie told Harry, who told Lyle, who told Julie, who told Lizzie, who told –"

"Drink your milk," I interrupted, offering her the glass.

She took a sip, shared the rest with Freya, and the two snuck under the bed and recited pat-a-cake.

"So now the children know," Mhayree closed her eyes and sighed. "Can you imagine if they told their school friends in town?"

"I doubt anyone would believe childish tales," I replied.

"And if word reached the Councillors, of children telling stories of their vampire families, what do you suppose would happen?" my mother asked.

"Hysteria, persecutions, and slaughter. Exactly as it was before," Saara said, standing from the bed to join Mhayree. "Our choice is obvious – we must go into battle against the Inservium. We always knew it would come to this."

"Battle? What do you mean?" I asked.

"The covens must become one, and, like the original Thirteen, fight the Councillors – kill them," Saara said.

"Saara, the children," my mother whispered, pointing beneath the bed.

"You want to risk your lives just because a group of children know I'm a vampire?" I mocked.

"Not only for that reason," Saara continued, "Now, they think you are dead, there is nothing to prevent them from replacing you with another vampire hunter."

"And what about Jacque? If we provoke the Councillors, there is no doubt they will kill him. Do you think, after all I've done, and all the people I have murdered – including your friends and family – I would let that happen?" I spat.

"And what about your sister? Would you risk her life for his?" my mother asked.

"That's not-" I said, before being interrupted by the chandelier hanging from the ceiling shaking as Amelie and Freya's childish giggles grew louder. My mother and

Mhayree, with worried expressions, looked upwards.

"Which one of them is doing that?" Mhayree said.

My mother frowned. "Girls, behave under there."

"Shh," Freya whispered, causing Amelie to burst out laughing. Again, the chandelier shook, almost dislodging.

"She's far too young. It can't be time," my mother said to herself. Crystal droplets fell from the silver arms and shattered across the floor. Amelie and Freya peeked their heads out from below the bed and crawled out.

"Careful!" Mhayree said, darting towards Freya and grabbing her. It was too late. The fragrance hit me – honey laced with essence of the sea. Blood gushed from the little girl's foot as she lay on the floor, sobbing. My mother and Saara tore pieces of fabric from their clothes and the bed linen, and crowded round her. As Mhayree consoled her daughter, Saara picked out shards of crystal from the child's soles. My mother and I gathered the remaining fragments scattered on the floor.

"This tastes nice. It's nicer than mama's bunny stew."

My mother, Mhayree, Saara and I turned to see Amelie dipping her finger into the pool of blood.

"No!" my mother yelled, snatching Amelie's hand away from her mouth. My sister, frightened, burst into tears and ran towards me.

As she buried her head into my chest, I heard her mumble, "It just looked nice."

"I know, sweetie. You were only a little curious," I replied, knowing too well the temptation of blood.

Mhayree and Saara stared at my mother as though awaiting her next move. A look of pity appeared on her face, and she moved towards Amelie, prised her away from me, and held her close. Mhayree, looking relieved, returned to bandaging Freya's foot.

Saara sat by my mother and stroked Amelie's hair. "How old is she?" she asked.

"Six," I answered.

As tears welled up in my mother's eyes, she muttered, "She won't survive this. Her little body won't take it. She will fail, like I did."

"What are you talking about?" I demanded.

"I will go to my mother and ask her if there has been anyone so young to go through it," Saara said, ignoring me.

"How can this be happening?" my mother said. "So soon after Elise?"

"Perhaps that is what triggered it," Saara replied.

"One day apart?"

"Maybe it's the Havasi and Arany curse," Mhayree interrupted.

My mother, horrified, stared at Saara.

"We don't know that," Saara said, holding up her hands as if trying to appease my mother. "But I will find out what I can."

"Is anyone going to answer me?" I said.

"I will not have her suffering as I do. She'll not be damned to live between worlds," my mother said. "You couldn't possibly understand how it feels to fail the transition."

Saara grabbed her by the shoulders and said, "You are strong."

"Strong! The fevers? Being trapped in my own head? How sheer existence is draining the life from me and yet will not let me die? Immortality without a purpose? You would let a child suffer this?"

"I'm sorry, mama, I didn't mean to make you upset," said Amelie, raising her head.

My mother laughed, dabbing her eyes, and replied, "No, no, no, these are happy tears, because Freya's foot is all better. Why don't you go over and play with her?"

Amelie launched herself towards Freya, and, as Mhayree drew them both closer to her, they nestled into her shoulders, falling asleep.

"The Councillors will come after her now," said my mother.

"We will hide her," assured Saara. "We can take her to

Suomi."

"No. Our children will not be separated from us," Mhayree said. "No man has the right to decide whose land belongs to whom. Every Phoenix vampire has the right to come home. Why should we run and hide?"

"And what if it was Freya?" my mother asked.

Silence fell. As I watched the two girls snuggle into Mhayree's arms, I thought about them growing into young women, facing the challenges of a new century. What wonders would they see? Perhaps they would travel continents, embracing new cultures. Perhaps they would become what society deems as "New Women" and strive for independence by joining the Suffrage movement. All the while, being hated and hunted for being born different. That is, if they were not killed first.

I knew it was a question of sacrifice. Somebody had to end up dead. After all the times the Inservium forced me to kill for them, it was now my turn to decide who was next. Jacque's life or Amelie's?

Or my own?

Simple choice.

"Nobody is going into hiding," I announced, "because we are going to fight."

My mother grabbed my arm. "We? No! You will not be fighting with us, it's too dangerous."

I took her hand and placed it upon her lap. As I released her, I said, "I am a murderer, mother, whether or not you choose to acknowledge it. Night after night, I stabbed, strangled, and decapitated people without guilt. Do you understand? I murdered dozens of people. And I don't remember most of their names. It meant nothing to me."

My mother bowed her head and, without looking me in the eye, said, "No, Elise, that was for Jacque-"

"I may have been a murderer for the wrong side, but-"

"But now, she will be a warrior," Mhayree said.

My mother lifted her head, looked at Mhayree and me

and sighed. As she stood up, the door burst open. Natashka, seething, muttered to herself in Russian whilst entering the room.

"The spell didn't work!" she exclaimed.

"What spell?" asked Saara.

"The spell, spell! Mhayree gave me a sample of Jacque's blood and asked me to locate him," Natashka answered.

I reached for my neck, searching for the necklace containing the vial of blood, and found it gone.

"But every time I went near it, it repelled me, and burst into flames. The damned stuff blocked me!"

"Where is my necklace?" I demanded.

"I snatched it when you were lying in the mausoleum," said Mhayree.

"*Zaya!*" Natashka squealed. "You look delightful. How was your transition?"

"It was-" I said.

"How do you feel?" Natashka interrupted.

"Well-"

"Oh, let me see your fangs."

Natashka positioned herself in front of me, with wide eyes full of expectation. I opened my mouth and half-grinned, fangs catching my bottom lip.

"Aww, they're perfect," Natashka said. "We will need to teach you how to feed. But right now, we don't have time. Have this instead." Natashka produced a goblet full of blood from behind her back, and took a drink before handing it to me. "I laced it with vodka, so you're not overwhelmed by your first taste of blood as a vampire. We'll save that for your first feed from a vein."

"More importantly, what about Jacque?" I replied, taking a sip. Natashka was right, it was nothing special. If anything, the alcohol outweighed any taste of blood.

She rolled her eyes. "The spell didn't work."

"They always work," said Mhayree.

Natashka spun around and stared up at the ceiling.

"Something – someone – is obstructing me."

"That can't be," said Saara. "Only somebody who knows our craft would have the knowledge."

"Well, I didn't do anything wrong," Natashka said. She pointed up, to the broken chandelier. "What happened there?"

"Nothing. Don't change the subject," my mother replied.

"How many people know about Jacque's kidnapping?" Mhayree said.

Natashka thought for a moment. "Everyone in this castle?"

"So not just the people in this room?" Saara said.

Natashka laughed. "With the gossip around this place? Everybody knows why Elise is here."

Saara knelt on the floor and placed her fingers over Natashka's temples. "Think."

Natashka sat silent, staring at Saara. Within seconds, her face fell. "Someone in the coven is working with the Inservium."

Saara, sullen and despondent, nodded.

"Who?" I yelled, leaping from the bed. Amelie and Freya stirred, yawning.

"Everything is fine, go back to sleep," Mhayree whispered. As the two girls settled into her shoulders, Mhayree frowned, warning me to be quiet.

"I cannot determine who," Natashka said. "If they can prevent me from finding Jacque, then it is certain they have taken precautions to shield themselves."

"I will find them," I said, storming towards the door. "Even if it means killing every vampire in the castle."

Saara sprung from the floor and held me back. "No, *kulta*, this is not the way. We fight the Inservium, not ourselves."

"I will not fight beside a traitor," I snapped.

Saara turned me to face her, and looked deep into my eyes. "We forgave and will fight beside you, despite what you have done. Do not punish the entire coven because of one rotten apple spoiling the harvest."

"Finally, one of you admits it – you consider me a traitor," I replied.

"No, Elise. You will be the one who trains us to fight," said Saara.

Confused, I broke away from her grip.

"Saara is right," Mhayree added. "I might be able to throw a punch or two, but your expertise is altogether different. Why else do you think the daughter of an original Phoenix would be sent here?"

"News of your rampage has reached the covens around the world," Saara said, eyeing me, impressed – and yet disturbed.

Natashka, clapping her hands, announced, "I know what we must do. *Zaya* and I shall go to the Inservium and hunt for documents – anything which will incriminate the Councillors. We can expose them and their corruption. And Mhayree and Saara – you can call the rest of the covens to arms."

Before anyone could object, Natashka grabbed my hand, dragging me out of the room. Mhayree and Saara followed, carrying the two children. Behind us, I heard my mother ask, "What shall I do?"

Nobody replied as the door closed.

CHAPTER SIXTEEN

In the Great Hall, Mhayree formed a quartz pentacle for me and Natashka to enter. Saara collected two cloaks from a closet and handed them to us for disguises. Natashka recited an incantation, set alight the crystals, and, in a flash, she and I stood in the middle of an abandoned road outside of town.

"You couldn't have gotten us any closer?" I asked.

"And risk being seen? You have such odd notions, *Zaya*," Natashka replied, as she negotiated her chair over the rocky road – avoiding muddy puddles and struggling against the uneven terrain. She looked up at the stars in the crisp, cold night sky and a tear rolled down her cheek. "Ahhh! I have not left the castle in almost eight years."

"Have you never been to town?"

"No," she said with sad eyes, "you will have to show me the way."

I listened to the silent breeze until a soft crashing of waves reached my ears. "The North Sea is ahead of us."

"Roughly one and a half miles away," Natashka replied, tilting her head to hear.

"Which means we are fifteen miles from town," I said, pointing in our intended direction.

We travelled all night, along the lochs and rivers, over the hills, and through the wilderness, until we reached the centre of town.

We spoke of Jacque and how we met. The first time I murdered, and how the guilt disappeared all too quickly. About her family and how they abandoned her at Castle Árnyék soon after she transitioned. As we entered the town square, returning to our human guises, dawn broke through the night sky, and men and women emerged from their homes. The streets came alive with bakers lining their shop windows with breads and pastries, laundry women filled giant copper pots with water, and street sweepers cleaned up horse manure. As we passed, every townsperson either gawped or aimed a sly stare at Natashka.

An old woman approached us and said to me, "Is this you out on a little walk?" I nodded in contempt. Under her shawl, her wrinkled face offered a smile tainted by condescension and pity. "Should she be outside, though, with normal folk?" she continued.

I opened my mouth to unleash a tirade against the woman, but Natashka clasped my elbow and guided me away. "Why didn't you let me say something to that old toad?" I said.

"As we say in Russia, *nu naxer*," Natashka replied, shrugging her shoulders, and mouthing a profanity to demonstrate the translation. "Besides, I have an unfair advantage, in that I could rip out her throat."

We laughed at the absurdity and entered the back gate of the Inservium grounds. Candles flickered through stained glass windows and green smoke escaped from the chimneys, signalling an initiation ceremony was in procession.

We made our way to the back door and found it to be locked. Natashka looked upwards to a chimney before checking for passers-by. "Wait here and I'll let you in," she said, lifting her arms. Within seconds, she turned into a bat and flew into the chimney. The door unlocked, and on the other side waited Natashka with soot covering her nose and cheeks.

We sneaked through the corridors, cautious not to alert the Councillors to our presence. The droning hum of chanting echoed through the marble walls, and the shimmering candlelight reflecting off the gold embellishments guided us through the labyrinth of passages.

"Do you really think Bothwell and his cronies would be idiotic enough to just leave a list of my murder victims lying around?" I whispered.

"Shh! We discussed this. What better way for the Inservium to ensure a Councillor stays in line than to record all his misdeeds?" Natashka replied. "For any Councillor involved in Jacque's kidnapping and your list of murders, Bothwell will have implicated them in writing. Secrets keep secrets."

"I always thought money kept secrets."

"Well, they didn't acquire all these riches by magic. If we can find the documents, all the better – but mostly, we need their weapons. Or rather, our weapons that they stole from us."

"I can definitely find those," I replied. "Follow me."

We turned a corner, and travelled the length of a dark passageway with only our sharpened eyesight to cut through the blackness. Glass panels displayed golden chests and polished amulets sprawled against greasy oil paintings of their Idol. Large arched doors lined the passageway, each one refusing to open as we rattled the handles.

"I could try to pick the locks. Or unbolt the hinges," I said.

"We don't have time. Our priority is to retrieve the weapons. Afterwards we can-"

A series of footsteps rumbled at the end of the passageway, moving towards us. In the distance, a candle flame flickered against the whistles of a Councillor, holding a candelabrum. Natashka and I backed ourselves against the wall with hopes of remaining unseen. As the footsteps drew closer, a tall, gangly man strode into view, with his black cloak billowing like an ominous shadow. He stopped five doors away from us, retrieved a key from his waistcoat, and opened a door. As he disappeared into a room, Natashka and I, looking at each other, sighed with relief. With diligence and swiftness, we crept past the doorways, easing our way towards the end of the passageway. We halted before reaching the room containing the Councillor to ensure whatever shenanigans kept him occupied prevented him from discovering us. Looking into a glass panel opposite the doorway, I saw his reflection dripping oils into a large incense burner, alongside powders and various other ingredients. Natashka and I took advantage of his distraction and moved forward. But as soon as I stepped in front of the threshold, a voice shouted in the distance, "Councillor Walters! The ceremony is commencing."

Councillor Walters turned to face the door and flinched at the sight of the two females in front of him.

"You're dead!" he said, staring and pointing at me.

"Hello," Natashka said with a disconcerting calmness.

The Councillor opened his mouth to scream and I rushed towards him, slamming him against stacks of wax-sealed scrolls.

"Councillor Walters!" yelled the voice again. Natashka wheeled into the room and closed the door behind her, being careful not to make a sound. I covered the Councillor's mouth with my hand, stifling his pathetic cries. Outside the room, we heard footsteps pacing the passageway. The Councillor called for Walters again and door handles shook, denying entry. Natashka and I looked at each other with nervous anticipation, awaiting the door to open. The footsteps grew louder as they approached nearer.

"Do something," I muttered to Natashka.

No sooner had she positioned her chair against the door like a barricade, the door handle turned. As the door creaked open, Natashka placed her hand over the latch and, with a silent motion, slid the bolt closed. Councillor Walters's muffled voice pleaded beneath my hand as he struggled under my weight. The door handle rattled once more, but held, keeping the monster outside at bay. Defeated, and no doubt confused, the Councillor retreated as the sound of his footsteps receded into the distance.

Again, Councillor Walters squirmed under my grip. Natashka raised her hand, causing the Councillor's body to rise a few feet off the ground. She moved forward and, with her other arm, reached for one of the scrolls and bit down on the wax, slicing through the seal. After examining the parchment, she tossed it into the corner.

"It's nothing," she said.

"Where do you keep the confessions? Details about the Councillors? How did you choose my victims?" I asked Walters, removing my hand from his mouth. He spat at me in response and Natashka waved her hand, twisting his arm behind his back. As he grimaced, I asked the same questions again. No response. Natashka and I drew back our lips to bare our teeth and snarled, releasing a guttural growl. Again, no response.

"It might have been more effective if our fangs had been out," Natashka said, pouting. Picking up the incense burner, she sniffed the contents.

"Garlic, hawthorn, and ashwood. Do you really think these will save you?" she asked, waving around the incense burner. "I've never understood the reasoning behind these silly superstitions. These won't ward off vampires."

Foolishly, I turned around, to inspect the offensive item.

"Don't!" Natashka shouted.

I looked round to Councillor Walters, and saw him reaching into his pocket and removing a vial of clear liquid. He released the cap and swallowed the contents moments before I could do anything to stop him. Natashka lowered her hand and dropped the Councillor to the floor. I grabbed the empty vial from his fist and sniffed the glass, detecting a distinct aroma of bitter almonds.

"Cyanide," I said.

Walters lay in a heap in the corner, clutching his chest as his breathing grew erratic. Natashka moved forward as I bent down to examine the body, finding the Councillor's skin developing a reddish tinge.

"There's nothing we can do," Natashka muttered.

"If there was, would we have done it anyway?" I replied.

Natashka raised an eyebrow in consideration without committing to an answer. Within minutes, Councillor Walters fell unconscious and his breathing ceased. I placed two fingers against the underside of his wrist and found no pulse.

"Well, this poses some problems," Natashka said.

"What do we do?" I asked.

"You're the assassin! Do you have any suggestions on how to hide a body?"

"The idea was for people to find my victims' bodies. So the Councillors knew I had done the job right."

Natashka turned up her nose and shook her head in disbelief.

"Besides, this one was a suicide," I continued. "We can use that to our advantage."

"Never have I heard such a chilling sentence. But alright," Natashka smiled.

As I propped the Councillor's body up against the wall, Natashka rifled through desk drawers. After retrieving a piece of parchment and quill, she sat at the desk and said, "I'll write the suicide note."

"Do you not think the other Councillors will recognise it's not his handwriting?" I asked, attempting to prevent Walters's head and torso from slumping forward.

Natashka ignored me and persisted with writing. The minutes dragged on as I paced the floor watching her arms flail in the air, in mock theatrics, whilst scribbling with the quill.

"Look, Sarah Bernhardt, you're not on stage," I said.

"Ah, the French actress! Mhayree knows her."

"Are you almost finished?" I replied, swiping the parchment from the desk and reading it. "Did you intend for it to sound like the ravings of a madman?"

"Well, he did join the Inservium," said Natashka, shrugging her shoulders.

I nodded in agreement and placed the parchment upon Walters's body.

"Wait!" Natashka interrupted. "We need to add his seal as a signature. Give me his necklace and the scroll I threw into the corner."

Removing the chain from around Walters's neck, I handed it to her alongside the two pieces of parchment. She placed the medallion on the desk and tore off the wax seal from the original document. As she positioned Walters's candelabrum under the seal, the heat from the flame melted the black wax onto the medallion.

"Hold the note flat," Natashka instructed me.

Whilst I spread the parchment across the desk, she flipped the medallion over, pressing the wax into the document and peeling it away to reveal Walters's embossed personal seal.

"Leave everything as it is. The messier the better. It makes the scene more believable," Natashka said.

With neither guilt nor remorse, we closed the door on Councillor Walters's lifeless body.

We continued through passageways and endless corridors, followed by the echo of the Councillors chanting a Latin requiem. Whilst their words filled my ears, my mind washed away proclamations of an all-seeing Inservium and praises to their Idol, as though drowning out falsehoods which no longer mattered. As we reached the end of a hallway, we turned into the sanctuary. Natashka placed her arm in front of me to halt my steps. We hid in a corner and witnessed the Councillors gathered in a circle, holding anointing oils and lifting their medallions towards their Idol's statue. On the outskirts, two Councillors swung gold-plated incense burners, the clouds of smoke masking the ensemble's prostrations and venerations. Their chants, along with the overpowering scent of hawthorn and ashwood filled the room. The crowd parted, revealing two men wearing brown Inservium initiation cloaks and kneeling in the centre. In front of them stood a Councillor, holding a jewel-encrusted goblet and raising aloft his medallion, as though offering it to an invisible deity. The two kneeling men declared their vows of fidelity, honour, and subservience to the Inservium and the Idol, and removed their hoods to sip from the goblet. As the brown cloth fell, it revealed their faces – my father and brother, Étienne.

"What the hell do they think they are doing?" I muttered.

"*Zaya*, do you know those men?"

When I informed Natashka they were my family, her brow furrowed. "Has he always been that small and fat?" she said. "He isn't how I remember."

I looked at her, confused, but found her to be distracted in her own little world.

"Natashka?" I said, breaking her reverie.

"He is, after all, the one who put me in this wheelchair."

"Of course he did," I replied.

Without taking my eyes off the men, I clasped Natashka's hand to reassure her of safety. I felt no surprise of her involvement in my father's experiments. But I knew for certain that whilst I stood beside her, he would never touch her again. I'd kill him first.

My father and brother stood, received their black cloaks as ordained Councillors, and the initiation ceremony ended. As the Councillors dispersed, Natashka and I lingered, awaiting the opportunity to move. We watched as Bothwell shook hands with my father and Étienne and invited them to join the Councillors in private prayers. My father smiled as though the offer included a cigar, whisky, and the keys to a seedy gentleman's club. Perhaps it did. Étienne, on the other hand, looked like a lost urchin, ensnared in a world in which he did not belong. I almost felt sorry for him. Bothwell wrapped his arm around Étienne's shoulder and guided him and my father from the sanctuary, leaving us alone in the shadows at last.

Neither of us moved. Natashka kept her eyes to the floor, looking sullen as her hands trembled to adjust her lace choker necklace. With our hands still clasped together, I stroked hers, to offer reassurance before taking the initiative to step forward into the room. Natashka pulled me back.

"I promise he cannot get you. We are far stronger than he could ever be," I said, coaxing her to move.

After deliberating for a few moments, she placed her hands on her wheels and edged herself forward into the sanctuary.

I led her to the hidden vault, unlocked its seal, and opened the door to reveal the array of weaponry, all of which had once been at my disposal. One by one, I removed daggers, chains, razors and whips, and handed them to Natashka. "Hide these," I said.

"Have you used all of these?" she whispered.

"Aye," I replied, inserting a silver dagger down the side of my boot.

Natashka raised her eyebrows with amazement before wrapping a whip around her thigh, concealing it under her skirt. As she struggled to find suitable places to put the razors and daggers, I said, "Perhaps you should think about wearing trousers. More pockets for practicality."

"They are an interesting alternative," Natashka said, and, with trepidation, she attempted to slide a dagger's blade down her bodice.

"Before you stab yourself, consider this one," I said, offering her another wrapped in a leather sheath.

She accepted and inserted it down her chest. "It's surprisingly comfortable," she remarked.

"I don't really notice anymore," I replied, filling my coat pockets with razors and chains. Once the vault was empty, I closed the door and beckoned Natashka to follow me. We retraced our steps and left the Inservium.

Outside, streaks of sunlight pierced the clouds, as snow floated to the ground. As we moved along the pathway, my footprints and Natashka's wheels left markings along the icy blanket. We continued, and the snow grew heavier, but neither of us shivered against the air's frozen chill.

"Natashka…" I said.

"Hmm?"

"Can I ask you something?"

"It happened over twenty years ago," Natashka said.

"My father?"

She nodded. "Mhayree and I were in Edinburgh – she thought it was time for me to see life outside of Árnyék. We were staying with friends, and one morning, walking along the Royal Mile, a man pushed me onto the road, and under the wheels of a carriage."

"And you survived that?" I said.

"Even in our human form, it takes a certain skill to kill a vampire. As you know," Natashka smiled.

I narrowed my eyes, unimpressed. "Carry on."

"Are you familiar with galvanism? Think Frankenstein."

"I've heard of the experiments," I said. "They run electrical currents through dead frogs to resurrect them."

"Well, when I awoke, I was tied down on a laboratory slab. Your father was standing over me, driving electric rods into my body, and obviously – as one would – I screamed out."

"And I'm guessing the idiot thought he'd brought you back to life."

Natashka nodded. "I'll never forget the way he looked – that sleazy grin – with his hands all over me. Like I was his play-thing. His pet."

Her voice trailed off. "He even cried."

Stepping closer, I placed my hand on her shoulder.

"But cheating death wasn't enough for him," Natashka continued. "For an entire day, he subjected me to experiments. Injections, electrocutions – all whilst I was awake and gagged – until finally he tried severing my legs from my body."

I gripped Natashka's shoulder tighter, knowing I'd drive a knife into my father as soon as the opportunity arose.

"But then Torrin found me," Natashka said. "I'm not sure how. He says it doesn't matter. And, of course, it was late into the night, so, as vampires, we were stronger. Torrin knocked your father out from behind, and I managed to break free."

"My father knows you're a vampire?" I said.

"No. He was unconscious before he could notice the transformation."

"Is that how you and Torrin met?"

"No," Natashka smiled. "I've known him for much longer. He let me feed from him until I was healed. But the damage to my legs was irreversible."

We both fell silent, watching the sun rise higher in the sky.

"Perhaps you should change the subject, *Zaya*," Natashka said.

I thought for a few moments before commenting. "You look strange wandering in the snow without a coat or cloak."

"Says the woman wearing trousers," Natashka replied.

"Says the Russian who can transform into a bat," I responded.

We laughed and turned back towards the Inservium to find the snow disguising our tracks and making our existence disappear.

We wandered through the streets, keeping out of sight of the townspeople, until a scraggy boy wearing a tweed cap and jacket appeared in the town square, waving a newspaper above his head.

"Vampires attack Councillors! Read all about it!" he bellowed.

Natashka and I stopped and stared at each other. An eerie silence befell the town square until, all of a sudden, almighty hysteria broke out. From every household and shop, people flocked in panic towards the boy. Women and men pushed and shoved one another to ensure they reached him first. Abandoned prams lay strewn across the cobbled paths as droves of chubby, bumbling nannies threw pennies at the boy's feet and grabbed their copy of the Daily Alba.

"Vampires! Vampires in Loch Fala!" shouted the boy, drawing screams and cries from the crowd. "Two Councillors dead!",

"I think they'll find it's now three Councillors," Natashka whispered to me as we hid in an alleyway.

I gave no reply, and instead watched as the townspeople erupted into a brawl. Horses reared as carriages overturned in the commotion. Starving looters ransacked the greengrocers, bakers and butchers, dropping cabbage leaves, pickled carcasses and meat pies. Ladies collapsed to their knees, wailing, as gentlemen bashed each other with canes to reach the front of the crowd.

"Councillors warn no one is safe! It could be you next, sir!" the boy yelled, pointing at a man grappling at the pile of newspapers on the ground. "Or your children," he added, playing to his audience.

As we peered around the alleyway, a young man ran past, tripped up and banged his head against the wall, falling unconscious.

"How fortunate," Natashka said.

I looked at her, shocked by her cruelty. She rolled her eyes and pointed towards the Daily Alba squashed under the man's arm. "What does it say?"

I crawled on my knees towards the man, pulling my hood over my face, and stole his newspaper. I retreated into the alleyway, crouched beside Natashka, as the boy in the square shouted, "The Councillors say only the faithful can be saved!"

We sniggered at the absurdity of the claim. "What do they think we're going to do? Pillage graves and create an army of revenants who rise from the dead each night?" Natashka said.

I unfolded the newspaper and rifled through the pages, ignoring the sensationalised front-page headline and grotesque portrait of a supposed vampire. As I skimmed through the sections, I glanced "Prayers for Protection," written by the Inservium, amulets for sale, to ward off vampire attacks – available for purchase in the Inservium, and requests for charitable donations, to aid the Councillors in their "invaluable" and "self-sacrificing" mission. I grunted in disgust, flicked over the page, and froze.

"Natashka!" I said, as a cold shiver ran down my spine. I turned the newspaper to face her and splayed the pages open.

"We have to go. Now!" she replied, grasping the

newspaper from my hands. She sat it upon her knee and, as I rose to my feet, a picture of a pale-faced, dark-haired girl, with a steely glare looked out from the page. Me.

From the town square, we heard the boy shout. "Come read all about it! Real vampire found. Elise de Volonté. Serial killer, vampire fakes death. When will she strike again?"

Natashka strained to smile at me. "Perhaps we move a bit quicker?" she suggested.

I nodded in agreement as a strange fear gripped me. If by chance one or two townspeople spotted and assailed me, I could fight them off no problem. However, the reality of staving off a full-scale, frenzied rabble would, without a doubt, end in my death – culminating with a stake driven through my heart and decapitation just like they do in novels. Silly superstitions.

"Transform," I muttered to Natashka, "and escape."

"No, *Zaya*. We stay together. You do not need to protect me," she replied, leading me into a backstreet, away from the crowd. "Tell me which way to go. It is up to you to get us home."

I navigated Natashka through the vacant, run-down slums, hidden behind the merchant buildings surrounding the town square. We negotiated leaky drainpipes, doped-up opium and gin addicts collapsed on the icy, cobbled streets, and the putrid filth amassed from animal and human faeces.

The young newspaper boy's voice echoed in the distance. "Vampires! Vampires in Loch Fala!"

We turned a corner, out of the narrow depths of the slums, and disappeared into the snow.

Chapter Seventeen

Natashka and I arrived at an abandoned farmhouse several miles outside of town, and found shelter inside a barn – the only purpose of which seemed to be providing a feast for woodworm. After forming a quartz circle around Natashka, I stepped inside, and waited for the incantation and flames. Within moments, we found ourselves standing in the middle of the Great Hall.

"We have a problem," Natashka said to Mhayree as the redhead strode across the hall and stood before us.

"I'm aware of that," Mhayree replied, holding up a copy of the Daily Alba.

"Where did you-" I said.

Mhayree interrupted, pointing her finger towards a set of doors and beckoned us to follow. "A lot has happened since you left."

She slid the doors open and we stepped inside the drawing room to find a crowd of people amassed in the centre.

"We don't allow humans in the castle!" raged Natashka.

"They are family. They won't hurt us," said Mhayree. "Attention, everyone. This is Natashka, and our new local celebrity, Elise. Now, I don't want you to worry, she only kills vampires." The room gasped in unison. "Me, on the other hand – two human Councillors and counting… this year. So, if anyone would like to take issue with her, please let me know first."

The room fell silent for a moment, before each man and woman, considering Mhayree's words, thought it best to look away as though busy with other matters.

I leaned into Mhayree and whispered, "Actually, I helped to kill the Councillors. And the body count just rose to three."

"They don't need to know that, dear," she replied then closed her eyes, exasperated. "Three?"

"We should probably talk, Mhayree," Natashka said.

I looked around the room of faces – both vampire and human alike – recognising many from portraits and photographs displayed in the houses of my victims. In a corner, the Red Woman chatted to a man wearing a navy-blue flat cap, with a Cockney accent – the one who sold me the Phantasma. She smiled at me, patted the man on the arm, and whispered in his ear, before the two walked towards me. Mhayree, with her hands on her hips, nodded her head in the direction of a moustached man, standing by the window.

"That is Freya's father," she said.

"Your husband?" I replied.

Mhayree glared at me, disgusted with the insinuation. "On paper, perhaps."

"I remember him."

"Hmm," Mhayree said, turning her back to the man.

"Does he know about you and my mother?"

"No," she said, frowning. "And please don't be difficult about it."

"You don't know me, Mhayree," I replied, leaning into her. "Just keep her away from my father."

A tap on my shoulder distracted me from continuing the conversation.

"Elise," said the Red Woman, as I turned to face her. "I believe you have met my great-nephew, Joseph."

I nodded, trying to hide my confusion as to how a man in his fifties could be the great-nephew of a woman who appeared to be thirty years his junior. "Aye," I half-smiled, shaking the man's hand. "As I remember, you recommended Little Girl of the Ashes to me. Very cryptic."

Joseph laughed, "I just do as I'm told."

"Very wise," chuckled the Red Woman.

"Are you a vampire?" I asked the man.

"No," he laughed. "I was never turned."

My face fell, scrutinising him. "Did you know I was a vampire?"

The Red Woman placed a gentle hand upon my arm. "There was no conspiracy, Elise. No harm was meant."

Out of the corner of my eye, I spotted Natashka glancing towards the three of us. "Is everything alright?" she enquired.

"Oh yes," said the Red Woman.

"No! No, everything is not alright. If you all knew I was a vampire, why didn't you just tell me? Why, instead of all these games? You knew where to find me," I said.

Natashka held her hands up, as if surrendering, and Mhayree turned around to join us. She stood in front of me, with gritted teeth, and muttered, "Think about it, you stupid girl! There was someone out there killing vampires. If we had told you the truth, it might have put you in danger. At the time, we didn't know you were the dangerous one!"

I moved forward, stopping an inch from her face. As we stared at each other, I said, "If you and my mother had told me, a lot of innocent people would still be alive."

"Enough," Mhayree warned, narrowing her eyes.

"It's your fault these people's relatives are dead." My voice hit a crescendo, silencing the entire room.

"*Zaya*, no. Don't do this," Natashka pleaded, pulling me back. Mhayree didn't react. Instead, she stood beside the Red Woman, whom she addressed as Hart, and enquired after her family.

Unclasping myself from Natashka's hand, I walked across the room towards the door. Amidst the silence and the stares, Mia called out, "Did you really kill seventy people?"

I turned around and found her, sitting reading a newspaper in the corner.

"No. It couldn't have been." I paused before uttering, "I don't know."

"What I take umbrage at is how ugly they make us look," said a regal-looking brunette woman, adorned with silver chains and dramatic rouged lips and kohl eyes. She sat on top of a dust-covered chaise longue, and flicked through a pamphlet. "I mean, hairy palms and faces? Drinking the blood of infants? And look at the crookedness of those fangs!"

"Apparently," interrupted a man wearing a top hat, clad in black riding boots, trousers and smoking jacket, "we can't enter cemeteries, we are the children born out of wedlock, and committed suicide during our lifetime." I remembered him from the night I killed his friend, Katja – the white-haired one. From under his long hair, an array of nose, lip and eyebrow piercings glittered against luminescent skin. He shook his head, and turned towards another male vampire. "Torrin, have you read this?"

The young man – the one Natashka fed upon when we first met – sat beside him and lifted a newspaper from a stack scattered across a pile of moth-eaten cushions and scoffed. "They say people born with red hair and blue eyes are more likely to become vampires."

The room looked at Mhayree. "What?" she said, as though daring anyone to answer.

Deciding not to wait around any further, I walked away. As I reached the door, I noticed, out of the corner of my eye, a short, unattractive woman swiping a finger along a cobweb-covered railing. "Doesn't anyone clean in this castle?"

She must be a human, I thought.

I walked the length of the hallway, listening to the familiar sounds of restless ghosts, stones falling from buttresses, and crows cawing in the towers. Sunlight beamed through the cavities in the walls and streamed across my face. I opened a door leading into the courtyard and stepped outside to embrace the heat of the winter sun.

"Enjoy it while you can," Natashka said, following me.

"I know," I replied, with a sad smile, remembering what she had told me after my transition. Within one century, maybe two, I'd never walk in daylight again and instead be forced to live for eternity in darkness.

"Two centuries is a long time," I recalled telling her.

"Not compared to forever," Natashka replied.

I stepped forward into the full body of the sun, feeling the heat wash over me. Icicles and sprinkles of snow clung to the tips of trees surrounding the castle. Sun rays skimmed across the frozen lake as steam emerged from the surface. Red and brown leaves succumbed to winter's chill and fell to the ground. Natashka edged beside me, holding a goblet. "Drink this," she said. "You look tired."

I accepted the offer and bringing the goblet to my lips, tasted the intoxicating, metallic saltiness of blood. After draining the contents, Natashka and I sat upon the snow, whereby she divulged the details of the humans' arrival to Castle Árnyék. All across Loch Fala, the Councillors preached of the vampire epidemic spreading throughout the island. Day and night, citizens endured the onslaught of questioning, as henchmen battered down their doors and brought them to confess or face torture in the Inservium vaults. Newspapers, flyers and posters declared warnings of vampire attacks, and offered rewards to anyone who captured one, dead or alive. Within three days, twenty or so innocent women and men received death sentences, with their final moments ending on the hangman's noose, the executioner's axe, or at the fires of a stake. Across town, market stalls and street charlatans sprung up overnight, trading in protection paraphernalia, antidotes for vampire attacks, and "ancient" Greek, Egyptian, and Babylonian texts unearthed in recent excavations and reproduced on the black market.

The families of suspected vampires either fled their homes and country, never to return, or pleaded their innocence, only to be exiled or coerced into accusing more families. Others – the families of real vampires – journeyed to Árnyék to reunite and find safety with their relatives in hiding.

"What do you think will happen to Jacque?" I asked.

Natashka took the goblet from my hand and frowned after attempting to swig from the empty cup. "I don't know."

"He's in more danger now than before," I said, standing up, and pacing around in the snow, before stopping in front of her. "Do you think he's already dead?"

"No," she said, wiping snow from my coat. "The spell I performed rejected my powers, but his blood wasn't dead. Jacque is still alive."

A tear fell from my eye. Embarrassed, I lowered my head, trying not to draw attention. As a lump rose in my throat, I swallowed hard and focused on the snowdrop stems emerging through the snow.

"I'm guessing a slice of *pirog* won't help this situation?" Natashka asked.

I laughed, feeling grateful to have a friend by my side. "If you were me, what would you do?"

Natashka replied without hesitation. "What wouldn't I do?"

Unapologetic of our violent natures, we remained silent, with mutual respect.

"We have to find out who the traitor is," Natashka continued. "The Inservium are just playing with the townspeople. All these executions and tortures serve no purpose than to cause hysteria and unquestioned devotion. They know who they are looking for, and somebody is giving them names."

"We will start training. Tonight. Besides, we need to be ready to confront my father."

Natashka frowned, scared.

"Together," I said, smiling.

She nodded in agreement, and we made our way back to the castle.

"Has this place ever tried to kill you?" I said.

She laughed. "Are you talking about what happened after

you killed Katja?"

"Aye."

"There is no need to worry, *Zaya*. It was a hallucination. The castle was preparing you for transition."

"The castle?"

"Of course," Natashka smiled. "It has many secrets. Your spider friend will be back, too."

"How do you know about the spider?" I said.

"I still haven't managed to bake some *pirog*. I might need to dust off the old baking trays," she said, ignoring me.

"Don't tell the humans – they'll only ask us to clean the place," I said, knowing it was pointless to ask more about the spider.

Natashka grinned. "The last time I used a feather duster, I turned it into a boa."

As we entered the castle, I heard rustlings in the woods, far off in the distance. I turned my head to search between the trees and strained to discern a doe scavenging for food.

"Elise? Are you coming?" Natashka asked.

"Aye, sorry," I replied.

"We should get some sleep before everyone gathers for training."

Taking one last look towards the woods, I noticed the doe had gone, and smiled at my own stupidity before entering the castle.

***

Midnight struck on the old grandfather clock in the music room. As I walked past, the door creaked open, revealing the dancing ghosts, yet again rising from the Underworld. One by one, the spirits appeared and readied their positions in anticipation of the piano striking up the music. I stood watching, wondering if I'd reach a day when I no longer felt guilty about their deaths. It's doubtful, I concluded, as the door closed, leaving me abandoned on the other side.

Step by step, I treaded the groaning floorboards, carrying a bag full of weapons Natashka and I had confiscated from the Inservium. Whilst passing a mirror, I watched myself transform into my vampiric form. It reminded me of the first night Mhayree escorted me through the castle and her monstrous body overpowered her human guise. As I continued my journey, I heard faint whispers of "vampire killer," "traitor," and "murderer," creeping behind me.

I looked around, searching for someone or something following me, and found only darkness. Upon a wall hung a portrait with a shadowy outline of a dark-haired girl, standing alone, dressed in purple velvet with an evil stare. At the bottom of the gold-gilded frame, a plaque read:

ELISE DE VOLONTÉ, 11TH MARCH 1879 –

Moving closer to inspect the portrait, its eyes followed me, and a wicked smile teased at the corner of the mouth. Its eerie resemblance drew me in, and as I reached out my hand, I swore its lips moved and muttered "death to de Volonté." For all the unnerving sights contained within the castle, my portrait terrified me the most. I edged away, almost tripping over my own feet, before running down the remainder of the hallway. All the while, the portrait's taunts and threats followed my every step.

As my pace quickened, I reached the doorway to a room in the east wing and heard familiar voices arguing inside. I bent down and peered through the keyhole.

"The covens will not come," Saara said, handing a letter to Mhayree. "They will not fight beside Elise."

Mhayree snatched the letter from Saara's hand. "I thought your mother was using her influence to encourage them to join us?"

"She's not the only original Phoenix. The others have sided against her," Saara replied.

"Well, it's not like we can ask the humans to join us,"

Mhayree added. "Most of them drank so much port they're comatose."

She ripped up the letter, threw the pieces in the air, and walked towards the door. I straightened up and entered the room, pretending to be oblivious to the conversation.

"You're here," Mhayree said, startled. "Good! The rest will be here soon."

"How many?" I asked.

"Twenty or so. We decided not to contact the overseas covens," Mhayree replied, smiling. "No need to cause panic when we can handle this ourselves."

At the back of the room, Saara, failing to be inconspicuous, swept the scattered pieces of parchment with her feet and concealed them under her long, crinoline skirt.

"Twenty? The Councillors outnumber us two to one," I declared.

Mhayree's smile wavered. "You have us," she replied, holding me by the shoulders.

I opened my mouth to protest, but Natashka entered the room, managing somehow to both manoeuvre her wheelchair through the door and apply kohl at the same time. Not far behind, my mother followed, holding five daggers in her arms. "This is all we had. Mhayree, I have your sgian dubh. Elise already has the laguiole. I have Gizella's sabre. And the rest are-"

"You're not fighting, surely?" I said.

My mother stared at me, enraged. "I may have failed the transition into a Phoenix, but I still have my uses. Do you think this is the first time the Inservium has attempted a Second Cleansing?"

"What do you mean?" I asked.

My mother leaned in towards me, in an almost threatening manner. "I mean-"

The door flew open as a crowd of vampires strode into the room. I counted each one, as they stood gathered beside a wall-mounted tapestry depicting the original Thirteen

Phoenixes. Including the newer vampires – Clara, the two lovers, and three I did not recognise – plus the older generations, our coven consisted of twenty-eight Phoenixes. The odds still did not favour us.

"Do not worry, *Zaya*," said Natashka. "You will train us well."

I nodded, feeling not altogether convinced, and invited everyone to form a circle in the centre of the room.

"She's not lining us up to kill us, is she?" sneered an Irish woman.

"Be quiet, Bridget," said Saara. "Or would you prefer the Inservium continued to kill innocent people?"

The room fell silent and I seized the moment to distribute weapons from my bag. Each person received a dagger, sword, razor, or iron chains, and took it in turns to pass them around. Tears welled up in the eyes of the older vampires as they caressed and examined the weapons in awe.

"Ilona Samsa's blade," said Mhayree, studying a sapphire-encrusted dagger. "This was stolen almost two hundred years ago."

"And this is my mother's sword," added Saara. "The silver hasn't even tarnished."

The pixie-looking vampire spun two chains in her hands and smiled. "Noemi and Emilia Bokori's weapons. They'll be glad to see these again when they arrive."

Mhayree and Saara looked at each other with furrowed brows, knowing too well that no one was coming to help. As the vampires reminisced about the history of each weapon – from those owned by the original Thirteen to ones passed down from generation to generation – I spotted Mia holding a ruby-encrusted dagger with a silver handle. I held my hand out in front of her and she placed the blade in my hand. "This one is a particular favourite of mine," I said.

The vampires glared at me.

"That knife," said Mhayree, "belonged to Katalin Arany. She used it to slice open hers and Gizella's veins whilst cursing them both."

I dropped the dagger to the floor, feeling sick and disgusted. "You mean cursing me and Jacque!"

I turned to leave the circle, but my mother stood in front of me and said, pointing to Mhayree. "Fight us."

I laughed. "You will get hurt. Or worse."

My mother held Gizella's dagger to my throat, and as I continued to mock her, Mhayree lunged at me with Ilona's knife. I ducked and side-kicked Mhayree in the ribs, forcing her to the ground. My mother grabbed my leg mid-air, and swiped the other with her foot, causing me to fall. She grabbed one of the Bokori chains from the pixie vampire and whipped it over me. I snatched Mhayree's sgian dubh, entwined the chain around it, and pulled to slam my mother into a wall. I sprung from the floor onto my feet as Mhayree threw a dagger towards me. Managing to catch it before it hit my chest; I slid it into my boot and yelled, "Enough!"

Mhayree stood up and helped my mother to her feet, kissing her as she did so. "Are you alright?" she asked. My mother nodded and hobbled back to the circle.

"Shall we begin?" said Natashka, motioning to me, as though awaiting a performance.

I studied the faces around the room, which were full of expectation. "This won't be like the brawl in the kitchen the other night," I remarked.

The vampires looked at one another, bewildered and nervous, until Mhayree stepped forward. "Form a line," she demanded.

"We'll start with the basics," I said, holding up a sword. "How to kill a man."

I explained the delicate details and nuances of the different weapons – how the serrated edge of a razor glides and slashes the throat with one swift motion, the correct way of lassoing a whip around a neck to cause an instant break or asphyxiation, and when to choose between a dagger or sword for up-close or distance combat.

"Why don't we use guns?" asked a man with his arm

around Mia. "It would be quicker and easier."

"Guns are loud," I said. "They draw too much attention."

The hand of a tall, slender, leather-clad woman shot up. "If we end up spilling the Councillors' blood, can we drink it?"

The entire coven stared at the woman in disapproval, and, with a tinge of sadness, she lowered her hand.

"If you intend to kill a man, you'll be spilling his blood," I said.

"Drink the blood of live Councillors?" Mhayree added. "Have some standards."

The woman, conceding, nodded.

"Next," I announced, "defence and how to use the body for attack."

I stood in the middle of the room and demonstrated a leg sweep, dropkick, and ducking and weaving. For me, the manoeuvres felt natural, however, it grew apparent the group did not share my abilities. Even Mhayree, who in previous encounters proved more than a match for my capabilities, laboured when trying to fight against my vampiric form.

"I'm sorry," I said after slamming her into the door, inflicting a deep wound.

She rubbed her head and blood seeped onto her fingers. "Not at all, my dear. Keep going."

I kneeled down beside her and whispered. "We are nowhere near ready. This could take months, or years."

"Have faith. You are your mother's daughter," Mhayree replied, pointing towards a corner. I turned around and saw my mother fighting against a male vampire twice her size. She twisted his arm around his back, bringing him to his knees and pretended to drive a knife through his heart. They both laughed, and once releasing her victim, she proceeded to give him advice about better defences.

"This is going well, *Zaya*, no?" Natashka shouted across the room whilst feeding from a young, doe-eyed, female vampire. This in turn attracted the attention of Torrin, who ceased training and confronted the Russian. She rolled her eyes, lifted her sleeve, and to satisfy him, offered a vein. As he bit down and consumed Natashka's blood, he stopped, appearing distracted, and looked out the window. Natashka whispered to him, as he shook his head, and left the room.

"Natashka has an interesting way of fighting," I commented to Mhayree.

"Hmm," she smirked.

In a corner, my mother knelt on the floor, holding a man in a headlock, and demonstrated how to break a neck.

"Mhayree, how did my mother learn how to fight?" I asked.

Mhayree's face fell. "It's to do with your father."

"What about him?" I asked.

She looked at me with pity. "It's nothing," she said, and walked away.

"Mhayree?" I called after her. She ignored me, choosing instead to launch an attack at Mia.

The coven trained through the night, combining successes with failures. For every time someone dodged a punch or swipe, someone else crashed to the floor, or battered against the walls. I remained in the background, waiting to be challenged. It grew obvious that nobody dared come near me, and so I slipped into the corner, out of sight. Amidst the darkness, I soon found myself fighting with my shadow – a backflip off the wall, a spin into a side-kick, a parry and a riposte with a sword, a high-kick into a somersault and a leg sweep. Behind me, I heard a burst of excited applause and turned around to discover Amelie and Freya sitting by the door. Amelie leaned forward, resting her head on her hands, and watched with an intense stare. Something about the way she smiled unnerved me, as though she was capable of leaping up and killing at any moment.

"Are we actually getting anywhere?" interrupted a male vampire, slumped against the window.

"Shh!" announced Hart, in her half-mangled red dress.

"I just managed to punch Saara in the face and swipe a knife across her stomach."

"And I dodged it," replied Saara.

"Once!" I remarked. "Everyone back to it. Now!"

Amidst the groans, Natashka lifted her arms, raising all the weapons into the air and circling them above the vampires' heads. "Anyone for decapitation?" she asked. Without hesitation, the group recommenced training.

As I walked towards Amelie and Freya, the two girls giggled and mimicked the fight moves. "Why are you awake?" I said, crouching in front of them.

"A man was looking in our window," Freya said.

"Don't be silly," I laughed, "how could anyone find us here? We're in the middle of nowhere."

"What are they doing?" Amelie asked, peering around me.

"Playing," I replied.

"That's what adults do at night," Freya informed us both.

"Indeed," I said, as though it was normal to be watching her mother bash a man's head into the floor. As I steered them out of the room, Torrin reappeared, dragging the bodies of two dead Councillors.

"They've found us," he said.

CHAPTER EIGHTEEN

Torrin dropped the two bodies at my feet. "Sebastian and I finished them off. We found them skulking in the courtyard," he said.

Mhayree and Natashka moved closer, enticing more of the coven to follow as curiosity got the better of them.

I ushered Amelie and Freya towards the door. Amelie strained to see what was happening. "Why is that man bleeding from his head? I can see his brain."

Mhayree knelt down to inspect the bodies and said to the children. "It's time to go back to bed, my dears."

My mother joined Mhayree.

"Mama?" said Amelie.

"Go back to bed," my mother replied.

"It's a game," I lied, pushing Amelie and Freya out the room and closing the door.

"How did they get past your enchantments?" Mhayree asked Natashka, grabbing one of the Councillors by the hair to examine his face.

"I don't know," Natashka answered, worried. "Only someone who knows magic could break the defences."

I leaned in towards Mhayree and whispered. "Someone in the coven?"

"Perhaps," she replied, eyeing the group with suspicion.

"More importantly," Mia announced, stepping forward. "How did they find us? This castle has been abandoned for two hundred years."

"The humans must have led them here," said Torrin. "I'm assuming accidentally."

"I need some samples of their blood," Natashka informed him, removing an empty vial from her pocket and a dagger from her bodice. She handed them to Torrin and slicing across the Councillor's wrist, he deposited the blood into the glass.

"What is that in aid of?" I asked.

"Come with me," Natashka replied, taking the dagger and vial from Torrin, and departing the room.

I followed, abandoning the coven to argue amongst themselves about conspiracies and intrigues.

Natashka led me through the castle, and transformed into a bat to take me down into the deep caverns of the earth, until we reached the undercroft.

"Where are we going?" I asked.

"My laboratory," said Natashka, reappearing in her vampiric form. "Nobody ever comes down here."

The whispers of men and women echoed from inside the walls. They called our names, teasing us to join them.

"Do you hear that?" I said, stopping to listen as the voices grew louder.

Natashka nodded without a hint of emotion on her face.

The ghost of a weeping woman, holding a baby, emerged from the shadows. Head bowed, watching her child, she drifted towards us. A cold chill swept over me, alongside an overwhelming feeling of grief and despair, as she walked through me and disappeared upstairs.

"The dead cannot hurt you here," Natashka said, stopping outside a door. "Wait here."

"What are you doing?"

"Just be patient," she replied, disappearing into the darkness.

I waited behind the doorway and paced up and down. The voices within the walls gravitated into the room and crept beneath a crack under the door. From inside, a violent stream of bangs shook the stone foundations and a flash of light pierced through the gaps between the door hinges.

"*Chert voz'mi!*" I heard Natashka yell in frustration.

A cloud of smoke leaked under the door, which preceded a further round of glass smashing, pots clattering, and muttered chants.

Over and over, the same sounds and flashing lights came from the room until – all of a sudden – silence.

The door opened, and Natashka appeared, with her hair in complete disarray and flecks of embers dotted over her dress.

"Is everything alright?" I said, trying to appear nonchalant.

Natashka nodded, patting her sleeves. I leaned over and removed a cobweb from her hair.

"The Councillors weren't alone," she said, holding up the bloodstained, empty vial. "The other three returned safely, back to the Inservium."

"How do you know that?" I asked. A loud bang caused the ceiling to quake, drawing no response from Natashka. "What the fu-" I exclaimed.

"Spell," Natashka replied.

"And it's reliable?"

Another bang.

"Always!" Natashka responded. "Our defences are down. The Inservium could arrive at any time."

"Then my sister is no longer safe," I replied.

Natashka nodded, sullen and despondent.

"We both know what needs to be done," I said. "Cast the circle, we leave now."

Natashka retrieved five crystals from an apothecary table and handed them to me. "What about the rest of the coven?"

"There is a traitor amongst them, they can't be trusted," I replied, laying the crystals on the floor. "And besides, they haven't trained enough to fight. They would be dead within an hour."

We entered the circle and Natashka clasped my hand. "I will take us into the Inservium."

"Won't they see us coming?"

Natashka bit her lip. "We're probably going to die anyway."

***

In an instant, the stone walls of Castle Árnyék dissolved, and transformed into the Inservium vaults.

"I don't know this place," I said.

"I aimed for underground."

Natashka and I negotiated the dark passageways, turning countless corners, unwary of being caught at any moment. Each time we reached the end of one corridor, we soon got lost in another. As we neared the upper levels, the muffled sound of Councillors' voices echoed in the distance. I removed my poignard and dagger from my boots and offered one to Natashka. She shook her head. "This one has already spilled Councillor's blood," she laughed, pointing to the knife down her bodice.

I smiled in agreement, not daring to imagine how much vampire blood the blade once spilled.

"Are you afraid?" I asked.

"Not particularly," she replied. "We've dealt with them before."

"True. I suppose there's nothing they can do to us."

"Not anymore," Natashka replied, patting my hand. "Are *you* afraid?"

I looked at her and for the first time in months didn't feel alone. "Not anymore."

Approaching the sanctuary, we wandered down the centre aisle with no fear of the Councillors discovering us. Let them find us, I thought, and let us hunt.

I drew back a curtain to an anteroom, and found it to be empty. Natashka searched the alcoves and vestries. "Nobody."

"We can try upstairs," I said. "I believe that's where their chambers-"

"Elise de Volonté!" cried a familiar voice.

"Bothwell!"

He moved towards us, with an unsettling calmness, keeping his eyes fixed upon me. "It has been such a long time. I heard you died. And then became a vampire. Tell me, which was worse?"

He stood before me, and moved a strand of hair from my face. "You look different. More refined, almost."

"Remove your filthy hands," I said.

He laughed. "Did the coven welcome you with open arms?"

I stayed silent.

"Hmm?" he continued. "Elise, the vampire murderess. Did you enjoy killing their families?"

I stared at him, but didn't move. Natashka's hand brushed against mine.

"It's very brave of you to come here all by yourself," Bothwell said.

"I'm not by myself," I replied.

Bothwell turned to Natashka, as though noticing her for the first time. "Shouldn't that be in an institution?"

I leaned into him and bared my fangs. As he recoiled, I slashed his face with my nails, and Natashka thrust a knife towards his abdomen. He grabbed the handle of the blade, evading the impact, and ran backwards, withdrawing a sword from his cloak.

"Councillor Bothwell!" shouted another Councillor, entering the sanctuary. Three more joined him, and flinched at the sight of Natashka and me.

"Vampires!" Bothwell yelled, pointing at us.

The four men ran towards us, wielding swords, and commenced their attack. Two of the Councillors brought down their swords around me, aiming for my head and chest. I struck both their blades with my dagger and poignard, deflecting the weapons, giving me enough time to side-kick one in the ribs, and slice through the other's throat. As the first lay on the floor, I saw Natashka's knife floating in mid-air as she fought off her assailants. One dropped his sword, providing her with the opportunity to thrust the blade into his heart, and levitate the fallen sword to defend against the other Councillor. My second opponent attempted to swipe at my ankles. I kicked his leg, and heard the bones break. Natashka disposed of her remaining attacker by bringing her knife around the back of his neck, and dragging it forward, to decapitate him. Three of the four men lay dead, with the other squealing beneath my boot. I aimed my poignard towards him. Natashka suspended her knife over his throat, and drops of sweat dribbled down his forehead as he trembled.

"Where is Bothwell?" Natashka asked me.

I turned my head, but saw no signs of the squirmy little toad.

"I was so close to killing him," I said.

"I know where he is," the trapped Councillor gurgled.

"Bothwell?" Natashka said, digging the blade further into his throat. "Yes, take us to him."

"No," he replied, struggling against the knife. "The boy. I know where the boy is."

"Boy? What boy? You mean–" said Natashka.

I dropped my poignard, grabbed the Councillor's chest, and pulled him forward until we were nose to nose. He winced as Natashka's blade scratched his throat.

"You know where Jacque is?" I spat.

"Yes," he croaked, avoiding my stare. "He is here."

I released the Councillor, and collapsed to my knees. Natashka spoke to me, but I heard nothing, and saw only her lips move. Deep feelings of guilt, resentment and shame took hold of me. All this time, the Councillors had imprisoned Jacque in the Inservium without me knowing.

***

The Councillor screamed.

"Enough!" I said. "If you thought watching her turn into a bat was terrifying, you should see her when she's hungry."

"I will kill you if you lead us into a trap," Natashka threatened him, as she returned to her human-like form. The Councillor led us beneath the vaults, hobbling along in front, his fractured leg strapped up with wood ripped from a pew, and strips of fabric from Natashka's skirt. I walked behind him, pointing a dagger at his back, as Natashka suspended one at his throat. The Councillor did not reply, only his erratic breathing and pounding heartbeat broke through the silence.

"Move it," I growled, shoving him forward.

We ventured deep into the bowels of the Inservium, where I lost all sense of direction, surrounded by unfamiliar territory. Nerves crept into my stomach as I thought of seeing Jacque again – smelling his scent, hearing his voice, and feeling his warm body against mine. His secrets didn't seem to matter, nor did my being a vampire. At least, not at that moment. As long as he came back to me.

We passed the torture chambers, filled with racks, whips, and thumbscrews. The overwhelming stench of sweat, pain, and human waste – alongside the sight of impaled, innocent men and women – nauseated me. Room by room exposed the Inservium's horrific capabilities, and I broke into a cold shiver imagining them subjecting Jacque to the same treatments.

We reached a cell, and the Councillor removed a set of keys from his cloak and unlocked the door. I pushed him aside and forced myself into the tiny, freezing room.

"Jacque!" I cried.

Amidst the squalor of the dark, windowless room, sat an empty straw bed. But no Jacque.

"Where is he?" I said.

The Councillor stuttered, unable to find the right words, as his hands trembled against the door frame. Enraged, I walked outside and drew my poignard across his throat, leaving him to die on the floor. As tears welled up in my eyes Natashka attempted to console me, but to no avail. I stumbled into the cell and collapsed onto the bed. Foolish idiot, never trust a Councillor, I thought.

"What is that?" Natashka said.

I looked up towards her, and she pointed to the corner of the bed. On top of the mattress, a piece of folded parchment sat, with a red wax firebird seal. I ripped it open and found within a letter addressed to the Councillors:

My Dear Councillors

The more attentive of you will have realised that the Honourable Jacque Angou is no longer under your care. In payment for your hospitality, you will find two of your brethren nailed to the walls in one of the cells. Do forgive the blood – disembowelment is such a messy business. If, for some reason, you find yourselves in need of Master Angou's company, please do let me know. I see you have a vast collection of torture implements, and it would be most enjoyable to try them out on you.

Katalin Arany

"*Zaya*?" Natashka asked, manoeuvring beside me.

I handed her the parchment and said, "She's back."

"Who?"

"His great-grandmother," I said, through gritted teeth.

"Katalin?" Natashka read the letter and closed her eyes. "Perhaps she heard Gizella is dead."

"All I had to do was save him," I responded, sitting on the edge of the bed with my head in my hands. "That's been my job for months, and she's taken him from me."

"At least you know he's alive. And, presumably, safe."

I nodded in agreement, knowing Jacque's freedom should bring me comfort. But it didn't.

"Although, judging by this note, she sounds violently

unhinged," Natashka said.

I frowned at her through my fingers. "You mean like me?"

Natashka, attempting to diffuse the awkwardness, said, "Perhaps you might like her."

Standing up, I looked at her in disbelief, and said nothing. Instead, I wandered around the cell, wondering how Jacque managed to survive these rancid conditions. He needed to come home – our home.

"We must find her," I said.

"No need," Natashka replied, shaking her head and giving the letter back to me. "She will find you."

"Good," I said, scrunching up the parchment, and tossing it into the corner. "Because I'm going to kill her."

We retraced our steps, arguing at every corner as to which direction to take. Stairwell by stairwell, I ascended – and Natashka flew – until we reached the surface, and the sanctuary.

The sound of swords clashing, and men and women yelling and screaming, awaited us. As Natashka and I emerged out of the vault, the body of a young Councillor slid towards us. Dead.

Around the room, Mhayree, my mother, Saara, Hart, Mia, and Torrin, alongside the other coven members, fought the horde of Councillors. Bodies of both sides lay across the floor.

Natashka transformed back from being a bat and sat beside me. She yelped as a Councillor gripped her by the hair and brought a sword down towards her chest. Without hesitation, I flicked my boot to release the dagger hidden within it, grabbed the handle, and sliced through the Councillor's jugular. His blood spurted onto Natashka, covering her hair, face and arms. She lapped up the drops running down her fingers, and said, "This one was dying anyway."

The Councillor collapsed onto the floor, the life draining

from him.

From all directions, black cloaks surrounded us as the Councillors fought the vampires. One by one, the Inservium succumbed to the strength of the Phoenixes as daggers and fangs ripped the Councillors apart.

I removed my poignard from my coat, and joined the battle. The indiscernible faces of Councillors flashed before me as my blades tore through them. Their screams turned to silence.

Beneath my feet, a river of blood seeped into my boots as I made my way across the carnage. Behind me, Natashka raised the Councillors who ambushed her into the air and hurled their bodies against walls and pillars.

A Councillor leapt in front of me and slapped me across the face. He let out a sinister laugh as his ring caught my cheek, causing it to bleed. I stabbed my dagger into his mouth and out through the back of his head. He stopped laughing.

In the corner, Mhayree dragged a man across the floor and stood on his neck, before bending down, and snapping it with her bare hands.

The dead bodies of the pixie vampire, the raven-haired woman, the American Clara Price, and the two lovers lay on the ground.

I stepped around Clara and spotted my brother, Étienne, skulking in an alcove. Shrouded in darkness, he peered out into the sanctuary. I turned to face him and saw, standing behind him, my father. Étienne stared. I imagined he was watching the horror stories from his childhood come to life. His confused expression turned to fear at discovering his fang-baring, blood-soaked warrior sister.

In the distance, I heard Natashka spouting Russian profanities. My mother – the only non-vampire on our side – stood on top of the altar, wielding a sabre. Just as she had demonstrated to me in Katja Ustov's house, she killed with swift, precise movements. Three, maybe four, Councillors attacked her in succession. Each of their bodies was dumped at her feet. One sudden strike against a Councillor's neck forced the sabre from her hand. It flew through the air, passing Natashka's face. She stuck out her tongue and licked the blood from the blade as it continued its journey mid-air. Before it fell to the ground, she grabbed the handle, and launched the weapon back towards my mother, who caught it without looking.

"*Zaya*, behind you!" Natashka yelled, whilst raising her arm.

I spun around to find a fat, middle-aged Councillor, suspended upside down above me, and aiming a sword towards my head. I stepped forward, gripped his wrist, and broke the bones. He dropped the sword. Before it landed, I cut his throat with my poignard.

Outside the windows, the dusky pink and orange hues of dawn streaked into the sanctuary. As the sunlight crossed over the vampires, our beautiful, monstrous forms gave way to our weaker, human-like guises. By then, another dozen Councillors entered the room to join the battle. Our strength waned, allowing the Councillors full advantage against us.

All around me, the coven members fought, and failed, to defend themselves.

"Raise them!" I yelled to Natashka, motioning to the vampires.

She lifted her arms, and the few surviving vampires levitated towards the ceiling. All except my mother, who avoided Natashka's aim. The Councillors stood in disbelief, as their prey escaped their grasps. High above me, Mhayree and Mia protested, and Saara threw down her axe, killing a Councillor in the process.

As the Councillors surrounded Natashka and me, I unleashed a tirade of bone-crushing high-kicks, vein-ripping bites, slashes, and stabbings. My mother proved to be the more elegant fighter in our family. I was not my mother.

Natashka bared her slowly receding fangs at the Councillors, provoking them to attack. Many of the men cowered. No matter, I killed them anyway.

"Leave my daughter," said my mother, as she limped towards us. "She is only a child."

The Councillors turned on her. She retaliated, and, with swift swipes, executed her assailants.

As she pushed a dead Councillor off her body, another seized the opportunity to grab her around the neck. I turned to see my mother choking and – whilst slicing a Councillor from groin to sternum with my poignard – drove my dagger into her attacker's eye.

Natashka's screaming pierced the air. A Councillor stabbing her in the arm with a switchblade caused the suspended vampires to plummet to the ground. Without hesitation, I tossed my dagger towards the Councillor's chest, where it landed in his heart.

The vampires scrambled to their feet – only a handful of us remained against the mass of Councillors – and charged into battle.

Natashka removed the switchblade from her arm, as my mother and I warded off our attackers. I could smell the blood gushing from the wound.

Mhayree joined my mother and disposed of three men in quick rotation. As she swung her arm around to stab an approaching Councillor, I ducked to avoid her sgian dubh. The blood from her blade spattered across my face, the taste of death filled my mouth.

Saara wielded her axe, severing limbs and heads with each swipe.

An Inservium sword struck a Councillor rushing towards me. I glanced backwards to find Mia withdrawing the weapon from his chest. "You're using their weapons to kill them?" I smiled, whilst side-kicking a Councillor.

"They did the same to us," she replied.

Hart cracked a whip across the Councillors' torsos and backs.

Natashka let out a faint whimper, as she grasped her

wounded arm. In vain, she attempted to lift her hand to raise the surrounding Councillors. She screamed in frustration, removed her knife from her bodice, and stabbed it into one of their legs. Before the Councillor collapsed, she retrieved the weapon and sliced it across his throat.

Whilst defending himself from an oncoming attack, Torrin slid up his shirt sleeve, and placed his wrist against Natashka's lips. As she bit into his vein, the smell of her blood disappeared as the wound healed.

A Councillor punched me in the gut, causing an insurmountable surge of pain, and leaving me gasping for breath. Hunched over, I clutched my stomach, and watched, petrified, as the steel of his sword swiped towards my neck. Mhayree grabbed my shoulders, pushed me behind her, and within seconds, the Councillor's body lay dead on the floor.

Across from me, a Councillor turned towards Torrin, and lifted his sword to strike. Natashka released her bite, and with a wave of her hand, threw Torrin across the room. With the other hand, she suspended the Councillor and bent his body backwards, until his spine snapped.

The sunlight grew stronger, and a myriad of colours streamed through the stained-glass windows. Geometric yellow, green, and blue motifs of their Idol shimmered against our blood-soaked bodies. Matted hair clung to red-stained faces, and the weight of our sticky, blood-encrusted garments restricted the most basic of movements. In that moment, it felt as though the sunlight sent a message – neither side shall win.

A pile of corpses surrounded my feet. I clambered on top of the bodies to kill another Councillor, and saw Étienne emerging from the alcove, holding a sword. Despite trembling, he moved towards the battle – gripping the blade too tight, like an amateur. Hart charged towards him.

"No!" my mother screamed. "Hart, don't!"

Étienne dropped the sword, and darted towards the safety of the darkness. Hart continued her pursuit. My mother pushed aside two Councillors and, although limping in pain, ran after her son.

One of the floor vaults opened, allowing Bothwell to enter the sanctuary. My mother, either ignoring or not noticing him, darted past, into the alcove. He narrowed his eyes and followed. I forced myself through the crowd, attempting to chase him. A greasy, blond Councillor with a scar across his cheek, bashed into me, knocking me to the ground. He spat in my face and kicked me in the ribs. Lying on the floor, my attention never wavered from Bothwell, until he disappeared into the shadows. A blade swooped down towards me and – as I deflected it – clattered against my poignard. I slammed my boot into the Councillor's kneecap and – whilst he collapsed – slashed my dagger across his throat.

As his body slumped against my legs, I climbed over him and headed towards the alcove. Inside, amidst the blackness, I heard my mother's and Bothwell's footsteps. His increased, as hers slowed down, succumbing to her leg injury. I tracked their steps to the end of a passageway until they faded. Unable to locate them, I turned a corner, and Étienne grabbed me, placing the point of his blade under my chin.

"Don't be a stupid boy," I growled.

"You are a monster, Elise. You seduce men and eat children," he said, shaking.

"You always did believe in fairy tales, Étienne."

He pushed the blade further into my skin. "Father told me."

"Been drinking again, has he?"

Étienne gripped me tighter and led me around a corner. "I'm taking you to Councillor Bothwell."

"Very well," I replied, masking my gratitude at being led to my next victim.

We reached the doorway of a private prayer room, lit with candles and its walls adorned with coats of arms and flags displaying the symbol of their Idol. Étienne and I remained outside. From a distance, I saw my mother, cornered by Bothwell. He pinned her against a wall and forced a kiss upon her lips. Overcome with rage, I shoved Étienne away from me. The poor boy looked too shocked by Bothwell's behaviour to stop me – or prevent himself colliding with a pillar. To my mother's surprise, I stormed into the room, with my dagger and poignard at the ready. Bothwell turned around and laughed upon seeing me.

"Isn't this wonderful?" he said. "Mother, father, and daughter, together at last."

My weapons dropped from my hands.

CHAPTER NINETEEN

My mother pushed past Bothwell and stood beside me. She clasped my hand and turned to my brother. "Run, Étienne. Before anyone finds you."

Étienne, his face growing pale, crept forward into the room. "She's his daughter?"

I launched myself towards him and punched his mouth. Terrified, my brother stumbled backwards and fell to the floor. My mother took hold of my shoulders and hauled me from him. "Go, Étienne. And don't look back."

She held me tight, as Bothwell walked up to my brother and helped him to his feet. "Your mother deceived us both. And your sister is beyond saving-"

"You kissed my mother," Étienne said.

"I loved her. I still do," Bothwell replied.

"Liar!" I yelled.

Étienne flinched and hid behind Bothwell.

"Don't listen to him, Étienne," said my mother. "I can explain."

"You mustn't blame your mother. She is a troubled woman – not even our doctors could help her," Bothwell whispered into Étienne's ear. "But I fear what she will do to you."

He gazed up at Bothwell, hanging on to his every word. "What will you do to them?"

Bothwell tilted his head. "Help them."

Étienne's brow furrowed.

"Go and join the Councillors. You'll be safe," Bothwell continued.

My brother smiled, bowed his head, and turned to leave. My mother released me and moved to run after him. Bothwell retrieved his sword and placed it at my throat.

"Choose. Your daughter or your son," he said.

My mother backed towards me, and watched Étienne leave the room. Bothwell laughed.

"Is it true?" I asked my mother. "Is he my father?"

She lowered her head and sighed.

"Did he force you?" I said.

Bothwell sucked his teeth and tutted.

"Did he rape you?" I asked, preparing to kill him.

"No," she whispered, unable to look at me.

"Did someone make you do it?"

She shook her head. "It was my choice."

Feeling nauseated, I stared at the stranger who called herself my mother. "How could you? With him?" I said, "You disgust me!"

"Elise, I didn't..." she trembled.

I grabbed her by the shoulders, and felt searing heat rising through her body. "Did you love him?"

"No!" she said. "It wasn't like that."

"She was pretty convincing," Bothwell remarked.

My mother lifted her head and glared at him. "That was the point, you narcissistic shit!"

"And you," I said to Bothwell. "As vile as you are, how could you be so cruel to me – your own daughter?"

Bothwell sniffed and stared at me. "Logic. We needed someone to carry out the murders. And your mother would never have disgraced her other children by having us reveal that you are a bastard. And that she is a whore."

I spat on Bothwell's face. He didn't react. The blade of his sword cut into my throat, causing a drop of blood to drip down my neck.

"She would never have risked exposing the Inservium as I could have outed her secret," said Bothwell.

"I didn't know Elise was the murderer," my mother

interrupted.

"Are you sure?" Bothwell replied, unconvinced. "Who else but another vampire – or a highly-trained Councillor, of course – could kill one of you."

My mother shook her head in desperation. "No. She didn't have it in her to murder anyone."

"And yet, she did," mocked Bothwell.

"Because of you!" my mother replied, pushing me out of the way, and, seizing the sword. As the blade sliced through her hand, she refused to let go, and allowed the blood to flow down her arm. Beads of sweat formed on her forehead and her breathing grew heavy. I moved towards her, to help.

"No, my love," she said, holding out her hand to stop me. "You have to let this fight be mine."

"My old friend. Have you learnt nothing about me?" said Bothwell. He removed a dagger from the inside of his cloak, and stabbed my mother in the stomach. She bent over, clutching the wound, and Bothwell whispered in her ear, "You knew."

As she fell to the floor, I rushed forward and held her. Bothwell took full advantage of the opportunity to escape. She lay in my arms, and a tear fell from her eye. Her blonde, matted hair covered the black circles around her eyes, and the colour drained from her lips as she fought to breathe. I placed my hand over her stomach to try and slow the bleeding. She cried out from the pain and took my hand in hers.

"*C'est bien*," my mother muttered.

"*Ça va aller*," I replied, cradling her tight.

"*Je suis désolé.*"

The sound of footsteps walking through the passageway drew closer. I sat upright and stared at the doorway, ready to attack anyone who stepped into the room.

"Mirella!" Mhayree yelled, as she entered, with Natashka not far behind.

"Mhayree, please help me!" I sobbed, relieved to see

223

them.

Mhayree ran, knelt beside my mother, and examined the wound. My mother struggled to speak as she and Mhayree looked at each other, heartbroken.

"Mhayree, help her," I pleaded. "Do something."

She wrapped her arms around my mother, remaining silent. Behind me, I heard Natashka crying. I turned to face her and said. "There must be some magic."

Natashka shook her head. "I'm sorry, *Zaya.*"

My mother squeezed my hand and smiled. Her breaths faded. Mhayree leaned down and kissed my mother on the lips. "I love you," she murmured.

My mother smiled one last time.

"Mirella!" Mhayree said, shaking the body. No response. "Mirella!" Mhayree tried again, before being overcome with grief. "Who did this?"

"Bothwell," I managed to say through the numb feeling rising in my chest.

Mhayree held my mother against her, and wept.

"Mhayree, he's my-"

"I know," she snapped.

Natashka, sniffling, placed her hand on my shoulder. "We cannot stay here. The Councillors will find us."

"No!" Mhayree said, shielding my mother from us.

Moments felt like hours as silence filled the room and none of us could find it in ourselves to look at the other.

"We cannot leave her here," I finally said.

"I will kill him," Mhayree mumbled to herself.

"Then, we must bury her," Natashka interrupted.

Mhayree stroked my mother's hair and said. "She will have the proper funeral rites."

"You know we cannot move the body that far," said Natashka. "The coven lost, and used the crystals to retreat back home. We have to bury the body outside."

I looked around the room, at the candelabra lining the walls.

"Do the rites here," I said, standing up and taking down two candles.

"We don't have time," Natashka urged. "We have to move fast; Bothwell may come back with other Councillors."

"We can barricade the doors. Between the three of us, we could give any Councillor who finds us a good fight," I said.

Natashka thought for a moment, before nodding. "The odds are not in our favour, but it is doable."

Walking around the room, I closed the two sets of doors, jamming them with flagpoles taken from the walls.

Mhayree stared at the two of us. "You would have her laid to rest here, of all places?"

"We have no choice, Mhayree," Natashka replied.

"She is my mother, and I should decide," I said, holding back my tears.

"Well I was her…" Mhayree answered, before breaking down again.

Natashka wiped a tear from her eye and lowered her head to mask the sadness.

"I can't do this on my own, Mhayree," I said.

She closed her eyes, shutting out the world. I kneeled down beside her, and – despite her protests – unwrapped her arms from around my mother. I lay the body on the ground, and stood up, keeping my eyes on the mixture of peace and sorrow upon her face. As I gathered the lit candelabra around the room, I placed them, one by one, in a circle around Natashka, Mhayree, and my mother.

Mhayree prepared the body with the grace and dignity befitting of a warrior. As best as possible, she wiped the blood from her face, and undressed her, folding each piece of clothing into a neat, precise pile. She removed a silver ring, entwined with a Celtic knot, from my mother's finger and placed it on her own. After I finished creating the circle, I sat beside the body, stripped the wedding band from her, and threw it across the room. Mhayree and I gave her one last kiss and stood by Natashka's side. As she raised her arms, my mother's body rose into the air.

Mhayree removed a dagger from her stocking and traced symbols of a sun and moon upon my mother's arms and legs. Natashka removed two gold coins from her pockets, and passed them to Mhayree, who placed them over the dead body's eyes.

"What will we use for ribbons?" I asked.

Mhayree lifted her skirt and tore a piece of white fabric from her petticoat. Natashka untied her corset and unwound the silver lace.

"Give me another piece of your petticoat and the dagger," I said to Mhayree.

She ripped the fabric with her bare hands and handed it to me. I sliced the blade across my palm, and stained the white petticoat with my blood. Natashka and Mhayree followed suit, drenching the fabric in red. We placed the makeshift ribbons over my mother's chest, and Mhayree proceeded to recite a funeral chant. Natashka instructed me to set the body alight. Candle by candle, the flames engulfed my mother. As the body burned, Mhayree smashed open a stained-glass window and the ashes escaped, free from this world.

Falling embers floated to the ground, spreading fire across the wooden floorboards.

I walked towards the door, picked up the weapons I dropped earlier, and removed the flagpoles. Natashka and Mhayree followed, and turned back to watch as the room set alight. As I opened the door, two Councillors stood waiting, brandishing swords.

"Wrong time!" I said, kicking him in the groin.

The Councillor fell to his knees, and I stabbed him. I turned around, finding the other Councillor impaled on a flagpole. The flames in the prayer room grew higher, spreading faster.

"What do we do?" Natashka asked.

"Let it burn," I said.

The three of us left the Inservium, listening to the screams of the Councillors in the distance.

CHAPTER TWENTY

The town's clock tower bell chimed seven o'clock. Natashka, Mhayree, and I sat amongst the snow, keeping ourselves hidden behind the trees outside the Inservium gates. Mhayree wrapped her arms around me as we both wept for my mother. Councillors ran in all directions, screaming, praying, and begging for water to extinguish the fire. We watched as the flames consumed the building, causing the golden symbol of their Idol to fall from the roof and smash to the ground.

"Is it safe for us to be here, Mhayree?" Natashka asked.

"Probably not," Mhayree replied.

"I'm not going anywhere," I said.

"No, no, neither am I," Natashka assured. "I only ask because I found some *pirog* in the undercroft earlier, and wondered if this was a good time to hand it out?" She removed the cake from under her skirt and offered a piece to Mhayree and me. We both refused – too grief-stricken and angry to eat.

Smoke billowed for miles into the air, turning the white sky a putrid grey. Shards of stained glass exploded into the surrounding graveyard, hitting – amongst others – my gravestone, and rocks and bricks crumbled to piles of ash as the walls of the Inservium collapsed. The remaining few Councillors fled, escaping through windows and jumping from the three storeys, attempting to find safety.

"It was all pointless, wasn't it?" I said.

"What was?" Natashka replied.

"The battle. We lost. My mother died for nothing."

"We lost this battle," added Mhayree.

Amidst the commotion, townspeople braved the freezing

temperatures and arrived carrying buckets of water and hoses. Natashka, Mhayree, and I snuck behind an oak tree to avoid being seen. In the distance, Bothwell stood with his arms folded, watching in disbelief, as everything he held dear disappeared before his eyes. As I leapt to my feet, with intentions of attacking, Mhayree grabbed my arm.

"Not yet," she hissed.

I tried to break free of her grip, but she hauled me to the ground, pinning me down.

"When?" I answered.

"Soon, *Zaya*," Natashka added. "If you go out there now, all you will achieve is getting yourself killed."

"It will make me feel better," I said.

"And what of Amelie? She has no mother, she needs you," Natashka replied.

"Especially now she is transitioning," Mhayree interrupted. I stared at her, confused. "You must have realised," she continued. "The signs have been there."

I struggled to find words, and instead sat in silence, fearful for my sister's future. Natashka placed her hand on my shoulder to comfort me – the gesture failed. When I turned to look at Bothwell, he was gone.

"We will find him," said Natashka.

I nodded, feeling not altogether convinced. "Have you always known he was my father?" I asked Mhayree.

"Aye."

"Why was my mother involved with Bothwell?" I continued.

"She didn't love him!" she snapped, before stopping herself.

"Then what was she doing?" I asked.

No reply.

A few moments passed until I grew impatient of Mhayree's silence. "Mhayree!" I yelled.

"Shh!" said Natashka, looking to see if any of the Councillors or townspeople had heard me.

"Mhayree!" I whispered, refusing to relent.

"What?" she growled. "Do you really think I want to discuss this now?"

"Tough!" I replied.

Mhayree groaned, and closed her eyes. "Before you were born, a few of us decided to bring down the Inservium. Your mother and I were amongst the warriors – that's the reason she knew how to fight… and kill."

"What has that got to do with Bothwell?" I asked.

Mhayree sighed and looked at me. "Mirella had a very specific job. She was to infiltrate the Councillors by starting an affair with Bothwell."

"Wait! I think I'm missing something," Natashka said.

"How long did it last?" I asked.

"About a year," Mhayree replied. "Then she fell pregnant with you."

Natashka took a giant bite of *pirog* and, with intense fascination, listened as Mhayree revealed my mother's secrets.

"That's when we decided she should marry Marius de Volonté," Mhayree said.

"Your father?" Natashka struggled to mumble, whilst chewing.

"Apparently not," I answered.

Mhayree kept her eyes fixed upon the blazing Inservium. "Of course, Bothwell wasn't a fool – he knew Mirella's child must have been his. I think it was a relief for him when your mother married Marius. By then, he knew he could use you against her…"

I pulled my coat around me – not for protection against the winter morning, but for an odd, comforting sensation – and felt the thread lining of the intertwined initials M and E.

"Go on," I urged Mhayree.

Mhayree leaned against the tree, twiddling her sgian dubh between her fingers. She continued to watch the fire and said, "When you were a little girl, Mirella decided to leave Marius. She managed to travel with you and Étienne from Paris to Munich on the Orient Express. Bothwell sent his henchmen to fetch her back. I was supposed to meet you in Budapest."

"Why did he care if my mother left?" I asked.

Mhayree placed her sgian dubh down her boot. "Control. After she came back, he convinced Marius to put her in the women's asylum to modify her behaviour. By the time I heard and made it back to Loch Fala, the doctors had sent her back home. I won't tell you the things they did to her."

"Why didn't he have her killed?" Natashka asked.

Mhayree rubbed her forehead, looking strained. "I don't know. Perhaps he wanted to keep her alive to torment her."

The three of us fell silent for several minutes. Try as they might, the townspeople and Councillors failed to extinguish the fire. Water turned to dustings of snow as soon as it hit the air, only to be melted by the heat from the blaze. From the wreckage, men attempted to salvage statues of their Idol. The Councillors seemed more interested in saving their riches, as they carried armfuls of jewels, gold chests, and silverware.

"Then, of course, he turned you into a murderer," Mhayree said, breaking the silence. "And now, he has her son."

"Where are Étienne and my father?" I asked, feeling a strange sense of concern for my brother.

"Bothwell?" Natashka said.

I grimaced at the name. "I meant Marius."

"Oh! Hart let your brother escape; I think she felt sorry for the boy. But your father evaded her," said Natashka. "They have both disappeared."

"That is a pity – I so much wanted to have a word with my father about his experiments on you."

"Some other time," Natashka smiled.

"Did Marius know about us being vampires?" I asked

Mhayree.

She laughed. "No. Bothwell discovered Mirella's secret – we don't know how – and whenever Marius grew disturbed by her symptoms, Bothwell assured him it was a sign of hysteria."

"I'm starting to think this Bothwell isn't altogether charming," Natashka said, whilst searching for more *pirog*.

"It all makes sense, now, how the Councillors decided on my victims," I said. "If Bothwell knew about my mother-"

"Mirella never told him anything about us!" Mhayree interrupted.

"No. But he would suspect anyone she associated with," Natashka added.

"Perhaps that is why he sent me to kill you, Mhayree," I said.

She thought for a moment, before shaking her head. "It doesn't account for everyone. Mirella only associated with a small circle of friends."

"Does anyone else think it's all too coincidental?" Natashka said. "Amelie is transitioning. Jacque's brother turns up unexpectedly. Elise transitions. I find the man who took Frankenstein a little too seriously. All within the space of a few weeks."

"I don't believe in coincidences," I said.

"Neither do I," Mhayree added. "I'm sure we will find out soon enough. Probably not today, though."

The Councillors ran across the grounds – treasures in hand – seeking refuge. The townspeople, in their stupidity, continued to collect water from nearby wells. Two men ran past the three of us. By luck, the looming shadow from the oak tree kept us hidden.

"There are too many people around, we need to leave," Natashka said.

Mhayree and I agreed.

We waited for a few moments, ensuring nobody saw us. As we moved away from the tree and crept onto the street, we heard the sound of the last Inservium wall collapsing.

Snowflakes started to fall and we quickened our pace, trying to decide the fastest route back to Castle Árnyék. We passed rows of townhouses, as men and women flocked from their homes, all too late to save their Inservium.

"You're going the wrong way," said a middle-aged woman, wearing a fur coat over a nightgown.

Mhayree narrowed her eyes, and the woman carried on her business.

We travelled a few miles through the streets and alleyways, with the smell of smoke suffocating the town. As families offered shelter to their poor, homeless Councillors, we hid out of sight. The streets emptied and horses calmly stood along the roadsides. Loch Fala descended into mourning for the Inservium. An eerie silence fell over the town as we turned a corner to where my old family house stood. Its windows were boarded up and a condemned notice fluttered on the door. I stopped outside the garden gates, and looked through the iron bars, still covered in chains and padlocks.

"Perhaps Étienne came home and is hiding out," I cried out to Natashka and Mhayree, as they continued along the path.

The two women moved towards me and waited beside the gate. Natashka removed her hairpins and handed one to Mhayree. "We shall see."

As Mhayree and Natashka tried to pick the padlocks, I scaled the bars to the top of the gate, and jumped into the garden.

"The locks are loosening," Mhayree said. "Go on inside."

I nodded – traipsing through the overgrown grass and weeds – and entered the house.

Walking through the empty hallway and drawing room, I called my brother's name. Along the walls, darker, square patches of wallpaper marked where the family portraits used to be. Silence replaced the ticking of the old grandfather clock; where once stood Marius's drinks cabinet, armchair, and the couch where he tried to sell me into marriage, now lay piles of dust and mould.

"There's nothing left of her here," I heard Mhayree say. I turned around and found her and Natashka behind me, looking around the room. When Mhayree realised she had spoken aloud, she continued. "Mirella, I mean."

Despite feeling a strange relief for the ghosts of the house resting in peace, I thought of my mother spending days hidden in her room with supposed hysteria, protecting her children from her drunken husband, and the trip we took on the Orient Express. She told me we were going on an adventure where I could eat cakes every day, and make friends with Princes and Princesses. Little did I know she was trying to save both our lives. Now I would never see her again.

"Was there any sign of Étienne?" Natashka said.

I shook my head, walked to the foot of the stairs, and shouted upwards. "Étienne!"

No reply.

"I'll go upstairs, to see if anything has been left behind," I said.

"Mhayree and I will check the other rooms and the garden," Natashka replied.

As the pair wandered through to the kitchen and dining room, I went upstairs and searched the bedrooms, the attic, and study. All traces of my family had disappeared. Amelie's toys, mother's dresser and sewing table, and my brother's insect collection were distant memories, as the rooms sat empty. A musty, damp stench greeted me as I entered my old bedroom. Traces of woodworm lined the wall panels and ceiling beams, and strips of wallpaper lay strewn across the floor. On one wall, faint markings of red and black caught my eye. I peeled back the remaining strips and discovered crayon scribbles of what looked like a spider, a young girl, with a circle of flames around her, and a giant moon with fangs. Perhaps the imaginings of children are closer to truth than the reality of adults. Looking at the picture, I remembered being seven years old and my father sending me to bed without supper for spilling his glass of whisky. I lay in bed, stomach rumbling, when a tiny house spider descended on its web and landed on my pillow. I spent the night making up stories and drawing on the wall. The next day, my mother ordered the room to be redecorated.

I wasn't sure if I was ready to forgive her for hiding the truth from me. Or if she had ever truly forgiven me. Already I struggled to remember the smell of her perfume, or the way she said my name. But I could still picture every time she promised to come back whenever she hid me in the cupboard as Marius hunted for her. And the relief upon her face as we stepped onto the Orient Express. All too quickly her happiness turned to fear as the Councillors approached us. In my eighteen years, I don't think I ever told her how much she meant to me. Now she would never be coming back. How was I supposed to bear eternity without her? In some ways it felt worse than losing Jacque. Perhaps I should forgive her after all.

As I stood up and turned to leave, a spider crawled between my feet and scurried beneath the floorboards. The house belongs to you now, I thought, closing the door behind me, and walking downstairs.

I heard footsteps coming from the library and stepped inside, expecting to find Mhayree. Instead, I discovered a man, with his back to me, wearing a black cloak, standing in the middle of the room. He turned around, and a familiar, cold stare greeted me – Bothwell. The surprised look on his face gave way to anger. "I hoped you had died in the fire."

"That's very unfatherly of you," I said.

"Where is the boy?"

"I don't know where my brother is."

"Not Étienne, you stupid girl. Jacque Angou."

"Don't you know? Perhaps someone has kidnapped him," I replied. "At least they didn't leave you for dead. Not like you did to me."

I removed my poignard and dagger from my boots, and edged towards him. He laughed and retrieved a sword from under his cloak. "Do you really intend for me to kill you and your mother on the same day?"

"No," I replied, continuing to move forward.

He laughed again. But then suddenly his face fell, as the library door closed. The floorboards creaked behind me, and the sound drew closer as Mhayree and Natashka joined my side, weapons in hand.

Nobody said a word.

I stepped forward, and Mhayree and Natashka followed.

Bothwell swiped his sword in the air to ward us off.

Natashka raised her hand, ready to throw him across the room.

"No," I said. "Give him a chance."

The three of us continued to move in on the Councillor.

He sliced the blade of his sword towards my neck.

I blocked it with my poignard.

Mhayree swiped at his throat with her sgian dubh.

Bothwell leaned back and dodged the blade.

With the handle of my dagger digging into my fingers, I noticed the stains of my mother's blood embedded in my nails. I looked at Mhayree and Natashka. In silent agreement, we knew our time had come.

Natashka suspended her knife in the air and thrust it towards Bothwell's chest.

He ducked, spun around, and struck his sword across Mhayree's ankle.

As she fell to the floor, she stabbed her sgian dubh into his groin.

He collapsed, and dropped his sword, cowering into the corner.

Mhayree struggled to her feet, and the three of us edged forward, backing Bothwell against the wall.

"It's not just me, you know. Others will hunt you, too. And the boy," Bothwell said.

"Then we will kill them, also," Natashka laughed.

I pressed my boot over Bothwell's chest, holding him down.

"Is there nothing you would say to me, daughter?" he smirked.

"No," I replied.

I placed my poignard across his throat.

Mhayree aimed her sgian dubh over his heart.

Natashka levitated her knife over his abdomen.

As one, the three of us sliced and stabbed Bothwell, ignoring his screams and pleas for mercy.

"For Mirella," Mhayree whispered into his ear.

Natashka motioned for her knife to return to her, turned to me, and said. "For you, too."

I pitied the old man. Nobody to love or mourn him. What a waste of human existence.

"Would you call it a dignified death?" I said, staring down at the wounds across his body.

"More dignified than he deserved," Mhayree replied.

"My mother would be happy," I added. Perhaps I was more like her than I thought.

We abandoned the corpse and departed the house. Opening the garden gate, I glanced back to look at the house one last time. I thought of Bothwell lying undiscovered – as the condemned notice fluttered on the door – and walked away.

The smoke rising in the distance travelled across the sky, over the rooftops. I hoped Jacque could see it – wherever he may be. I searched up and down the streets, wondering if, perhaps, he hid in one of the houses.

"Elise, we must go," Mhayree said.

"You go on ahead," I replied. "I will follow you soon."

"No, *Zaya*, you do not know the way," Natashka said.

"I'll find it. There is somewhere I have to go. Alone."

As I moved to leave, Mhayree caught my arm. "He won't have gone home. It's not safe for him there. Or you."

"And what if his brother is there?" Natashka said. "You don't know what he's capable of."

"I'm not going home," I said, releasing Mhayree's grip.

"It's not safe for any of us to be here. You must come with us," Natashka pleaded.

I said nothing, and instead turned around.

"*Zaya*!"

"Wait!" Mhayree demanded, tucking my hair behind my ear. "Stubborn, as always. So, I'm going to help you. Do whatever you have to do, and once you are finished, wait outside my house. Revenik will be waiting with the carriage."

I smiled in silent appreciation.

"Just remember to come back to us," Mhayree added, before leaving me.

I continued to journey along the street. Behind me, Natashka cried out my name. I didn't answer.

CHAPTER TWENTY-ONE

"Elise…" Natashka's voice faded into the distance. For a split second, I almost turned back to join her and Mhayree, but before every new beginning, an ending must be resolved.

Placing my hood over my head, I walked the length of town, passing Dante's and the linen shop – where a pile of fresh bedsheets waited on the counter for me. Through the window, Mrs Ruthyard – unaware of the fire destroying the Inservium – scowled over her half-moon glasses, and waited, in vain, for me to collect the goods. The blaze continued to fill the sky, as the flames spread into the streets.

Men and women were running around, hauling furniture from their houses, and bribing carriage drivers to take them to port.

"I'll pay you double a year's wages."

"I'll give you any one of my daughters."

"I'll give you two of my daughters, and my wife."

Amongst the bustle, a woman carrying a Spaniel bashed into me. "You must get away my dear," she sobbed. "The whole town is going to burn down."

"I'll be fine," I replied.

"Did someone steal your dresses?" she said, looking at my clothes. "You can have any of mine if you'll help us leave."

"That's the last thing I'd want," I said, walking away.

"What do you want, then?" she called after me.

Jacque and my mother, I thought, disappearing into the crowd.

All around me men were yelling at each other, and

239

instructing their wives to take only the bare necessities. Women had their faces buried in handkerchiefs, wailing and praying to their Idol to save them. Some had children clutching at their skirts, others had pickpockets stealing whatever trinkets were close to hand. Amidst the commotion, a man bumped into me, pulling my hood back, screamed and pointed at me. "It's her! The vampire!"

"The one from the newspaper!" another man shouted.

The crowd turned to look at me, and the deafening sound of screaming erupted throughout the whole street.

"No, there's been a mistake!" I yelled.

"She'll kill us all!" said a woman holding a baby.

"Grab whatever you can. She must be stopped."

"No, really!" I struggled to shout over the screams, as a group of men backed me against a wall of a house.

Towering above me, a sea of faces looked on with hatred and disgust. The men brandished makeshift weapons; made from anything they could get their hands on – stones, walking sticks, small tables.

"Kill her!"

As a suitcase flew towards me, I removed my poignard from my coat, and held it against one of the men's throats. "I don't want to do this," I said. "I don't want to hurt you."

"Idol help us all!" the man screamed, trembling as the colour drained from him.

The women stepped back, shrieking and flapping, but the men stood their ground.

"I'm not going to kill you," I whispered to the man. "I just need you to help me get away."

"It's just one vampire, we can take her," called out a woman's voice.

"Listen to me," I said to the man, easing my blade away from his throat. "Nothing will happen to you."

"If there's one vampire, there'll be more."

"Kill her!"

"Who's going to do it, then?" I yelled, grasping the man

and using him as a shield. "Who's brave enough?"

As I edged towards the drainpipe, dragging the man with me, the crowd launched bottles, bricks and stones at me, but nobody actually had the guts to come near.

"I'll do it," I said, pressing my poignard against the man's jugular.

Suddenly, I felt his full weight upon me, as his body went limp; he fainted. I dumped him on the ground, and the crowd drew closer, trampling over his body.

Taking hold of the drainpipe, I felt myself being pulled down, as a mass of hands grabbed at me, tugging at my legs, coat, and waist. Trying to release their grip, I batted them away and climbed higher and higher.

A chair flew overhead missing me by inches.

"Idiots!" I shouted. "I'm not going to hurt you!"

Two butcher knives came hurtling towards me. One bounced off a window and the other struck my coat, pinning the material to the wall.

As I removed the blade, an earth-shattering shriek broke through the crowd.

A woman's mangled body, halved in two, collided with the wall.

Then, the sweet, overpowering aroma of honey and salt hit me. Blood. One by one, the men and women screamed out in agony, as a sword sliced through them. Like a hot knife through butter, the blade tore heads from necks, torsos from limbs, and hearts from chests. The crowd parted, with dead bodies lining the street.

There she stood – poised and graceful as a bird, with feral eyes, and a cruel, poisonous smile. She moved as though pirouetting, brandishing a sword, and killing in swift succession. Katalin Arany.

Those who tried to escape were cut down where they stood. No one was spared, not even the children.

As the last man fell, she bent down, and licked the blood from his face. Wiping her lips, she walked towards me, looking me up and down. "Hello, Elise."

Watching her, I realised how much Jacque resembled her. Both in looks and capabilities. "I know who you are!" I said, and jumped from the drainpipe, to stand in front of her.

"Good, it will save time," Katalin replied, with a deep, Hungarian accent.

Staring at the bodies, I saw a little girl lying with her throat slit, and holding her mother's hand. "Did you know you were killing children?"

"Do you think I have a problem with that?"

I slapped her across the face, but she didn't flinch. Instead, she laughed, and sucked a bit of blood from her hair.

"Where is Jacque?" I said, pointing my poignard at her. "Where have you taken him?"

Katalin ran the blade of her sword along mine, and smiled. "Come with me," she replied, turning away.

"No."

She faced me and smirked. "Who else is going to take you to Jacque?"

"Do you really expect me to trust you?" I said, pushing my blade towards her chest. "After what you have done to me."

Katalin grabbed my wrist and bent it back. Despite the searing pain running up my arm, I refused to give her the satisfaction of seeing me lose control. As I clenched my other hand into a fist, and thrust it towards her face, she wrapped her fingers around my throat, and squeezed.

"Don't do that," she said, bearing down on me. "I could be on the other side of the road before your body even hit the ground. If this is about the curse, then I suggest you come with me."

"Why don't you just kill me instead?" I croaked, feeling my grip around the poignard loosening.

"You are sweet, but you are stupid," Katalin said, releasing me. "Now, come with me. Jacque is dying."

"Get in!" Katalin demanded, shoving me through the door of Poska's Inn.

Inside, one of the barmaids sat with her feet up on a table in the middle of the empty inn. As soon as she saw Katalin, she stood up, selected a bottle from behind the bar, and began pouring a thick, red liquid into a glass.

"No," said Katalin, holding up her hand. "I don't have time to partake in whatever pauper you obtained that from."

The barmaid pushed the glass towards me, where the scent of blood caught my nostrils.

Before I could do anything, Katalin took my hand and pulled me towards the stairway. "Don't let anyone else in," she called over her shoulder.

The barmaid nodded, keeping her head low, and decanted the liquid back into the bottle.

Climbing the stairs, Katalin's grip on my hand grew tighter as we approached the landing.

"Is that barmaid a vampire?" I asked. "Is Poska?"

"Don't ask questions," she said, standing outside one of the four doors in the hallway. "Wait here."

"Don't think for a minute I trust you," I replied.

"I can see why he likes you," Katalin said, with a slight smile, before entering the room and shutting the door in my face.

Whilst alone, I paced up and down, taking note of every window and door which could help me escape if the need arose.

Within moments, the door reopened, and the distinct stench of blood washed over me. Out stepped the young man with the phoney English accent who I'd saved from the trainee Councillors.

"Rémy?" I said.

He didn't answer, and instead ushered me inside. Edging

forward, I entered a cold room with mouldy brickwork poking out from underneath the bright yellow wallpaper, grand mahogany furniture crammed against every wall and corner, and Katalin, sitting in a rocking chair, holding the hand of a man lying in bed, wrapped in blood-soaked sheets.

Jacque.

He lay, half-unconscious, mumbling incoherently, and groaning as the fever and pain took hold. His sunken blue eyes looked unfamiliar without their kohl lines, his dark hair sat, lanky and greasy around his emaciated shoulders, and his skin was black and blue from the number of cuts and bruises. He looked older, somehow, with deep lines across his brow, and grey flecks in his overgrown beard.

I stood, numb, uncertain how to react.

"You have a choice to make, Elise," Katalin said. "Save him, or let him die." She peeled back the sheets, to reveal a deep knife wound in his side, seeping with pus, and smelling like rotting flesh. "I reached him just in time, before the Councillors killed him."

As I moved towards Jacque, Rémy grabbed my shoulders and held me back. With one swift elbow to his stomach, he let me go.

"Uh uh!" Katalin said, holding up her hand. "You choose first."

"There's no choice to make," I said.

"Very well, I'll save him by turning him," Katalin replied, standing up. "But, on one condition."

"Which is?"

"The two of you can never be together. You have to leave him."

As I watched Jacque's breathing get shallower, I sensed Katalin walking towards me. "You're mad," I said. "I'll turn him myself."

She laughed, with a hint of viciousness, and turned to face Jacque. "You can't. Arany and Havasi bloodlines can never join. If you bite and consume his blood while he is human, then the curse will kill him."

Rémy stood beside his brother and placed his hand across his forehead. "We're running out of time."

"Do you think he could ever look at you the same way?" Katalin continued, walking away from me. "Knowing you're a murderer, killing countless people. Do you think he would still love you?"

"Why are you doing this?" I said. "Why do you hate us so much?"

"I don't hate Jacque. He's my family, don't be ridiculous."

Katalin sat on the edge of the bed and Jacque winced in pain. "Save him," I said.

"Are you sure?" Katalin replied, sliding towards his body.

Rémy, undoing the buttons of Jacque's shirt, said, "There's no point in wasting time, we know she'll choose to save him."

"Now now, let's not be hasty," Katalin said, pulling back the collar to expose Jacque's neck.

"Katalin!" Rémy said, narrowing his eyes at her.

She held up a hand to silence him, and stared at me. "There's more. Jacque gave the Councillors the names of the vampires."

I frowned and pulled out my poignard, wanting to stab it through her chest.

"What are you planning on doing with that?" she laughed.

"You're a liar," I said, moving towards her. "Jacque would never do that."

"Bothwell said he would kill you if he didn't tell them."

"Why should I believe you?" I replied, pointing the poignard at her.

"He also blocked the coven's spells," she continued. "Maybe he didn't want you to find him. Maybe he doesn't love you after all."

"Don't!" I said.

"And he brought down their enchantments upon the

castle so the Councillors could get in," Katalin said. "I'm so happy I taught him magic when he was a child."

"My sister was in that castle," I replied.

"Just imagine what the Councillors would have done to her. You could say Jacque was a traitor."

"Oh, for crying out loud!" Rémy yelled. "It's true. Enough of this."

Katalin stood up, and pressed herself against the blade. "Are you really thinking of killing me? Who would save Jacque?"

"Him," I said, pointing to Rémy.

"I can't," he replied. "I'm not a vampire."

"Yet," Katalin said, glaring at him, before turning to me. "Do you still want me to save him? It *is* Jacque's fault that all those innocent people are dead."

Lowering my weapon, I collapsed onto the bed and, taking a deep breath, closed my eyes, knowing that this wasn't mine and Jacque's time. "I'm so tired."

A flutter of hot breath and strands of hair brushed against my cheek, as Katalin leaned into me. "Choose," she whispered.

"Save him," I sighed. "I've got my chance of redemption; he deserves the same."

"And what about you?" her deep voice seeped into me.

"I'll leave. For good."

As Katalin moved away, I opened my eyes to find her, crouched over Jacque, and pulling him towards her.

"Elise," Rémy said, standing by the door. "It's time to go."

"Just a few more minutes," I replied. "I need to know he's all right."

"No, you have to leave now," he continued, with a hint of desperation in his voice. "She won't do it if you stay."

Taking one last look at Jacque, I stood up, and moved to leave. As I reached the doorway, I turned back to see Katalin sinking her fangs into his neck. Jacque's body convulsed as his blood dripped down his throat, with the Arany matriarch pinning him to the bed. Rémy grasped my hand and pushed me into the hallway.

"Don't come back, Elise. She'll kill him if you break the pact," he said, closing the door.

Leaning against the wall, I told myself I had done the right thing. Jacque was safe. Hopefully. As I moved towards the stairwell, another door opened behind me.

"Finally," said a familiar Russian voice. "*Zaya*, you do drag these things out."

Turning around, I saw Natashka coming out from one of the adjacent rooms. I ran and wrapped my arms around her. "How long have you been here?"

"I may have been eavesdropping," Natashka replied, squeezing me. "And I may have followed you. That little barmaid is too easily bribed. A compliment here, a compliment there, and I was upstairs before I knew it."

"What am I going to do?"

She tilted her head and thought for a moment. "Pact or no pact, we'll find him again."

"She'll kill him."

"Not if we get to him first. Then we'll kill her."

I sat on the floor, with my head in my hands, trying not to think about what was going on in the room beside me. "Perhaps we should try just now?"

Natashka patted my shoulder. "If I thought that was an option, *Zaya*, I would have come in and turned him myself. Honestly, I don't know how she is managing to suffer the sunlight. She is stronger than we could ever have imagined."

"I hadn't thought of that," I replied.

"She should have been living in darkness years ago. We need to find out more."

I nodded, reluctant to admit defeat.

"Let her have her big, bad moment," Natashka continued. "And then, when we're stronger, we'll find them both. Right now, Amelie needs you. So does Mhayree, even if she won't admit it."

Twiddling my poignard between my fingers, I turned to Natashka and gave a slight smile. "How about we go after the Councillors instead, then?"

She looked at me as though a new game rallied her spirits.

"Starting with Marius de Volonté," I continued. "I believe he owes you a debt."

Natashka's eyes widened, all too willing to accept the challenge.

We took each other's hands, and made our way towards the staircase, prepared to travel to the ends of the Earth to avenge our kind.

Two survivors. Two warriors.

CHAPTER TWENTY-TWO

PRESENT DAY

Sirens, delivery vans, and double-decker buses animated London's cosmopolitan landscape. A black cab pulled up in front of the row of flats adjacent to Jacque's, and two young men stumbled out onto the street. One of them fell to the pavement. Sitting on Jacque's balcony, I could smell the stench of booze and cigarettes waft into the air as the pair staggered into their flat.

All through the night, Jacque read my diary, whilst I watched, outside his bedroom. Only once did he almost catch me. After finding the diary, he searched every room, looking for the intruder. Hearing him approach the window, I launched myself onto the guttering and climbed onto the rooftop. As he went back inside, I wrapped a whip around the drainpipe, and scaled back down onto the balcony.

Midnight. The human Jacque succumbed to his vampiric monster. Magnificent but cruel, his red eyes glowed against the darkness, fangs gnawed against his bottom lip, and death possessed his body. Feeling my gums receding and the blood draining from my face, I knew the moon had taken her son and daughter. Vampire to vampire. Phoenix to Phoenix. The night had claimed us both.

Page by page, Jacque absorbed my secrets, confessions, and heartbreaks. Sometimes he paced the floor; other times he sat on the bed with his nose buried in the book. The hours grew intense, as his emotions flicked between burning anger – where he kicked the sparse amount of furniture dotted around the room – to laughter, and despair. It would be a lie to say that as I watched him, I didn't feel compelled to barge inside and rip the pages to pieces. But it never happened.

Jacque turned the last page of the diary, tossed it into the air, and harpooned it against a wall with a dagger he removed from his belt. In one swift move, he leapt to his feet. He stood in front of the new hole in the wall, and examined the blade. As he turned around and crept towards the window, I mounted the balcony and prepared to somersault to the ground.

"Elise?" he called out.

I froze, and looked towards the concrete pavement beneath me, contemplating whether to jump and run away or enter and face him.

"I saw your reflection in the dagger," he said.

Decision made.

Realising the pointlessness of avoiding the situation, I stepped off the balcony and approached the windows.

He didn't move.

I turned the handle and walked into the bedroom. Finally, we stood face to face.

Silence.

He stared at me, as though searching for the innocent girl in the portrait kept in his bedside drawer. As casual as he tried to appear, the look in his eyes gave away the confusion and apprehension he felt.

Still silence.

I stood, hands on hips, with the weight of my swords and daggers pressing into me, reminding me of the henchman I killed less than a week ago. I wondered if the shock Jacque felt upon seeing me was anything like mine after finding him. Now, nothing remained but two strangers doubting if they'd ever truly known each other at all.

Jacque edged forward and stood before me, bearing down, into my face. I remained still, not wishing to provoke a response from either of us. My palms grew sweaty, and I found myself unable to look at him. Out of the corner of my eye, I saw Jacque smile and, despite resisting, I reciprocated.

He leaned in, pulled me closer, and sank his fangs into my neck. A sharp pain shocked me, until subsiding to a pleasant sensation of being consumed. As Jacque released me, I returned the favour, by grabbing his t-shirt, ripping the collar, to expose his neck, and biting his throat. He flinched, before scratching his fingers across my back, and licking the drops of blood running down my shoulder.

As I tasted his blood, it felt as though no time had passed between us. Memories of the last hundred and twenty years faded into the ether. Once again, I was his Elise, and he was my Jacque. Nothing else, in that moment, mattered.

Of course, the reality proved different.

I released my bite, and whispered, "How have you been?"

Jacque laughed. "After all this time, those are the first words you say to me?"

I narrowed my eyes, grinned, and kissed his lips.

"I've been good," Jacque muttered between kisses, as the blood covering our mouths mingled together. "How about you?"

I paused, and kissed him again to deflect the question, before offering a non-committal, "Uh huh," and reaching for his waistband.

"I've missed you," he said, inhaling my scent. "You've changed."

"I had to," I replied.

Jacque removed my coat, and, as it fell to the floor, my weapons scattered across the room, distracting us.

"Still killing people, I see," he said.

"I am a murderer, Jacque."

He placed his foot under the bed, and slid out a box of swords, hatchets, and maces. "So am I."

He watched me, trying to gauge my reaction. Judging by his confused expression, I showed none, and managed to conceal my lack of surprise. I kneeled down to inspect the

251

weapons – spinning them between my hands, slicing them through the air, and feeling their weight.

"Where did you get these?" I asked, admiring a blade inscribed with runes.

"Katalin gave them to me."

Unimpressed, I flung the sword back into the box. "Oh."

As I stood up, and proceeded to collect my coat and weapons from around the room, Jacque sighed and said, "It was a long time ago."

"I'm amazed she had any weapons left. I thought she gave them all to my sister," I snapped.

"Don't start!" Jacque replied.

"How is your Katalin?"

Jacque rolled his eyes. "My Katalin? We're related, Elise, get over it."

"And whose side are you on?" I said looking him up and down.

"Excuse me?" he said, folding his arms.

I held up my hand in contempt, not wishing to hear any more. Jacque took no notice. "We're all fighting the same fight."

"I don't kill humans just to piss off the Inservium, like your Katalin!"

"No," Jacque mocked. "You only kill Councillors… and, at one point, vampires."

Taken aback, I glared at him. "Don't you dare! Neither of us were innocent in that, remember?"

Jacque leaned against a wall, looking ashamed. "I didn't mean that."

I raised an eyebrow, unconvinced, released my diary from the wall, and placed it into my coat pocket. I tossed Jacque's dagger across the room, and it landed, embedded into the floor between his feet.

"Nice aim," he said.

"I missed."

He eyed me with suspicion, and I turned to leave.

"Why did you come to find me, Elise?" he said. "Why now?"

I stopped and faced him. "I promised I would find you."

"Yeah, so I read," Jacque smiled.

For a few moments, I fell silent, and moved towards him, before continuing. "And it's taken me this long. We've been searching since the day you were bitten."

"We?" Jacque asked.

"Natashka and me," I answered.

"Ah, of course!"

"She is looking forward to meeting you."

"Should I be worried?"

"It depends on what you do."

Jacque, seeming to ignore me, wandered around the room, removing clothes from drawers and throwing them onto the bed.

"I see you have been rummaging in my things," he remarked, whilst opening a drawer.

"Hmm?" I said, attempting to sound nonchalant.

"Were you looking for my cigarettes again?" Jacque replied, and patted his jeans' pocket.

I snorted in contempt, for both his filthy habit and the accusation.

He lifted the small portrait of me hidden amongst a pile of socks. "It was face-down. I always face it upwards."

I turned away, annoyed with myself for making such a simple mistake – in over a century of hunting Councillors, I never allowed for carelessness. Looking at my reflection in the windows, I saw the portrait soaring through the air, and land – faced upwards – on the bed.

"Amelie gave me your address," I said, breaking the awkward silence.

No response.

"I didn't know you two were so close," I added.

Jacque opened the wardrobe and grabbed a rucksack. "We're not. I've never met her. It must have been her husband who told her where-"

"You mean Rémy!" I exclaimed. "You can say your brother's name, you know."

No response.

My phone vibrated inside my coat pocket. At first, I ignored it, but the incessant buzzing refused to relent. Exasperated, I pulled it out, and saw Natashka's name flash on the screen.

"Hello," I said, answering. At the other end, the pounding beats of a nightclub played in the background. "Haven't you left yet?"

"No, *Zaya*. Can you chat just now?"

I glanced towards Jacque, who was preoccupied packing his clothes. "Hmm… a little."

"Is he there?" Natashka said, excited.

"Aye."

"Put him on the phone."

"No!"

"Yes!" Natashka demanded.

"No!"

"*Zaya*."

"No!"

"I'll bake you some *pirog*."

"You've been trying to use that bribe for over a century," I said, noticing Jacque's hand outstretched towards me, and motioning for the phone.

Pushing away his arm, I shook my head, but it was no use. He stuck out his tongue and kept flicking my nose with his finger.

"*Zaya*."

"Will the pair of you just leave me alone," I said.

"No," Jacque replied, flipping my hair over my face.

"*Zaya*."

"Oh fine, here," I said, passing the phone to Jacque.

As he chatted to Natashka, I leaned against the wall, and chewed the side of a ragged fingernail, pretending not to listen.

"Uh huh… I see," Jacque said.

A muffle echoed from the other end.

"No, she didn't try to kill me," he laughed.

Another muffled echo.

"Right… Uh huh… I'll remember that," he replied, looking concerned. "I'll hand you back to Elise."

"Are you satisfied now?" I enquired, holding the phone to my ear.

"Somewhat," Natashka answered.

As I fiddled with the dagger sized hole in the wall, Jacque removed a couple of books from a drawer and packed them into the rucksack.

"What is it you're actually doing?" I asked him.

"Packing," he answered.

"Obviously, but-"

"*Zaya*, are you paying attention?" Natashka said.

"Aye. Of course," I lied.

"Good, because Mhayree has just walked into the club."

"Shit."

"She's with Saara, Hart, Romia, and Freya," Natashka whispered.

I moved towards the windows, and stepped onto the balcony to continue the conversation in privacy. On the other end of the phone, Natashka mumbled an order of a Black Russian to a waiter. Inside, Jacque wandered room to room, gathering his possessions.

"Why is Romia De Rossi with them?" I asked Natashka.

"Is it not obvious?"

I waited for her to explain. Silence. After several moments, I realised she was anticipating my response.

"No," I said, frustrated.

Natashka slurped her drink, and babbled. "This straw is proving ineffective."

"Uh huh…"

"This tastes much better without it!"

"Natashka…" I urged, encouraging her to focus.

"Well, she is one of Emilia Bokori's daughters; perhaps she is looking for her great-great… whatever… cousin."

"You mean Jacque," I responded, watching him hide a dagger inside his boots, and cover it with the leg of his jeans.

"Well, his mother is related to Emilia's sister, Noemi Bokori."

"Aye, and his mother married into Katalin Angou's family. I know all this," I replied.

"Maybe Emilia is taking a vested interest in the war and joining us," Natashka answered, taking a gulp of her cocktail.

"Or both of the Bokori sisters are siding with Katalin. Maybe Saara and the others are, too."

"I'm not sure there are only two sides anymore. I've lost track of whose family is allied with whose."

"Anyone who is with Katalin is against us. It's that simple."

"Spoken like a true descendant of Gizella," Natashka said.

"Perhaps."

"What about Jacque? Do you trust him?"

"We'll see," I replied, looking over my shoulder to ensure Jacque wasn't listening. "He's admitted to killing people. But we already knew that."

Natashka's voice faded as the music grew louder. "Do you regret seeing him?"

"No," I said. "I don't know."

"So nothing happened?"

"Not really," I said, sitting crossed legged on the concrete. "Just a bit of fun. You and I have more important things to consider. Like that email from Lana."

"And Mhayree? Do we know whose side she's on?"

"Well, if it's not ours, I may have to kill her this time."

Natashka did not respond.

"Have they seen you?" I asked.

"No, not yet," Natashka said. "I am thinking of finding them before they find me."

"Be sure to welcome them to London for me," I said. "I will try to find out more from Jacque as to why Mhayree was at his flat last week."

"Good idea. I'll see you soon, *Zaya*."

"Just one more thing."

"What?"

"Where the hell have I to meet you?"

Natashka snorted, trying to stifle laughter. "I'll meet you on the South Bank, outside the Dungeons."

"Is that supposed to be our usual haunt?" I asked, confused.

"Think about it," Natashka replied, before hanging up the phone.

I leaned on the balcony railing and looked across the street. Within the houses shrouded in darkness, the human occupants slept, oblivious of vampires roaming around the metropolis. In a few hours, when the sun rises, men and women would awaken, scoff down their morning toast or cereal, gorge on caffeine and dash off to the daily grind of business meetings, shopping sprees, and congestion charges. Meanwhile, the city was hosting a war between vampire coven factions, with in-fighting involving the Inservium and an ancient grudge between family bloodlines. I envied the humans.

I stood up, adjusted my poignard attached to my belt, and re-entered the bedroom.

"I have to go and meet Natashka," I called to Jacque, who was disconnecting plugs in the next room.

"Should I be worried about her threats?" he asked.

"What threats?" I answered, smiling to myself.

"The kind that gentlemen do not repeat."

"Aye."

Jacque emerged from the lounge, looking unnerved, but remained silent. He opened the wardrobe, removed a leather jacket, and threw it onto the bed.

"Have you ever heard of a Mhayree de Loire?" I asked.

"Yes, we've been friends for a few decades."

"I heard she was in town, that's all," I said, trying to sound casual. "Have you seen her recently?"

"She visited last week. Why?"

"What a coincidence, we are all in the same place at the same time."

"Indeed," Jacque replied, putting on a black beanie. "Although, she has been here for years."

"How did you meet her?"

"Through friends."

"Which friends?"

"Not Rémy or Amelie, if that is what you mean."

To avoid sounding desperate for information, I kept quiet and decided to let Jacque lead the conversation. I wandered around the room, watching him cover his sparse amount of furniture with dust sheets.

"Mhayree tells me that you and Natashka went on a hunting expedition," Jacque continued.

"We've been on many," I replied.

"This one involved your father."

"You mean Marius de Volonté?" I said, grabbing a corner of a dust sheet, and helping Jacque to cover the chest of drawers.

"Yes, dear old Marius."

"That is a story for another time."

Jacque nodded. "Another diary?"

I laughed, but revealed nothing, trying instead to direct his attention back to Mhayree.

"You do know Mhayree was supposed to take care of Amelie?" I said.

"Maybe not mention Amelie to Mhayree," Jacque warned, whilst taking one last look around the flat.

"Feeling guilty, is she?"

"What Amelie did was not her fault."

"And what about Freya?"

"She's trying to make amends," Jacque said, removing a cigarette from his pocket.

Upon seeing my disgusted expression, he sighed and placed it back into his jeans. Whilst putting on his jacket, he turned to me and said, "Are you ready?"

"For what?" I replied.

Jacque smiled, shoving two Hungarian daggers into his belt. "To fight."

He secured his rucksack over his shoulder, picked up a silver gilded knife, and added, "I heard you're quite good at it."

I raised an eyebrow in modest agreement and – accepting the conversation about Mhayree was over – headed towards the windows, motioning for Jacque to follow. "Well, come on, then. We've got Councillors to track down."

We stepped onto the balcony, leapt over the railing, and landed on the ground. As dawn loomed over the horizon, we returned to our human guises, and travelled across the streets of Camden, knowing only danger and death awaited us. Loss begets loss. Murder begets murder. Hand in hand, we would face the Councillors, and avenge every vampire man, woman and child, whose blood they spilled. We would be persecuted and hunted, until only one was left standing.

Acknowledgments

Most of you probably don't know how Girl of the Ashes came into existence. In total it took four years to write and edit, several re-drafts, and countless name changes for Elise. Along the way, many people offered their support and encouragement, including friends, family, support team, and my characters who sometimes like to start midnight conversations in my head.

I would like to give particular thanks to my mum who never doubted me and told me from the age of five that I should be a writer. I wanted to be a popstar. She was right.

I need to give massive credit to Victoria, Gary and Connor who kept me going, made me laugh (when I should've been writing!) and loved me no matter what. Big thanks for being my editors!

Finally, I need to mention Sylvia, without whom this book would not have been published. Thank you for the opportunity and for giving me a chance.